Ignore that

Well since you're a boy
I thought this was the
perfect book for you :)

BETTER
READ
IT! ꙿ

Also you're
welcome

From
Elayna :)

Tut

THE STORY OF
MY IMMORTAL LIFE

ALSO BY P. J. HOOVER

Solstice

Tut

THE STORY OF
MY IMMORTAL LIFE

P. J. Hoover

A Tom Doherty Associates Book
New York

TUT: THE STORY OF MY IMMORTAL LIFE

Illustrations on pages 48, 93, and 233 by Erik McKenney

A Starscape Book
Published by Tom Doherty Associates, LLC
175 Fifth Avenue
New York, NY 10010

www.tor-forge.com

Library of Congress Cataloging-in-Publication Data

Hoover, P. J. (Patricia J.), 1970–
    Tut : the story of my immortal life / P.J. Hoover. — First edition.
        p. cm.
    ISBN 978-0-7653-3468-8 (hardcover)
    ISBN 978-1-4668-1475-2 (e-book)
    1. Tutankhamen, King of Egypt—Juvenile fiction. [1. Tutankhamen, King of Egypt—Fiction. 2. Middle schools—Fiction. 3. Schools— Fiction. 4. Immortality—Fiction. 5. Horemheb, King of Egypt— Fiction. 6. Mythology, Egyptian—Fiction. 7. Adventure and adventurers—Fiction.] I. Title.
    PZ7.H7713Tut 2014
    [Fic]—dc23

                                                              2014015848

Starscape books may be purchased for educational, business, or promotional use. For information on bulk purchases, please contact Macmillan Corporate and Premium Sales Department at 1-800-221-7945, extension 5442, or write specialmarkets@macmillan.com.

First Edition: September 2014

0 9 8 7 6 5 4

For Christine M.,
who shared the entire journey,

and for Katie M.,
who remains Tut's first and most unyielding fan

CONTENTS

CONTENTS

Tut

THE STORY OF

MY IMMORTAL LIFE

1

WHERE I CRASH THE WRONG PARTY

EGYPT—THOUSANDS OF YEARS AGO

My enemy taunted me from the end of the dark tunnel. I knew it as soon as I heard the chanting. A small voice in my head told me not to go down the tunnel. Told me that I would die if I did. But I ignored the voice. I was the pharaoh, after all. The great Tutankhamun. I battled Nubians and wrestled crocodiles with my bare hands in the Nile River.

Okay, the part about the crocodiles wasn't true, but the Nubians thing totally was. I could do this. I'd been searching for the Cult of Set for over a year now. And I'd finally found them.

Why? Because Set was the Egyptian god of chaos and storms and all things dark and terrible. His priests carried out their master's godly bidding, filling the world with Set's chaos.

They'd stopped the flow of water into the crop fields. They'd vandalized tombs in the Valley of the Kings. They'd even tried to have me poisoned on five different occasions. Thank the gods for my food tasters. But this was my kingdom, and I had to protect it. If that meant rooting out dissenters, then so be it. I stepped inside.

At the end of the tunnel was a giant wooden door. Light shone from under its base. I froze when I heard voices amid the chanting and held my breath as I peered through an exposed knothole.

Three priests surrounded an altar. One wore a jackal mask, complete with spiky ears and razor teeth. One wore a mask like an ibis, which was this bird I always saw out in the Nile, with a long beak that had been sharpened into a spike. And one wore a mask like the god Set.

Set looked like some sort of monster pieced together from every ferocious animal in Egypt, with fangs the size of throwing knives and claws that could skewer kabobs. Anything that involved long hooks or knives or people with masks freaked me out—which pretty much summed up every ceremony ever held in Egypt, but that wasn't what made the world shrink around me.

On the fourth side of the altar stood my uncle Horemheb.

I'd recognize him anywhere, with his skinny little arms and long stringy beard. I think he kept it so long because his head was as bald as a beetle's behind. He'd been my most trusted advisor since my dad had died and I'd become pharaoh five years ago, yet here he was, clearly part of the most dangerous cult in Egypt.

"Mother of Horus," I whispered.

Laid out on the altar were all sorts of sharp, pointy things. The priests and Horemheb took turns picking up objects and chanting, all the while swinging incense around until smoke filled the air. Their words sounded like a bunch of nonsense, until Horemheb raised both hands above his head and started praying. What he prayed for chilled my blood.

"Deliver me my throne," Horemheb said.

His throne? It was my throne. He acted like he was trying to take over. But I'd been doing everything he asked. I'd been bringing the gods back to Egypt after my father had royally messed up the entire religious balance of Egypt. I'd been signing the decrees he asked me to sign. I'd even agreed to the whole moving of the capital city back to Thebes, though it was going to be a complete pain in my backside.

"Grant me my rightful place, Great Set," Horemheb prayed. "I am the true heir."

The priests repeated every word he said, including the stuff about him being true heir. But Horemheb wasn't the true heir. He was only my father's brother. I was Akhenaton's son. The heir. The rightful pharaoh.

"I have done your bidding, ridding Egypt of the heretic," Horemheb said.

The heretic? Horemheb had to be talking about my father, seeing as how most of Egypt viewed him as a heretic once he declared his favorite god the only true god. But it sounded a lot like Horemheb was saying he'd killed my father.

"Grant me permission to rid Egypt of his son, too," Horemheb said.

It was like someone had punched me in the stomach. Horemheb *had* killed my father, and he was going to try to kill me next.

I'd trusted him. Listened to his advice. Taken his guidance. And he'd done nothing but betray me and my family. My death was next on his to-do list. I clenched my fists. There was no way in all the realm of Anubis that I was going to let that happen. I'd have Horemheb killed instead. Do away with the entire Cult of Set. The only thing to do was to go back and get the palace guard. Bring them here and have Horemheb arrested and charged with treason.

Except then the incense coming through the cracks got super thick. My nose twitched, and I sneezed.

Within seconds, the door flew open, and the priest with the ibis mask grabbed my arms and yanked me into the room.

"The boy king," Horemheb said. "Set has delivered him to us just as we prayed for."

"Guards!" I yelled. They'd be here any second.

"The young king's presence here is a message from great Set himself," the priest wearing the Set mask said.

It was no message from a god. It was just me being in the completely wrong place at the completely wrong time. And where were my guards? Now was a horrible time for them to start giving me privacy.

"Your moment has come, Great Lord," the jackal-headed priest said to Horemheb.

Great lord? I was the great lord, not Horemheb.

"Guards!" I yelled again. I got a sick feeling as control of the situation slipped through my fingers like sand. The guards should have been here by now.

Horemheb laughed a deep, terrible laugh that made my scalp prickle. "Your guards won't come, Boy King. I'm afraid your time has run out."

I tried to run, but the three priests grabbed me and hauled me over to the altar.

"How dare you?" I fixed a death look on Horemheb. He would pay for this. I could list at least fifty divine decrees he was breaking. Not only would he be imprisoned, he'd be executed.

"I dare because I must," Horemheb said. "I've bided my time. Watched while you ran the country into ruin just like your father. Tried to reason with you and your childish ways. But I can watch no more. Egypt must be saved from your heresy."

Horemheb believed every word he was saying. I had to make him see the truth.

"I'm not a heretic," I said. "I like all the gods. Even Set."

That part was a lie. I hated Set. He'd betrayed his brother Osiris just like Horemheb had betrayed my father and was betraying me now.

"I went along with your suggestions," I said. "I had my father's name removed from all the monuments. I restored the temples." I struggled against the priest who held me, but he gripped me so hard that I thought his fingers might poke through my skin.

"It's not enough! All trace of the heretic must be removed from Egypt, including his son," Horemheb said. "Set's will must be done."

Around me, the priests started chanting. Horemheb grabbed a long knife off the altar and took a step toward me. I elbowed the jackal-headed priest, hard enough that I knocked him to the ground. I shoved the ibis-headed priest into my uncle. This whole mess couldn't be happening—except it was.

I ran.

Behind the altar was an archway leading to a tunnel. I took off down it. I didn't care where it went. All I knew was I had to get away from Horemheb before he killed me. Otherwise justice would never be served.

"Guards!" I screamed. Where were they? "Guards!"

"You can't fight the will of Set!" Horemheb yelled from behind me.

I kept running, panting as I wound through one stone passageway after another. Finally the maze of tunnels ended and I was out in the desert. The sun beat down from above, making me visible to anyone. Except there was no one around. I looked around to get my bearings. I was out in the middle of the Valley of the Kings, and just ahead was the entrance to my tomb. I ran for it.

With what I knew now, Horemheb couldn't let me live another day. I dashed into my tomb. The entrance had been left open since it was under construction, and Osiris must have been on my side because the first thing I saw once my eyes adjusted to the dim light was a shiny gold sword hanging on the wall.

Wait. It was my favorite hunting sword. Why was it already in my tomb? I used this thing every week. This was a "to be added after my death" kind of object.

"Very good, Tutankhamun. You picked the perfect place to die," Horemheb said from behind me.

I grabbed the sword and faced him, putting on my best pharaoh look in an attempt to intimidate him. But who was I kidding? Horemheb was a psychotic, Set-worshipping murderer.

"You're upset I killed your family, aren't you?" he said.

"My family? You killed my family?"

"Each and every one," Horemheb said. "Your father. Your mother. And your brother."

His words hardly registered past my hatred. "You traitor. How could you?" Horemheb had ruined my entire world.

He stepped closer, and light from the torches glinted off his thick gold bracelets. "Because your father was a heretic. If not for him angering the gods, my son Sadiki would be alive now."

"Sadiki died from the plague," I said. I used to play with him all the time, back when my dad was pharaoh. The plague had passed me over, but Horemheb's son wasn't so lucky. If he hadn't died, he'd have been fourteen just like me.

"My son died because of your father's crimes against the gods," Horemheb said. "And crimes against the gods are punishable by death."

"You'll be executed for treason." I still couldn't believe this was really happening. I'd been so blind. For the last five years, Horemheb had fed me lies. He'd pretended to help me while plotting my death. The whole thing was like a nightmare.

"I won't," Horemheb said. "You'll die, and I'll take the throne like I should have in the first place."

"You! Ha! You were never worthy of the throne," I said. "You're nothing but the son of a lowly consort. You're hardly even royal blood."

I must have struck a nerve, because Horemheb lunged at me with the knife. I jumped to the side. Except my tomb was tiny. There was nowhere to jump to. I fell against the entrance and barely had time to roll out of the way as the outer door to the tomb came crashing down. It made my bad situation worse. I was now going to be stuck in here forever.

"I was doing everything you asked," I said, trying to distract him, still gripping the sword, preparing to strike back. All I needed was one good shot at him. I'd trained with the best of the palace guard in all types of fighting since I was five years old.

"You were doing nothing." Horemheb's voice echoed off the hard limestone walls, making it all the more evident it was just him and me, sealed inside tons of rock. "I warned you about a religious revolt, but you refused to listen. And now here it is, Boy King. Welcome to the revolution."

It couldn't be a revolution. The priests hated me, but the people loved me.

"You're wrong," I said.

Horemheb laughed with a grating noise that made it sound like sand was stuck in his throat. "Why do you think the guards didn't come save you?"

It was a really good question. They hadn't done anything. And where were they now?

"They will," I said.

"They won't," Horemheb said. "Your entire palace guard was killed. And even if you manage to find a way out of this tomb, there's no throne for you to return to. You've officially been relieved of your royal duties."

"You can't do that!"

"I already did," he said.

I rushed forward, sword in hand, ready to take off his head. But Horemheb was more nimble than his gawky height led me to believe. He kicked the sword out of my hands. It smacked into a torch on the wall and fell near the tomb door. And then he thrust his knife forward.

I skipped to the side just in time, knocking the only other torch from the wall, and casting the tomb into darkness. Deeper into the tomb I fled, down a passageway, ignoring the shouts from behind me, until I ran smack-dab into a wall. My head spun, but I hurried to my feet . . . only to trip over a giant pile of walking sticks. There had to be at least two hundred of them. I stood up and immediately fell over a chariot wheel. Great Osiris, this place was loaded with stuff, cast all willy-nilly everywhere. There had to be a weapon around here somewhere.

"There's nowhere to hide, Tutankhamun." Horemheb's poisonous voice taunted me.

He was right. My tomb was tiny. That had been Horemheb's idea, saying my humility would please the gods. I ran for the burial chamber and squeezed past the sarcophagus. Images of me covered the walls, looking all regal with my long, brown hair flowing in waves behind me. Above the sarcophagus, on a shelf, sat the four Canopic jars that were supposed to contain my stomach, intestines, lungs, and liver. The tomb builders had already painted the sarcophagus with an image of my face. The peaceful look was exactly the opposite of how I felt right now. I had to find a sword.

I dragged my eyes away and came face-to-face with Anubis.

"Holy Amun!" My yell could have woken a mummy. But then I realized Anubis was just a statue. It was the fact that he didn't move and didn't answer that gave it away. Still, his golden jackal eyes followed me as I slipped around him, daring me to invade the treasury he guarded. Which, of course, I did.

Torches lit the treasury room. Shadows bounced off the walls, reflecting light off everything. The treasury was loaded— floor-to-ceiling gold. Not that this impressed me, but for anyone who'd never seen the stuff, it was enough to cause temporary blindness.

"Oh, Great Pharaoh! We thought you would never come."

I looked down and almost tripped over the army of little men congregated there. There had to be hundreds of them. It looked like they were made of baked clay, and each stood about six inches tall. Some master painter had probably spent the last two years painting each of them differently, varying clothes and hairstyles and even eye color. There were blue ones, golden ones, even solid black ones. They were my shabtis, placed here to be my servants in the afterlife—where I would end up soon if I didn't find a way out of this mess.

"We are here to serve you," the shabti in front said. Maybe he was their leader; his clothing was painted golden, he towered over the others by at least an inch, and he looked like he might be made of granite. "Give us your command."

I guess if I really had been mummified and in the tomb, an army of servants—one for every day of the year—would have been convenient. But now wasn't the time. I had bigger things to worry about than stepping on small clay men.

"Thanks for offering, but I'm kind of busy right now."

They all fell to the ground. Only the leader dared lift his head to speak. "How have we offended you, Great Pharaoh? Shall we take our lives? We only wish to serve."

I shook my head. Really, timing was everything. "No, it's nothing you did."

The leader's face didn't move.

"I swear. I just need to find a way to kill Horemheb. A knife or something."

At this the leader's head perked up. "A weapon! Great Pharaoh would like a weapon." He snapped his granite fingers, and three battalions of ten shabtis ran off into the piles of treasures. It wasn't ten seconds later before they returned, loaded down with twenty different knives and swords and things. Now I was beginning to see why the priests put these little guys in tombs after all.

"Will any of these do?" the leader asked.

"Submitting to Set is the only way, Tutankhamun." Horem-heb's voice sounded like it was just on the other side of the sar-cophagus. He let out a laugh that chilled every follicle on my skin. "As a favor, I'll make sure you are properly mummified."

I figured I better hurry if I wanted to keep my guts out of Canopic jars. I bent down to examine the weapons. Like the sword, they were mine—things I used on a regular basis. Part of me wanted to grab them all and shove them into my tunic, but I didn't figure that would help. So I grabbed the longest, pointiest knife of the bunch.

"And this, Great Master," the shabti leader said.

Two shabtis stepped forward, holding a golden box over their heads. They flipped it open, and inside I saw the scrolls of the *Book of the Dead*. It was the single most powerful religious object in Egypt. The priests swore that spells from the *Book of the Dead* actually worked. That the spells summoned the power of the gods. But I'd never seen the magic or the power of the gods. All I'd seen so far was death.

I took the scrolls. "What am I supposed to do with these?"

"Use a spell, Great Pharaoh," the leader said. "'The Judg-ment of the Dead.'"

"The spells don't work." Amun knows, I'd tried enough times.

"They will," the shabti leader said. "You must have faith in the gods."

Since I had nothing else, I figured I might as well give faith a shot. If the spell actually worked, it would give Horemheb a one-way ticket to the afterworld. And when his dead heart was judged by the gods by placing it on a scale and weighing it, there was no way he'd pass on to the Fields of the Blessed. He'd be eaten by the crocodile goddess, Ammut. I, on the other hand, would be free to find a way out of this tomb and figure out what I was going to do about Egypt.

"Faith in the gods," I said. "I'll give it a try. May you live your days in the Fields of the Blessed." I wasn't sure if shabtis went to the Fields of the Blessed, but it seemed like the right thing to say.

"We are here to serve you, Great Pharaoh," the leader said. "Give us your next command."

"Nothing now." Unless the shabtis could disembowel Horemheb and magically transport me out of here, I needed to do it myself.

I ran into the burial chamber and set the box on the sarcophagus, flipping it open. I uncurled the scrolls, found the right spell, and started chanting the words, making sure I pronounced each word correctly. I wanted to give the gods every chance to help me.

Nothing happened.

"You understand that I had to do it, don't you, Tut?" Horemheb sauntered into the room, acting like he was already pharaoh in my place.

I wasn't sure what he was talking about: killing my family, ousting me from the throne, or destroying every bit of trust I had in the world. I started the spell again. I chanted faster.

"When my son died, I was lost," Horemheb went on. "But

the gods found me. Set found me. He saved me from my despair. He showed me the future. I fought him at first, telling him it wasn't right. That your father shouldn't die. But Set insisted. Just as he insists I kill you now."

I kept chanting even though at this point, the chance of the spell working was about the same as the sphinx coming to life. Horemheb lunged for me, grabbing me and pushing me against the sarcophagus. The scrolls fell from my hand. The lid of the sarcophagus slid open, and I just had time to look in at the golden coffin before Horemheb was on me, pressing me against the mummy case. The aroma of perfume mixed with incense crept up my nose until I forced myself not to breathe.

"Do you like what you see, little Tut? Are you ready to take your proper place inside?" Horemheb had me pinned like a scorpion under a knife.

Great Osiris, please don't let him mummify me. Anything but mummification.

"What's wrong?" Horemheb asked. "Don't you want to join your father in the afterlife?" He pressed his knife into my side.

"Don't you dare talk about my father." I managed to get the words out even though my throat had constricted to about the width of a grain of sand.

A drop of Horemheb's disgusting sweat fell into my eye. I tried not to blink. That knife could be in my side faster than a cobra.

"Akhenaton was a fool to anger the gods the way he did. He brought about his own end." Horemheb twisted the knife into my tunic.

"I told you not to talk about him. You're unworthy to utter his name."

The *Book of the Dead* had failed me. The gods had failed me. I only had one option. I fumbled until I found the handle of my own knife, and I prepared to strike.

But Horemheb struck first, tearing his knife into my side.

My body reacted before my mind. I raised my knife and struck back.

2

WHERE I TALK TO THE GODS

I fell to the ground, vaguely aware of Horemheb falling to the ground across from me. The world slowed down. Giant drops of blood fell onto the scrolls of the *Book of the Dead*.

This was it. I was too late. I was going to die, and my only consolation was that Horemheb was going to die also. As I stared up at the painted ceiling, black mist filled the air, and words from the *Book of the Dead* twisted around in my mind. Days passed in that moment. Years. Time had no meaning. My body separated from reality and drifted.

The god Osiris glided up to me. I knew it was him because his skin was dark green and he had a funny pointed hat with some ostrich feathers perched on his head. The two harvesting tools he was always holding were tucked under one arm. At his feet, palm fronds and flowers sprouted from the ground, and insects trailed after him by the thousands. They swarmed me just as he reached down with one hand and pulled me to my feet.

"I can't be dead," I said. Horemheb was back in my tomb. What if he wasn't dead? He'd rule Egypt and get away with his crimes. "You have to send me back."

"You assume I can," Osiris said.

"You're a god. Can't you do that?"

"You tell me, Tutankhamun. Do you think I have the power?"

I'll be the first to admit that I haven't been the most reverent pharaoh. The gods had done nothing for me so far in life except take away my family. But here was Osiris in front of me. And if there was a chance that he was real, I had to take it.

"I think you have the power," I said.

Osiris grinned, so I figured it was the right answer.

"I knew you believed in me," Osiris said. "Horus always said you were a good kid. Said there was something special about you."

I highly doubted the gods were spending much time discussing me. I nodded so Osiris wouldn't think I was being rude and so he would get on with making me alive again.

"Are you ready for your future?" Osiris asked, waving his crook and flail in the air in front of him like some sort of witch doctor.

"I'm ready."

No sooner were the words out of my mouth than Osiris began chanting. A glowing orb appeared on his palm. It pulsed light like the beating of a heart. I couldn't stop staring at it, not even when he thrust his hands forward and shoved the object deep inside my chest.

I snapped back to reality. I was in the tomb, on the floor. Light poured from my chest, illuminating the ceiling above me. Energy filled me. The pain where Horemheb had stabbed me was gone. I touched my stomach, but the blood was gone, too. There was no wound. Osiris had healed me. He'd put the glowing object inside me.

I jumped to my feet. Horemheb was still on his back, and black mist pooled in the air above him. But the place where I'd stabbed him was gone, too. And just like me, there was a light coming from his chest. Maybe Osiris had healed me, but Set must have healed Horemheb also.

The black mist grew and filled the air, making the light coming from my chest bounce around everywhere. Horemheb got to his feet.

I ran for him, knife back in my hand, but this time, when my knife cut into his flesh, it healed over instantly. Horemheb started laughing. And then he took his knife and retaliated. My chest pounded, but not on the left where I usually felt my heart beating after running. This was in the center, where Osiris had put the glowing object. I pushed Horemheb away. Not only was there no pain in my side, I healed as quickly as Horemheb had. That stopped Horemheb's laughter.

It seemed that, thanks to the will of the gods, I couldn't kill Horemheb. The good part seemed to be that he couldn't kill me, either. Horemheb looked as shocked as I did. His hands covered his own chest, but light exploded around his fingers. And then he started praying.

"Great Set, you have granted me your favor. Curse my enemy and this tomb forever. Grant my freedom. Allow me, your humble servant, to rule the world in your name."

At his words, the black mist thickened and spread everywhere like it was alive and a thick sulfur smell filled the air, almost making me gag.

I felt a tug on my sandal and looked down.

"Osiris has granted you a way out," the shabti leader said.

"Out! I can't leave Horemheb here alive."

But the shabti leader wrung his little hands. "You must. He's invoked the wrath of Set. You heard the prayers. The gods have cursed these walls."

I shot one last look behind me. I could come back for Horemheb. Bring some help with me. He could have lied about the palace guard being dead. About the whole revolution thing. Even if he couldn't die, he could be arrested and tortured for the rest of eternity for what he'd done.

The leader of the shabtis took my silence for a yes.

"This way," he said, rushing for a tunnel.

"Where are we going?" I ran behind him, making sure I didn't step on his battalion. Given that they were only six inches tall, shabtis could run fast. And they did seem to stay out from underfoot.

"A door shown to us by Osiris himself," the leader said, stopping when we reached the end of the tunnel. "It's here."

"Set is answering my prayers, Tutankhamun," Horemheb

said from what sounded like only steps behind me. "Soon you will be dead!"

I glanced down. "If you don't mind hurrying—"

The leader moved aside. "You must pass through."

The tomb was solid stone. This was nothing but a dead end. "How?"

The shabti leader only bowed to the ground. "Please, Great Pharaoh. You don't have much time."

I felt the wall. It was solid rock. But the little shabti was insistent. So I closed my mind to sanity and remembered what Osiris had said.

"I have faith, Osiris," I prayed. "Show me the way out."

The thing in my chest pounded. I stepped forward, ignoring the fact that I was trying to step into solid limestone blocks. And something amazing happened. I passed right through.

"Gods be praised!" I was halfway through the limestone, but I turned to look at Horemheb tearing down the tunnel after me. There was no way in all the realm of Anubis that Horemheb could be allowed to be free.

"Tut, this is not over. Do not leave like a coward," Horemheb said.

"This is over," I said. "You can rot in here for eternity!"

I launched myself the rest of the way through the stone wall and looked at Horemheb one last time. There was no sign of him. Or the tomb. The whole thing had vanished, like it had been covered up by decades of sandstorms. I scanned the horizon, looking for the palace, the capital city, anything. But my Egypt had disappeared, and with it, my future.

3

WHERE I GO ON THE WORST FIELD TRIP EVER

WASHINGTON, D.C.—PRESENT DAY

Riding a school bus is torture when there are assigned seats. The last mile on the bus, stuck next to Seth Cooper, felt like five centuries instead of five minutes. I'd bet my one-eyed cat Horus's other eye that Seth hadn't washed his hands twice since September. And don't get me started on his breath. It smelled like he ate dead fetal pigs for breakfast two months ago and hadn't brushed his teeth since.

I hurried off the bus, praying I wouldn't be paired up with him for the entire field trip. There were things moving in his greasy red hair.

"Don't stick me with Tut," Seth said to Mr. Plant, our World Cultures teacher.

Seth hated me. Nobody ever hated me. I couldn't understand it.

Mr. Plant ignored Seth and started calling out pairings. I braced myself, waiting for the bad news.

"Tut, you're with Henry," Mr. Plant said.

Wait, what? If I was lucky enough to be paired with someone besides Seth, why did it have to be Henry Snider? Ever since school started two months ago, he'd been trying way too hard to be my best friend. He sat next to me in every class we had together, which was five out of eight, including lunch and Advisory. He kept asking me to get together and do stuff, like go to the movies or play video games. He talked constantly. It was bad enough that we were already science partners. Why couldn't I get paired with the cute new girl who'd been sitting in the back of the bus?

"We're going to every exhibit," Henry said, pushing his glasses up higher onto his nose. His shaggy blond hair was going in every direction, like he'd been caught in a sandstorm. Even though it was chilly out, he wore plaid shorts, faded gray Chucks wrapped in duct tape, and a short-sleeved purple shirt that read, SAVE PLUTO. There was nothing about Pluto that deserved to be saved. It never should have been called a planet in the first place.

"Maybe you are," I said. I'd seen all these exhibits a million times. Or at least all but one.

"Partners," Henry said. "It means we stick together, through it all. Fight the fights. Defeat the foes. I got your back. You got mine."

I wasn't sure what he thought was going to happen on this field trip. Maybe the zombie apocalypse? He'd probably seen too many cheesy horror movies.

"I got my own back. Thanks," I said.

Henry tried to bump my fist. He missed and ended up punching me in the arm instead.

This is one of the problems with being immortal in eighth grade. I'd be this age forever. Other kids, like Henry for example, would get older each year. They'd move on, go to high school, be old enough to drive. I never would. I didn't see much point in making new friends each year.

"You're welcome, compadre," Henry said.

Great Osiris, help me. I'd have skipped today if Gil hadn't insisted I come. Just thinking about this whole exhibit was starting to make my skin turn green. Yeah, green. It's this weird, thanks-to-Osiris thing that happens to me when I get nervous. But in my defense, these were the King Tut treasures we were talking about. Last time I'd seen them was in the seventies. Back then, I'd been the first in line. Big mistake. I was depressed for years. All my stuff being paraded around the country, like some carnival, and I couldn't have any of it. But the worst part was the memories it brought back. Memories of Egypt and my family and happiness.

"Seth, you're with Tia," Mr. Plant said.

No way. Seth got the new girl? And I was stuck with Henry?

Tia wore baggy cargo pants, combat boots, and a bright pink athletic shirt. She had eyes that were as blue as lapis lazuli, which were stones used in all sorts of stuff from ancient

Egypt, and a giant pink streak ran through her short dark hair. Her wrists were layered in bracelets, and at least five different necklaces hung from her neck. But the thing that won me over was the way she *accidentally* jabbed her elbow into Seth when she marched over to join him. He winced and opened his mouth to say something but stopped himself. It was almost like they knew each other and already despised each other. Seth had that effect on people.

"Someone told me she got kicked out of Catholic school for fighting," Henry whispered to me.

"Who?" I asked, pretending I wasn't just staring at her.

"Tia," Henry said. "They say this is her third school so far this year."

Seeing as how we were only two months into the school year, Tia's troublemaking skills must be the thing of legend.

My chance to ask anything else about her was cut off when Mr. Plant blew his whistle. Yes, whistle. I felt like a two-year-old.

"First, the project," he said.

Everyone groaned. Homework was bad enough. A three-week-long project was worse than hauling rocks around in the blazing hot desert to build pyramids for dead kings.

"Your partners assigned here will be your partners for the project. Your job is to study the artifacts you see today and then pick one to present to the class. You'll be graded not only on your research but on your originality, creativity, and presentation skills. The project will count for fifty percent of your final grade."

"You're in luck," Henry said. "My presentation skills are awesome."

That made sense. He did talk constantly, so he had plenty of practice.

"And now, I'd like you to meet our tour guide." Mr. Plant motioned to a redheaded guy with yellow eyes standing next to him. I guess the tour guide was taking the whole King Tut exhibit thing pretty seriously. He was dressed in some toga-looking loincloth tunic that actually resembled the real thing. Maybe he'd patterned it off the images from my tomb. It had been all the rage back in the day. Now he just looked like some kind of Halloween reject.

The tour guide caught me staring and smiled. My nerves prickled to the very edges of my skin. Coming to this exhibit was a horrible idea. I should have faked being sick today.

"Are you feeling okay?" Henry said. "You look green."

"It's the lighting," I said, and tried to make the green go away.

Henry pulled his wiry glasses from his eyes and cleaned them with the bottom of his Pluto T-shirt.

"No, you still look green," he said once he slid his glasses back onto his nose.

Mr. Plant blew his whistle again and we followed him up the stairs in two lines, me next to Henry and Seth behind us next to Tia. When Mr. Plant got to the King Tut exhibit entrance, he put the whistle to his mouth like he was going to blow it again.

Our tour guide yanked it from Mr. Plant's mouth and

threw it across the room. "Do not disturb the tomb of the pharaoh," he bellowed.

"Tomb of the pharaoh," Seth said from behind me. "I heard he was a puppet ruler. That he was too incompetent to make a single decision on his own."

I bit my tongue. I didn't need to justify myself or my rule to some smelly eighth-grade loser.

"I know you've all been waiting for this day," Mr. Plant said, scowling at our overdramatic tour guide.

"Not really," I muttered. It wasn't too late. I could pretend to twist my ankle. Or act like I passed out.

"Are you kidding?" Henry said. "This is the best field trip ever. Even better than that pumpkin farm we went to back in third grade."

I hadn't been in third grade with Henry, or at all, for that matter, so I couldn't agree or disagree.

Henry ran his hand over the gold-painted entryway they'd built specially for the exhibit. Above it hung a sign that read,

Death Shall Come on Swift Wings
To Him
Who Disturbs the Peace of the King.

It was the curse that had been inscribed outside of my tomb. A chill blew through the air, which had to be part of the exhibit. I scanned the area looking for hidden fans but didn't see any.

"I think the curse is hooey," Henry said. His messy blond hair was blowing from the fans, covering one of his eyes. He tried to push it out of the way, but it only blew back.

"Me, too," I said, even though I was living proof that the curse was real. "It's propaganda, created by archaeologists." I left it at that. My true opinion of archaeologists wasn't relevant. And curses were definitely real. They were the most favorite, best weapon of the gods.

"I think they made it up to keep people out," Henry said. "Do you have any idea how much stuff was buried with King Tut?"

"How much?" Tia asked, kicking her combat boots against the gold column. The whole exhibit entryway shook but didn't collapse.

I hadn't realized she was listening in on our conversation, but she was hanging on Henry's every word, flipping one of her necklaces around in circles on her finger. It looked like it might be a cross, but then I noticed the loop at the top and realized it was an ankh pendant, which was one of the most powerful symbols in Egyptian mythology. She must be way into this field trip, too.

Henry flipped open his notebook like he'd written it down. "I Googled it," he said, talking louder now that he knew he had an audience. "There were chariots. And walking sticks . . . a whole collection of them."

Every word out of his mouth made it clear he'd totally geeked out over the field trip. It was flattering in a way, the reality that most of the world thought I was some kind of rock star. Still, the fact that the priests decided I needed that much stuff in the afterworld was pathetic. I'm not sure what they thought I was going to do with everything.

"What do you think King Tut needed walking sticks for?" Tia asked, craning her neck to see into the exhibit.

The tour guide scowled at her and shifted so she couldn't see past him.

"I heard he was a hunchbacked, bucktoothed pansy," Seth said.

Wait. He was talking about me. How dare he! If only I had the power to smite him. The only reason I'd had so many walking sticks is because they'd belonged to my dad before me.

"That's not nice," Tia said, hitting Seth on the arm with her wrist full of bracelets.

Seth flinched like it hurt. No wonder she'd been kicked out of school for fighting.

"Before we enter the exhibit, it is imperative that nothing should be touched," the tour guide said. "Doing so would invoke the wrath of the gods."

I forced myself not to groan. The wrath of the gods. That wrath had been invoked thousands of years ago. Touching a few of my old possessions wasn't going to make them any angrier.

The tour guide opened the doors. I hesitated. It wasn't too late. I could leave. Except everyone started pushing forward, trying to be the first in, and I was shoved along with them. Seth bumped into me, I'm pretty sure on purpose. Hunchbacked and bucktoothed? Who was he to spread those lies about me? They'd been started by my enemies after my reign as a way to lessen my popularity.

The tour guide stopped in front of the first item. "This is the actual chair the boy king sat in while eating his meals."

My face heated up. The chair was small enough for a five-year-old. I felt like I was two feet tall. If I had to be immortal, why couldn't I have been eighteen? Or twenty-one? Why did I have to be fourteen? It was perpetual puberty.

"King Tut must have been a midget," Seth said, loud enough for everyone to hear. Even Henry laughed.

I balled my fists to keep from punching Seth. "Maybe he just liked the chair." Why hadn't I had a new one built when I was still pharaoh? Now the entire world thought I was short.

"Does this sound descriptive enough?" Henry asked, showing me his notebook. He'd written, TINY PHARAOH CHAIR across the top of the page.

I grabbed the pencil and scratched out the word *tiny*.

We moved on to the next object.

"The funerary chest," the tour guide said, stepping in front of a curtain.

He pulled aside the curtain, revealing a white marble chest with hieroglyphs etched along the sides. This was where my guts would have been neatly tucked away had I actually been mummified, which thank the gods I hadn't.

My scarab heart—that's what I called the thing Osiris had

stuck in my chest—started pounding. I'd found out early on that it's what kept me immortal and gave me special powers from the gods as long as I kept it charged with energy. I tried to calm it.

The tour guide flipped a light on, revealing the four Canopic jars inside, each with an image of my face carved on the top.

A palm frond sprouted from under my feet. Seconds later, it was joined by five more.

"Whoa!" Henry said. "What is up with that?"

Everyone looked.

What *was* up was the powers of Osiris. Osiris was the god of plants and bugs, and lucky me, I had special powers over plants and bugs. Things like palm fronds and roaches appearing out of nowhere. Yeah, I know what you're thinking. Powers over plants and bugs. Big deal. But I've found some clever ways to make use of the powers, like mind tricks to make people forget the crazy things that happened around me. And then there was the way I could create swarms of gnats around people who irritated me. Like Seth.

Normally I had control over my powers. Perfect control.

I took a deep breath. Tried to stay calm. "What do you mean?" I asked. And then I incanted my memory spell. It struck faster than a viper. Everyone's face clouded over and resettled as their short-term memories were adjusted.

Henry picked up one of the leaves. "Hey, cool. They added plants to the exhibit. You think these are the kind they used to have back in ancient Egypt?"

"They're exactly the same kind," the creepy tour guide said. He was only inches away. "Aren't they?" he asked me.

Uh, that was weird.

"How would I know?" I said. "It's not like I've been to Egypt."

The tour guide only narrowed his eyes.

"I'll add it to our report," Henry said, dropping the palm frond and writing in his notebook. He'd titled the page, Death Box with Creepy Little Box People Inside. It did sum up the funerary chest pretty well.

The tour guide stepped away. "Our next item is new to the exhibit, recently uncovered in Egypt just outside the tomb. We're honored to be the first to display what surely must be the most valuable of the King Tut treasures."

This got even my attention. I'd always figured my sarcophagus was the most valuable thing in the exhibit. The tour guide moved into the next room, and the whole class followed.

"It's probably another stupid sculpture of King Tut's ugly face," Seth said, like he was one to talk. "He must've been the most stuck-up pharaoh in existence to have so many pictures of himself around."

Not the most stuck-up, but definitely one of the best looking, which was kind of the reason there were so many images of me. Except none of the artists could get me just right. Either my eyes were too small or my teeth too big.

"He was kind of cute, for a pharaoh," Tia said, pulling at the pink streak in her hair.

"You have horrible taste," Seth said, but I didn't care. I was stuck on her "cute" comment.

The tour guide stopped next to a thick red curtain. I prepared myself. I would keep my powers in check this time, no matter what was behind the curtain. My scarab heart tensed in anticipation.

The tour guide grasped the velvety material. "I present to you the most powerful Egyptian god in existence." He pulled the curtain aside. "The god Set."

It was a short, gold statue of the god I most despised. It had definitely never been part of my tomb. And the most powerful god in existence? Horus would choke on catnip if he heard that.

"Go, Set!" Seth said, making some stupid victory motion with his arm.

I couldn't take it anymore. This tour was officially one of the worst days in the last century. Eighth grade was bad enough without the added worries of my scarab heart flaking on me. I ditched the tour and the ominous statue of Set, using the bathroom as an excuse.

"What about our project?" Henry said as I was leaving the exhibit hall. Everyone was busy jotting down notes about the fictitious relic.

"Take good notes," I managed to say. "Except no way are we doing our project on that statue." I hated Set. He had no place in my exhibit. He was the reason behind every problem in my life. My scarab heart pounded in my chest, and I was pretty sure my powers would burst from me, growing vines over the entire museum, if I didn't get away from the exhibit.

I left the room and sat by the giant elephant in the museum rotunda and waited. I was not returning to the exhibit ever again.

4

WHERE I MAKE
A MONUMENT EXPLODE

et's work on our project today," Henry said once we got off the school bus. He'd talked about the exhibit for the entire bus ride, writing stuff in his notebook and asking my opinion on everything from how many crocodiles I thought lived in the Nile to whether servants really were buried alive in pyramids. I wasn't sure why he thought I'd have the answers.

Our project was so far from my mind, I almost laughed aloud. All I could think about was the energy slipping from my scarab heart with every second that passed.

"Not today," I said. "I have things to do."

"Things like what?" Henry asked.

Great Amun, he was nosy.

"Just things," I said. Things like recharging my scarab heart.

It was nearly drained. It skipped around in my chest like some kind of dying fish.

"The deadline for the project's gonna be here before you know it," Henry said, showing me his notebook where he'd circled "Three Weeks" at the top of the page.

"We have plenty of time," I said. Anything could happen in three weeks.

Henry didn't look convinced, but I hurried away, leaving him outside the front of the school, so he couldn't nag me about it anymore.

I texted Gil to let him know I'd be late so he wouldn't worry about me, and then tried to decide which obelisk to use for recharging. The Washington Monument was out. It has enough cracks and flaws that sucking energy out of it was like drinking a milk shake through a straw with a hole in it. A better choice—actually a near-perfect example—was one of the five brand-new ones that had been put up in the last year around the District. They were taller than the Capitol building and made my heart jump in anticipation every time I saw them. Horus swore they were the work of Set. Part of Set's grand plan to take over the world or something ridiculous like that. But Horus was full of conspiracy theories. The government claimed they were memorials to dead heroes. That explanation worked for me. I decided on the obelisk in the middle of Dupont Circle.

I hopped the Metro, even though it was standing-room only. My stomach grumbled, but eating would have to wait until I'd recharged. On a good day, my scarab heart made me feel like I could slay a Tyrannosaurus rex. Right now, I don't think I could have summoned the energy to squash a bug. My powers were virtually gone.

Invisible energy sizzled in the air around the obelisk. It drew me toward it as I came up from the Metro station. All I could think about was recharging. The obelisk was the perfect collector of immortal energy. My scarab heart leapt in anticipation.

It was rush hour, so the streets were packed with cars and people filled the sidewalks. I crossed the street, barely waiting for the light to change. How had my heart gotten so low? It had to be the anxiety from the field trip. Once I got to the traffic island, I fought to keep from running up to the obelisk because I didn't want people to think I was strange.

The thing was enormous. So huge, twenty schoolkids could have sat around it and had their picture taken. But there were no schoolkids around today. Only some stinky homeless guy crashed out near the base. There was some sort of black graffiti painted on the obelisk behind him, but I couldn't see what it said since he was pressed up against the limestone base. I plugged my nose because he smelled like dirty socks, and skirted around him to the other side. The immortal energy called to me. So fresh. So powerful. I couldn't wait any longer.

I put my hands on the obelisk.

The connection was instant. Raw energy pulsed through my heart, filling it. I devoured it, feeling my powers grow and replenish with every second that passed. It pumped out of my heart and through my arteries, reaching every single part of my body. And then it returned to my heart and collected. Great Osiris, it felt good to be an immortal.

I stepped back, basking in the glory of recharging . . . and the obelisk exploded.

I flew backward, landing on my butt on the crowded sidewalk. Around me, cars screeched to a halt and started blowing their horns. People screamed and ran away from the traffic circle.

Some woman with a giant flowered purse ran up to me. "Are you okay? Are you hurt?"

No, I wasn't okay. This had never, in the three thousand years I'd been recharging my heart, happened before.

"I'm fine," I said, and got to my feet, brushing limestone dust off my jeans and windbreaker.

"You could have been hurt," she said, clutching her purse so it didn't get swept away in the crowd. "You could have died."

"It just surprised me," I said. "It's all okay."

Except it wasn't all okay. Limestone dust filled the air so thick that I couldn't even see where the obelisk had been. Mixed in with the dust was black mist putting off the overwhelming scent of sulfur. It was the same odor and the same kind of black mist I'd seen three thousand years ago when I'd been fighting with Horemheb.

With a final assurance that I wasn't hurt, the woman finally scurried away, getting swallowed by the crowd. The police and fire trucks would be here any second. I could already hear the sirens.

By some miracle the homeless guy was still asleep, but I

rolled him out of the way so I could get a closer look at the graffiti behind him. I held my breath to keep the smell of singed limestone and the sulfur mist out of my nose. Someone had drawn something on the base of the obelisk: an image of the scepter of Set with some hieroglyphs next to it. Since I knew Egyptian hieroglyphics better than my ABCs, I recognized them the instant I saw them.

Horemheb.

The hair on the back of my neck stood up, and the world slowed down around me. General Horemheb was in Washington, D.C.

It had been almost a hundred years since my tomb had been opened by archaeologist Howard Carter, and in all that time, there wasn't a sign of my uncle. I'd hoped—okay, actually I'd prayed—that somehow Horemheb had been destroyed when the tomb was opened. That maybe dung beetles had eaten him. Or he'd been buried in a sandstorm. But deep down, I knew better. If I was immortal, he was immortal. It meant you got to live forever. Which was fine for me, but not for my murderous uncle. He didn't deserve immortality. He didn't deserve anything but death. And now he was back in my world.

Immortal life was looking up.

"I'm going to kill Horemheb," I told Horus once I got back to my town house. My scarab heart was pumped full of energy, and the man who'd killed my family had finally surfaced after three thousand years. Revenge was going to be mine.

Horus stared at me from the futon, flipping his tail back and forth.

"And how exactly are you going to do that?" he said.

That was the only problem with my plan: I didn't have one. Since Horemheb was immortal like me, then there was no way I knew of to *actually* kill him. The only upside of that was that there was no way for him to kill me, either.

"I'm working on it," I said.

"Hope you have a direct line to Bes, then, because you're going to need some luck," Horus said.

Sadly, praying to the god of luck was my only option at the moment.

I guess this would be a good time to mention that Horus isn't really a cat. Well he is a cat, but not only a cat. That's just the form he prefers to stay in most of the time. He's actually a god, son of Osiris and Isis who, without getting too technical, are the king and queen gods. Oh, and also, Horus can talk. Sometimes too much.

I collapsed on the futon, brushing aside scarab beetle exoskeletons on my way. After three millennia, I knew Horus well enough to know that he had no intention of cleaning up after himself.

"Couldn't you at least eat the shells?" I asked.

He licked his paw. "Too crunchy."

I grabbed for a scarab shell, but the leader of the shabtis—I called him Colonel Cody—jumped on my wrist and tore it away. Scarab beetles follow me everywhere, even without me having to summon them. It was all thanks to Osiris. The fact that Horus ate them just made for a win-win situation.

"Please, Great Pharaoh, allow your undeserving servants to do that for you," Colonel Cody said.

So I let go. Who was I to argue with the shabtis? I'd found the shabtis—or they'd found me—after my tomb was opened back in 1922. I wasn't sure how I ever lived without them.

Horus licked his paw again. "See, the shabtis will clean up. They're meant to serve us."

"Me," I corrected. "They're meant to serve me." After all, they'd come from my tomb.

I want to point something out. I'm not just some egotistical jerk who likes to order people around—even if they are only six inches tall and made of clay. I'd asked the shabtis not to fall on the ground when I spoke. I'd asked them not to threaten to take their own lives if the toilet didn't get cleaned five seconds after I'd used it. But after years I'd finally come to the conclusion that they had to act this way; the spells written all over them bound them to me forever.

"Is Gil home?" I asked. He'd want to know about this Horemheb thing, too.

"He was," Horus said. "But then he went out looking for you." He squashed a beetle between his teeth, squirting the inside into his mouth and tossing the shell back onto the floor.

Gil was the only other immortal I knew of, because I was definitely not counting Horemheb. But unlike me, Gil got lucky and was eighteen forever. Gil lived here and pretended to be my brother and legal guardian, which kept Social Services away.

"I told him I was going to be late," I said. I wasn't sure why he thought he had to go out looking for me. I'd texted him and everything. "When will he be back?"

Horus scowled. "You think he told me?"

"Not really." Horus and Gil tolerated each other at best. At worst, they fought over the best ways to protect me—not like I needed protecting.

I looked down at the shabtis. Those not cleaning up the beetle remains stood at attention under the coffee table. "Can you get me a soda?" My throat was parched.

Colonel Cody threw himself to the ground. "Nothing would give me more pleasure." He snapped his fingers, and two shabtis I called Lieutenant Virgil and Lieutenant Leon ran off to the kitchen. They were painted solid blue and were almost always the ones who brought me drinks or snacks, like that was their specialty.

Since our town house was smaller than my tomb, the two shabtis were back in less than a minute. Lieutenant Virgil balanced a glass full of ice on his blue head, and Lieutenant Leon held a soda. They set the items on the coffee table and returned to their perch below.

"Back to Horemheb," Horus said. "Tell me about the obelisk."

"How did you hear—?"

Horus stopped me with a paw in the air. "Tut, seriously, do you think I'm an idiot? I'm a god. What part of that don't you understand?"

"But it just happened like a half hour ago."

Horus sighed. "The explosion stunk up the entire city. I can smell Set's sulfurous stink from miles away."

I'd smelled the sulfur, too, right after the obelisk blew up. I waited. I knew what was coming next.

"I told you Set was behind the obelisks," Horus said. He crossed his front paws and looked at me with his eye. And I do mean eye. Set had ripped out his other one ages ago.

"Whatever," I said. This wasn't the time for I-told-you-so's.

A low hiss came from Horus's throat. "Not whatever, Tut. You need to start listening to me. If you'd believed me when I said the Cult of Set was behind the obelisks, this never would have happened."

"Stop treating me like a child," I said.

"Why shouldn't I?" Horus said. "You've been acting like you're fourteen for the last three millennia."

I took a sip of my soda. "That's because I *am* fourteen."

"Well, maybe it's time you grew up."

"That's not the point," I said.

"And what is?" Horus said. "Horemheb? So he's back. What makes you think you can kill him now? Didn't you already try that once?"

"This time is going to be different. I feel it inside." I tried to keep my scarab heart calm inside my chest. "So how can I kill an immortal?"

"You can't," Horus said. But he'd stopped moving his tail. Horus never stopped moving his tail. Not even when he slept.

"What aren't you telling me?" I asked.

"Nothing, Tut," Horus said. But his tail still wasn't moving.

"I know you're lying. You stopped moving your tail and that's what you always do when you lie."

"I don't lie," Horus said.

"You did just the other day when you were talking to Gil. Remember? He asked you about the beetle shells under his pillow and you told him you had nothing to do with it."

Horus started flicking his tail back and forth again. "That wasn't a lie. The shabtis put them there."

"You told them to."

"That's a technicality," Horus said.

"Still, there is some way to kill an immortal, and you're not telling me what it is," I said.

"Why would I not tell you?" To Horus's credit, his tail only stopped moving for a microsecond.

"I don't know," I said. "It seems to me that you'd want Horemheb gone as much as I do. He's in allegiance with your sworn enemy. Getting rid of Horemheb would be a huge blow to the Cult of Set. Both of our problems could be gone."

"I don't have any problems."

"Right. Set isn't a problem."

Horus said nothing.

"He's a huge problem. You know it. He ripped your eye out. Or did you forget about that little incident?"

Horus's ears flared back. "I did not forget about that little incident. Nor will I ever forget about how he killed my father. Ever."

"Then tell me how to kill Horemheb," I pleaded.

Horus bared his pointy teeth at me. "There is nothing to tell, Tut. And we're done with this conversation."

"Whatever." I stormed out of the room. Horus was a big, fat, kitty liar. His non-answers had told me what I needed to know. There was a way to kill an immortal, and Horus knew what it was. And I was going to find out.

5

WHERE HOMEWORK
IS LIKE A VIRUS

I tried to pretend things were normal the next day at school, but my life had taken a wrong turn down Crazy Street. All I could think about was Horemheb. And the obelisk exploding. And the secret I knew Horus was keeping from me.

"Can you work on our project *today* after school?" Henry said when he sat down next to me in World Cultures. He had a black shirt on that read, PLUTO: NEVER FORGET, and in addition to his notebook, he had ten different-colored Sharpies clenched in his fist.

Ugh, the project. That was just one more thing to add to my growing list of annoyances in life. Maybe it was time for me to drop out of school. Gil was the only reason I was here in the first place. He bet me I couldn't go a week without asking the shabtis to wait on me, and sure enough, he was right. I'd failed miserably after two hours and ended up back in public school.

"I'm kind of busy today," I said. Making friends wasn't my top priority in life. Been there, done that. If someone wanted to be my friend, they could help me get revenge on Horemheb.

"Too bad, amigo," Henry said as he arranged the Sharpies on his desk. "We need to get it done. Unless you want us to fail."

If Henry flunked eighth grade it would only mean one more person who understood the tortures of repeating the same subjects time and time again.

"We're not going to fail," I said.

"Maybe you will fail," Seth said from behind me. "You could be the oldest kid in eighth grade." He snickered like he'd made a funny joke.

If only he knew.

Tia stomped up in her combat boots just then and sat down behind me, next to Seth. The chair on the other side of me was empty, but she completely ignored that.

"Who's the oldest kid in eighth grade?" she asked.

"Tut," Seth said. "But he's also the shortest."

I gritted my teeth and let the short comment slide.

Tia had on basically the same outfit as yesterday, except her shirt was lime green and the streak in her dark hair had magically changed to match. If it was possible, she had more jewelry on. In addition to the ankh pendant, she had a feather pendant and a circle pendant that looked an awful lot like a sun. All three were Egyptian symbols. I was going to ask her about it when Henry opened his mouth.

"So, today after school?" Henry said.

"I guess," I said, against my better judgment.

"What's today after school?" Tia asked.

"We're working on our project," Henry said.

Tia punched Seth in the arm. "We should work on our project today, too."

Which is how it worked out that at four o'clock that day I was sitting on the second floor of Martha Washington Public Library next to Henry with Tia and Seth across from us. By the time I dragged myself there, half our class was already deep into project research.

"I think we should do the creepy death box," Henry said.

"It's a funerary box," I said.

"Funeral. Death. Same thing. What are you guys doing your project on?" Henry said.

Seth was picking dirt out from under his fingernails, and Tia was playing with the ends of the green streak in her hair. They didn't have a notebook or a pencil between the two of them.

"What project?" Seth said.

"World Cultures, idiot," Tia said. "Remember? We're supposed to pick some object from the King Tut treasures and present to the class on it."

"Oh, that," Seth said. "We're doing that kick-butt statue of Set, the most awesome god ever. It was either that or one of those ugly statues of the boy king."

I let pass the way he emphasized *boy king*. Whoever came up with that title should be executed. I also let pass the ugly comment. But most awesome god ever?

"What do you know about Set?" I said. How was it that Seth, who didn't know how the sun managed to come up each morning, knew who the god Set was?

"I know he destroyed anything that got in his way," Seth said. "Unlike those other pansy gods who made flowers and stuff grow."

My scarab heart begged for retaliation, but I held it in check. The last thing I needed was some vines or flowers sprouting in response. Even with my efforts, a bunch of roaches crawled out from under the bookshelves. Tia slammed her combat boot down on a nearby roach, leaving a giant smear of guts all over the tile.

"Maybe we should get some books," Henry said, scooting his feet away from the guts. "Before they're all gone."

Anything to get away from Seth.

But Tia stood up before I had a chance to, yanking Seth along with her. "What's the Dewey decimal number for King Tut?" she said.

"Nine-thirty-two point zero one four," I said, failing miserably at keeping any pride out of my voice. The number of books written about me was beyond flattering.

"Got it." She winked at me and then was gone.

I sat in stunned silence, watching her stroll away. I tried to imagine Seth wasn't right there beside her, because it ruined the whole image.

"Come on, Tut," Henry said, and then he was off, following them.

"I'll save the table," I called.

Henry gave me a thumbs-up. "Good plan."

Five minutes later, all three came back empty-handed. Henry looked like his world was collapsing around him.

"Where are the books?" I said.

"They're all gone." Tia slumped into her chair and went back to fiddling with her jewelry.

"All the books are gone?" I said. There were so many. It wasn't possible.

"Yep. Every single one," Tia said.

Henry put his head between his hands. "We're gonna fail."

"What about the Internet?" I said.

"No Internet. Don't you remember?"

I shook my head. I guess I'd missed that part of the project explanation.

"Let's just go steal a book from someone," Seth said.

"We're not stealing a book," Tia said.

Seth pointed to Joe Hurd at the table next to us. Between him and his project partner, Brandon Knauss, they had six books on King Tut stacked up.

"There's no way they need all those books," Seth said, loud enough for Joe and Brandon to hear.

Joe opened his mouth like he was going to snap out some witty reply, but his face turned a sort of funny gray color and his eyes got all watery. He jumped to his feet and covered his mouth and ran.

"That was weird," Tia said.

The King Tut book Joe had been looking at lay open on the table. Brandon reached out to pull it over to himself, but Seth was faster.

"We'll look at it while he's gone." But no sooner had Seth grabbed the book than he dropped it on the linoleum floor like it burned him, making a loud boom that echoed around the entire library.

Dust lifted up from the book. At least, I thought it was dust until I noticed that it was black and swirling around in circles and smelled like sulfur. But before this had time to register, Brandon threw up all over the floor and the book.

We jumped up from our table to get out of the way.

"It's the curse of King Tut," Henry said, grabbing his notebook like he was going to record the whole incident in purple Sharpie.

"It's not the curse of King Tut. It's probably food poisoning," I said. The curse had no interest in the public library. It had bigger things to worry about. Things like Set and Osiris and battles for immortal dominance. I looked back to the book. Whatever black stuff I'd seen there was gone. And the only smell remaining was the contents of Brandon's stomach.

"You saw what happened. He was reading the King Tut book and then he threw up," Seth said.

I couldn't believe Seth was actually agreeing with Henry.

"And what about all these bugs?" Tia stomped on another roach. Her jewelry clinked together like musical instruments.

Wait, she thought it was the curse also? This was the problem with propaganda. It spread faster than a sandstorm and it never went away.

"What about them?" I said. "There are bugs everywhere."

"They're part of the curse," Seth said.

"There is no curse," I said.

"Right," Seth said. "And mythology isn't real, either, is it?" He acted like he'd said something clever and waited for my response.

What did he think I was going to say? That mythology was real? That all the Egyptian gods were among us, even if we had no clue where most of them were? Sure, I knew where Horus was, seeing as how he lived with me, but otherwise, I hadn't seen a god in the last century.

"Of course it's not," I said.

Given the mess on the floor, librarians started clearing us out. I texted Gil to come pick me up. His reply came fast.

already waiting out front he texted, like he'd known something was wrong. He must've talked to Horus. I could imagine the lecture I was going to get.

can you meet me in back? I texted back. I knew the reaction he'd get from Henry, Seth, and Tia, and I wanted to avoid it.

No response. I hoped that meant yes.

"Well, I guess I'll see you all tomorrow," I said, heading toward the back door.

Henry looked at me like I was speaking ancient Greek. "What about our project?"

"What about it?" I said. "The library is closing."

"When are we going to work on it?" Henry said.

I shrugged. "I don't know. Soon?"

His face kind of relaxed. "Okay, see you soon."

Which was not what I said at all.

Gil leaned against his black Mercedes, reading something off a scrap of paper. Like normal, he was decked out from head to toe in black. Black jeans. Black leather coat. Black hair. I'd never asked, but I bet he wore black boxers just to complete the look. He had a couple of scratches on his face, because Gil picked more fights than an alley cat.

"Why were you already here?" I asked when I reached the car.

Gil crumpled up the paper he was holding and dropped it to the pavement. It burst into flames. That's another thing about Gil. He got his powers from Nergal, a Sumerian god who had command of war and the sun in all of its destructive glory. Gil could do all sorts of cool things, like throw fireballs and melt metal. Me? I had roses and earthworms.

"What happened when you were recharging?" Gil asked the second the car doors shut.

"Where'd you go last night?" I countered. I'd still been awake when Gil got home, but I'd pretended to be asleep so I wouldn't have to hear his lecture. My conversation with Horus was bad enough. I heard them arguing down in the family room, and decided staying in my room was a good idea. And then I'd heard Gil storm out of the town house.

"I talked to Horus." Gil blew his horn and pulled out into rush-hour traffic. "I'm sure you heard. I haven't seen Horus that agitated in years, and that's saying something. After that I went out to check the obelisk."

"Did you see the name on the base of it?" Just thinking about it made shivers run up my spine. Revenge was going to be mine.

"Horemheb," Gil said. "Horus told me, but I thought maybe it was some kind of joke."

"Would I ever joke about Horemheb?" There were lots of things I'd joke around about, but revenge was not one of them. Gil knew how important it was to me. If anyone understood, he did. Just like my family had been killed, Gil's best friend had been killed. It was what bound us together thousands of years ago. Gil had met up with me not long after I'd escaped from my tomb. He told me the gods had sent him to protect me. Yeah, after the whole tomb fiasco, I wasn't too crazy about any mandate from the gods. Not to mention I didn't need protecting. So I'd ditched Gil first chance I got, leaving Egypt and heading to China.

Gil had followed. He found me stacking rocks, helping build the Great Wall of China. So I left again.

I'd tried everything: changed my appearance, hid among the people. But something changed along the way. It took centuries before I realized it. I was still hiding from Gil, but I expected him to find me. I wanted him to find me. It became a game. Until the time back in Greece when our immortality had almost been discovered. We'd had to flee, and while we were trying to escape, some kid got killed because of us. We never talked about it after it happened, but the games and the hiding stopped. And from then on, Gil and I roamed the world together, settling down wherever we wanted and living our immortal lives.

"If he's really back," Gil said, "then we need to find a way to keep you safe."

"Keep me safe? Are you kidding? Don't you see? This is the perfect opportunity."

"For what?" Gil turned the final corner to our street and started looking for a spot.

"To kill him." It was so obvious to me. How could Gil not see that?

"There's no way to kill an immortal." Gil didn't look at me when he said it. Instead, he got way too interested in parallel parking in front of our town house.

"That's what Horus reminded me of last night," I said. "But he's wrong. There must be a way."

Gil shook his head. "Horus is right. It can't be done." He answered way too fast. And I was overwhelmed by the feeling that he, like Horus, was lying to me. And maybe Horus wouldn't tell me, but Gil would.

"But . . ."

"But what?" Gil said.

"If it can't be done, then why do we have to worry about protecting me?" I asked.

Gil didn't have an immediate answer. I'd caught him.

"Well?"

"We just do," Gil said. "I'll talk to Horus about strengthening the shields around the town house."

"Seriously?"

"What?"

"That's all you have to say?" How was it that both Horus and Gil were keeping secrets from me?

"There's nothing else to say, okay?" Gil said. "Horemheb back means we need to be more careful."

Gil was wrong. Horemheb back meant revenge.

"Anyway, I'm going out to get us dinner," Gil said. "Any preference?"

My only preference was finding a way to kill Horemheb. I'd have to do it without Horus or Gil. I wasn't sure how I'd do this, but I'd do whatever it took. Talk to other gods—if I could find them. Pray to Osiris. Maybe I had to go back and visit my tomb. There could be some kind of clue there. Whatever it took, I would do it.

"No preference," I said, and Gil sped off to get us dinner.

6

WHERE I NEARLY MUMMIFY AN INTRUDER

"Gil is out of his Sumerian mind," Horus said before I'd even finished closing the door behind me. He paced back and forth on the top of the futon, and his spotted hair stood on end. Around the room, the shabtis were frantically working to contain the uneaten beetle population.

"You're both out of your minds," I said. "I can't believe neither of you are taking this Horemheb thing more seriously."

Horus leapt from the futon and confronted me by the entryway. "What did Gil tell you?"

I shoved my way past him into the family room. "Same as you. That there's no way to kill an immortal."

"It figures," Horus said.

"Of course it figures," I said. "Because you're both lying to me."

Horus flicked a scarab beetle across the room. Its feet started twitching the second it rolled onto its back, but a purple shabti named Lieutenant Roy ran over and flipped it right-side up.

"I was hoping he'd tell you," Horus said.

Time stopped as I processed his comment. "Tell me what? How to kill Horemheb? Because I know there's a way. If there weren't, then why would Gil be so concerned about protecting me?"

"He wouldn't be," Horus said.

My scarab heart hummed in my chest. Horus was going to tell me the secret he was keeping.

"Then tell me how to do it," I said.

Horus jumped to the little perch by the door that allowed him to look out the peephole. Once he was sure the coast was clear, he did some sort of waving, circular thing in front of the door with his paw.

"What are you doing?"

He landed back on the ground and started pacing again. "Putting up a ward. It'll let us know when Gil gets close."

I had no clue Horus could do that. He was full of surprises. "He's only getting dinner. You better hurry."

"You're right." Horus stopped in front of me. "Keep in mind that there's only one reason I'm about to tell you what I'm about to tell you."

It didn't take a genius to figure it out. If Horemheb was

back, that could only mean the Cult of Set's strength would increase. And if the Cult of Set got stronger, Set got stronger. Horus would never let that happen. To say Horus and Set despised each other would have been putting it mildly. There was this whole thing with a scratched-out-eye and torn-off . . . well, let's just not mention that part, but it had ended horribly.

"Set," I said.

"Set," Horus agreed.

"Horemheb is going to come after you," Horus said. "You know that, right?"

I knew it. He'd made that clear with the obelisk.

"Let him come." I'd finally have revenge.

"You need to be careful."

"I get it," I said. "Just tell me."

"I'm not kidding, Tut."

"Neither am I. And if you don't tell me soon, Gil will be home."

Horus's eyes flicked to the door. "You can't tell him about this, Tutankhamun."

Whoa. Had he really pulled out the full-name thing?

"I won't tell him," I said. "I promise."

Horus fixed his eye on me.

"I promise. I swear."

"Promise made," Horus said, and my chest tightened. When promises were made to the gods, they couldn't be broken.

"What do we do?" I asked.

"So for starters, you'll need power from the *Book of the Dead*. There's a spell you'll need to use."

Every bit of energy in my scarab heart tingled. A spell from the *Book of the Dead*. As had been proven so well back in my tomb, I didn't have the power to use the spells. Only gods did.

"How much power?" If Horus granted me power over the *Book of the Dead*, I could do almost anything except kill someone. *Book of the Dead* spells couldn't be used for death. Horus had only granted me power once before, back during the Crusades. Some ridiculous fight had broken out between the gods and Horus needed me to perform a couple of miracles. In my immortal lifetime, the only thing that felt better than recharging my scarab heart was using the power from the *Book of the Dead*.

"Enough power," Horus said. "You want revenge on Horemheb. And I want to stop Set. I have a plan, but you'll need a spell to make it work."

Energy jumped in my scarab heart. My immortal dreams were about to come true. I'd dreamed about revenge from the moment I discovered Horemheb was part of the Cult of Set. He'd killed my entire family. He had to die.

"Fetch the *Book of the Dead*," Horus said to the shabtis.

Colonel Cody immediately looked to me. "Shall we do as the cat says?"

"He's a god, not a cat," I said.

"Yes," Colonel Cody said. "Shall we do as the god cat says?"

"Absolutely," I said.

"Very good, Great Master," Colonel Cody said, and snapped his fingers.

Four shabtis climbed to the top of the bookcase and returned moments later balancing a giant wooden box covered in gold. Horus insisted we keep the *Book of the Dead* out of reach so no spells would be cast accidentally. The *Book of the Dead* was funny that way. It obeyed the will of the gods, but it also had a mind of its own.

"Open it, Tut."

Horus didn't have to ask me twice. I ran my hands over the engravings on the top, remembering when life had been normal. I'd never thought about revenge back when I'd been pharaoh, because Horemheb had fooled me. I'd never be fooled again.

"How many spells will I have?" I asked, anticipating the power running through me.

"One," Horus said. "It's all you'll need."

"One! You're kidding, right?"

"Why? What were you thinking?"

"Ten." That would be ten chances to fight Horemheb.

Horus put up his paw. "Not a chance, Tut. Ten spells could kill you."

It was easy to forget how much energy using the *Book of the Dead* required. How much it drained me the last time I'd used it. And it wasn't just the draining. It was the way it left me feeling like I wanted more. Needed more. Like I would die if I didn't get it.

"What about seven?"

"You only need one for the plan to work."

"What if something comes up?" I said. "It can't hurt to give me a little more. How about five?" I could handle five.

"Two," Horus said.

"Four."

So we settled on three. Three powerful spells from the gods to do away with my immortal enemy.

I flipped the box open and unrolled the scrolls. And then I braced myself.

Horus dug his claws into my hand. I'd been expecting it, but it still made my toes curl. We needed my blood for the power to transfer to me. I held my hand over the scrolls and let blood drip onto the thick, yellow papyrus. It vanished instantly. And then Horus said the words of power and I repeated them, making sure I didn't get a single one wrong. I'd tell you what they were, except they said things about pulling entrails out and owing debt to the god of feces and stuff like that. Not pretty.

Pain stabbed through my head, and every bit of air was sucked out of my lungs as the energy poured into me. My scarab heart pounded so hard, it felt like it was going to erupt from my chest. I fell to my knees and the shabtis circled me, but Horus hissed at them to keep back. They'd never seen me receive the power of the gods. Colonel Cody would probably want to take his own life for the pain I was going through.

No sooner had I repeated the final word than the pain vanished. I shoved the golden box and scrolls aside. With the power of the *Book of the Dead* running through me, I felt like I could face ten Horemhebs. Twenty. Bring them on.

"Tell me what I need to do," I said. I was ready.

"Right," Horus said. "So there's this knife. The gods know about it, but they don't like to talk about it."

My impression of the gods was that all gossip was good gossip, as far as they were concerned. For them not to talk about something was as rare as the creation of intelligent life.

"A knife? And Gil doesn't know about it?"

"Gil knows," Horus said.

"So what's the problem, then?" I asked. "Why can't I talk to him about it?"

"Because the knife is dangerous," Horus said. "You know how he is. He'd never let you try to find it."

"What kind of knife is it?" I asked. Gil was protective and all, but that seemed extreme.

"The same knife that was used to kill Osiris," Horus said. "A knife that can kill an immortal."

The knife that killed Osiris? I'd never really believed in it. I always thought it was more one of those figurative things. Like a symbol for death instead of an actual object.

"It really exists?" I asked.

"It really exists," Horus said.

"That kind of knife could kill Horemheb," I said. My mind buzzed with the image of me finally getting my revenge.

Horus scowled. "That kind of knife could kill you."

Which explained the secrecy. Gil would freak for sure if he thought I was looking for a weapon with the power to end my existence.

"Where is it?" I asked.

"I don't know," Horus said. "I'm not allowed to know."

"Not allowed to know?" Though I'd never tell him, I kind of thought Horus knew everything.

"Don't ask," Horus said. "Just go to the Library of Congress. You're looking for a scroll. But the scroll is invisible. Use spell number sixty-eight to reveal it. Got that? Spell sixty-eight."

"Sixty-eight," I repeated.

"Do we need to write that down?" Horus said.

That's when the doorbell rang. I wanted to mummify whoever was out there. This wasn't a conversation I wanted interrupted.

"Shall I do away with the intruder, Great Pharaoh?" Colonel Cody asked from under the coffee table.

I shook my head. "No. Go hide somewhere until I get rid of them." And my army of shabtis filed off into the coat closet.

I pulled open the door without bothering to see who it was. Foggy Bottom was a safe neighborhood, and who'd have a chance against an immortal anyway?

"Henry? What are you doing here?" That was the last time I opened the door without looking through the peephole first.

"I thought we could work on our project." Henry dropped his giant backpack to the ground and pulled out a book on King Tut. My shiny golden face stared back at me from the cover.

"Our project?" I couldn't believe he was here. His timing was horrible.

"Yeah, I found us a book. My parents had it at home. Can I come in?" He looked past me, into my sanctuary, and his eyes were filled with amazement.

Horus glared back at him with a scowl like a pirate.

"Uh, yeah, sure, I guess." I moved aside so Henry could get

through the door. And that's when I saw the van in the street—deep red, like it had been painted in blood, with some kind of golden designs on the sides of it. Some guy I'd never seen before with red hair sat in the driver's seat. And in the passenger seat was Seth Cooper, in all his greasy-headed glory. Smiling at me. How did Seth know where I lived? No one knew where I lived. I slammed the door.

"How'd you find out where my town house was?" I asked Henry. It couldn't have been the Internet. Even though it was a huge pain in my butt, I'd removed all references to my present-day self. Or, at least two of the shabtis had done it at my command; Captain Otis and Captain Otto were master hackers.

"That new girl, Tia," Henry said. He made himself at home, dropping his backpack on Gil's favorite chair. His collection of Sharpies spilled out onto the floor.

A small scratching noise came from the closet. The shabtis had to know to stay hidden, didn't they?

"She told you where I live?" I said. How did not only Seth Cooper, but some girl I'd never met before yesterday, know my address? It wasn't even on Google Maps.

"Sure. Why? Is your address secret or something?" Henry started flipped through the King Tut book. It had so many sticky notes at the top that it looked like an accordion.

"Of course not," I said. "Anyway, this isn't the best time."

"It's never a good time for you," Henry said. "Let me guess. You have other plans?"

Talking to my cat about a mythical knife wasn't something I could share. "I was just about to eat dinner."

Henry pulled a couple of grease-stained bags out of his backpack. "I thought of that, so I brought dinner. That way we can crank out this project."

"You got White Castle?" With revenge on my mind, my appetite was extinct.

"There is no substitute," Henry said, putting up his hand to high-five me.

I did a halfhearted high-five in return.

"I almost stayed at White Castle to eat, but they must have some kind of insect problem," Henry said. He glanced around the town house at the scarab beetles running rampant, but managed to stop himself from saying anything about them. "Once they clear up the bug problem, we could go eat there sometime."

These were the kind of comments that made me feel weird. I mean, a year from now, Henry would be fifteen and I'd still be fourteen. Five years from now, Henry would be nineteen and—yep, that's right—I'd still look fourteen.

"Sounds like fun," I heard myself say. It was like a strange part of my brain controlled my voice. I could stop it most of the time, but every once in a while, it would let a comment like that out.

"Great," Henry said. But his eyes weren't on the bag of hamburgers. They roved the room, scanning the walls and tables and . . . well, pretty much every other bit of space. "What's up with all this stuff?"

It's not like I was a hoarder or anything. But after three thousand years I'd gathered my fair share of souvenirs. There were fans and statues and amulets everywhere. Hanging from the walls, resting on every table, stuffed in the drawers.

Horus opened his mouth, and for a split second I thought he was going to talk. Which would have been a disaster. So I kicked a scarab beetle, and like any good cat, Horus followed it and pounced.

"Just treasures," I said, like it was no big deal.

"A feather fan collection?" Henry said.

"Those are real ostrich feathers."

So some of the stuff was junk. And it's not like I got the shabtis to fan me or anything. Well, not too often. But there were some cool things, too. And important things. Like my *Book of the Dead*. Which was still sitting in the middle of the coffee table next to the King Tut book. I prayed Henry wouldn't ask about it. And then I prayed Henry would leave.

He didn't. Instead, he grabbed a sword off the wall. "Are these real teeth?" He held it up, and the teeth hanging from it rattled together.

I nodded. "From Africa. It's really old, so be careful with—"

Before I had a chance to finish, Henry swung it around ninja style, jumped, and landed a few feet away, nearly swiping Horus's tail off.

Horus whirled on him and hissed.

I took the sword from Henry and hung it back on the wall. "It's kind of like a hobby, I guess."

"Sword fighting?"

"Collecting things." Sword fighting had, at some point, been a hobby for me, too, but I opted against mentioning that.

Another shiny object hanging on the wall caught Henry's attention. "You have an antique star chart? Is this real?"

Not only was it real, I'd drawn it myself, hundreds of years ago, after spending decades watching the movement of the planets. The paper had yellowed, even behind the protective glass. I'd have to get it represerved one of these days.

I shrugged. "I don't know. It's just something I picked up at the thrift store."

Henry jabbed a greasy finger onto the glass, and I tried not to cringe. The shabtis were going to be frantic after this visit. "Where's Pluto? It should be right here."

I studied the map to act like I didn't know. "Maybe it hadn't been discovered yet?"

"Dude, you have to add it. I am a huge Pluto fan." Henry had yet another Pluto shirt on. This one read, PLUTO: DWARF PLANET MY A**.

"I figured," I said. "But it's not a planet."

"It should be," he said. "I started this online petition to get it replanetified."

"That's not even a word."

"It will be once the petition gets accepted. You just watch and see." Henry grabbed a hamburger and sat on a faded green camel seat on the other side of the coffee table like he was all settled in to stay for the evening. He took a bite, but a big chunk of the meat fell onto the wood floor. And that's when I heard the closet door rattle.

I ran over and slammed myself against it a millisecond after it started opening. Inside, I heard small scrapings at the door.

Henry stopped mid-chew and stared at the closet. "What's in there?"

"Another cat." I shot Horus a look of pure satisfaction. "I take turns locking them up."

Horus glared back at me and then leapt onto the camel seat next to Henry, staring at Henry with his one good eye until Henry moved.

I opened the closet door a crack. "Do not come out," I ordered in an almost inaudible whisper.

"But master . . . ," Lieutenant Roy said. "Your visitor's food—" He looked like he was about to collapse from the strain of my town house not being immaculate. How did he even know . . . unless he'd left a shabti in the family room as a lookout?

"The food can wait," I said, and then shut the door. When I turned back around, Henry was staring at me.

"Were you talking to someone?" he asked.

"Just the cat. Try not to drop anything else, okay?"

Henry nodded but didn't take his eyes off me as I picked the food up off the floor. And then he grabbed another burger and ate it in one bite.

"So can't we work on this project some other time?" I said. I needed to head to the Library of Congress before Gil got home.

"We're already behind." Henry picked up the giant King Tut book. He was just about to flip it open when Horus pounced on a bug that had crawled up Henry's leg.

"Aaaaaahhhhhh!" Henry screamed. His jeans ripped, and he jumped like he'd been mortally wounded, dropping the book to the floor with a loud boom.

"Horus!" I yelled.

His claws were still attached to Henry's upper leg, but Horus didn't care. With expert precision, he peeled the scarab beetle out of its exoskeleton with his teeth and ate it. And then after a loud crunch, Horus spit the shell out on one of Henry's duct-tape-covered gray Chucks.

The closet door cracked open. I shoved it shut and kicked it. Then I swatted Horus away from Henry's thigh.

Henry collapsed. There was only a little bit of blood. His normally messy hair was a disaster, and his wire-rimmed glasses sat crooked on his nose.

I cringed. "Uh, sorry about that."

"What a horrible cat," Henry said, straightening his skewed glasses.

Horus hissed.

Henry wiped at the blood with his fingers, and his hands shook. Almost getting disemboweled by a cat can do that to you. At least he started to breathe again.

Horus jumped off the futon and headed for the fire escape.

"Wait," I said. Horus had vital information I needed.

Horus rubbed up against a golden cat statue in the corner. I joined him, praying the shabtis wouldn't pick that moment to show themselves.

"How do I find the scroll?" I whispered. I pretended like

I was scratching behind his ears so Henry wouldn't think I was totally crazy.

"Talk to Colonel Cody. I briefed him while you were busy entertaining your guest." He said the word *guest* in the same way he would have said *rodent*. Or *pest*.

"Wait until he leaves," I said. "I'll get rid of him."

Horus rubbed against a catnip toy near the windowsill. "Too late. Gil will be home any minute. And Bast is waiting."

"Bast? Are you kidding?"

"We have a date."

A date! Here I was worried about battles between the gods, and Horus was going on a date?

"It can't wait?" I asked.

"It can't wait." When he wanted to, he could almost disguise his voice like a meow. Either that or I'd lived with a cat for too long. And then he really did meow. This meant our conversation was over.

I gave up. When it came to Bast, Horus completely lost his head.

"Might I say your spots look especially clean tonight," I said. And it was true. Horus was a good-looking cat—an Egyptian Mau. Sleek. Spotted. Regal. Even with the missing eye.

Horus flicked his tail and jumped onto the fire escape and into the night.

Now to get rid of Henry.

"What's Bast?" Henry asked. He'd smoothed his hair back to its normal messy state.

"Not what. Who," I said, hoping he hadn't heard Horus talking in return.

"Okay, who?" Henry said.

"She's this cat Horus goes to see from time to time." I patted the golden cat statue. "She looks like this."

Like lots of other stuff, the statue belonged to Horus. Having an idol of a powerful goddess around couldn't be a bad thing.

"She's shiny," Henry said. "So where are your parents?"

"I live with my brother. But he's out right now."

"Where?"

Great Amun, Henry asked a lot of questions.

I shrugged. "Getting dinner."

Henry eyed the closet door, but it was still closed. "Just you two live here?"

I nodded at the loft, to Gil's bedroom door, which was painted solid black with a giant red X in the middle. My door, on the other hand, was painted gold, at the insistence of Colonel Cody. He'd tried to use real metal, saying it was the only thing befitting a pharaoh, but I convinced him paint was acceptable. "Yep. That's his room."

"Why a red X?"

"It means 'Do Not Enter.' He figured it was a universal sign."

"And do you ever go in when he's not home?" Henry said.

"No."

Henry gave me a you're-full-of-complete-hooey look.

"Okay, fine. A couple times. But don't you dare tell him."

Gil loved his privacy. He'd lock himself in his room and listen to music or play video games for hours. He never even let the shabtis in to clean his room.

"What happened to your parents?" Henry asked.

A lump in my throat formed before I could even think about it, and my scarab heart sped up. This was another reason I didn't want friends. They made you talk about things you'd left behind thousands of years ago. "They're dead."

"Dead," Henry said. "Wow, I'm sorry."

It was one of those awkward moments when neither person knows what to say, so Henry got up and started inspecting one of my feather fans.

"Yeah, it stinks," I finally said. "But that's the way things go." I never had visitors, so I wasn't really sure how to get rid of Henry.

Just then, a shrieking alarm sounded three times. Horus's ward. The door opened, and in came Gil, carrying Chinese food containers.

"Why the ward . . . ?" Gil started, but then he saw Henry. "Who's this?"

At least Henry saved me from having to make up excuses about Horus's ward. He'd accidentally yanked three feathers out of the fan when the alarm went off. I took the fan away from him and set it on the table for repairs. The shabtis would get to it later.

"This is Henry. We're working on a project together," I

said, as I saw Lieutenant Roy make a dash between Henry's feet, grab a beetle shell, and run back out of sight. I held the three errant feathers in my hand. "Henry, meet my brother, Gil Jones."

Gil cracked a grin. "His older, smarter, and better-looking brother." He took off his black jacket and tossed it on the floor, then dropped the Chinese food containers onto the coffee table next to the scrolls and King Tut book. Bits of rice spilled out everywhere. Colonel Cody would probably ask permission to dump beetle shells in Gil's room tomorrow while he was in the shower.

I stifled a groan. "Older for sure. How about more annoying? You left that one out."

"Right. You are more annoying." Gil nodded at the White Castle bag. "Any left?"

"No," I lied. There was only one burger left, and I was hoping to eat it.

Gil grabbed for the bag anyway. "How'd you find out where we lived?"

Suspicion clouded Henry's face. "You guys act like it's some state secret."

"We don't tell a lot of people," Gil said.

"But people already know," Henry said. "Like that new girl."

Gil narrowed his eyes. "What girl?"

"Tia," Henry said. "She just came to our school."

With every word Henry spoke, concern grew on Gil's face. It was time for Henry to go.

"Well, thanks for the food," I said.

"Oh." The smile fell off Henry's face. I felt kind of bad, but seriously, I was immortal, and . . . well . . . Henry wasn't.

"It's getting late," I said. Not like I needed to justify myself.

"Not really," Henry said. "What about our project?"

"Henry could come back tomorrow to work on the project," Gil said.

What was he thinking? Was he trying to encourage people to come over more often? Maybe we should just have a party and reveal to the world that we're immortal.

"Sounds like a plan," Henry said. "So tomorrow, meet back here?"

I decided not to let him get too hopeful. "Tomorrow's bad. We'll have to do it another time." There would be plenty of time for school projects after Horemheb was dead and gone.

"The library should be open again tomorrow. We could meet there after school," Henry said. And then he reached for the coffee table. Right for my *Book of the Dead*. "Hey, what's this?"

I yanked the scrolls out of the way just in time. Henry still had blood on his hand from where Horus had scratched him, and it almost touched the scrolls. That would have been a disaster. We hadn't used the *Book of the Dead* in ages. Power licked off it. It was hungry. Anything could have happened.

"Just a side project I'm working on." That was one way to look at the whole Horemheb thing—a side project to kill him while continuing to lead my normal, immortal life.

"It almost feels like there's heat coming off the paper," Henry said, holding his hand over the top of it.

"It's just hot in here," I said. Ancient magic did have that property. And I was going to use it. Three spells—that had to be enough.

7

WHERE I PLAY TRIVIAL PURSUIT WITH THE GODS

No sooner had the lock clicked behind Henry than the shabtis were out of the closet and cleaning. I was pretty sure Henry wasn't carrying the bubonic plague, but the shabtis didn't let that stop them from disinfecting everything. Lieutenant Roy led the cleanup effort, running frantically from one side of the town house to the other, making sure no spot was left untouched.

"What are the scrolls doing out?" Gil asked. "That could have been a disaster."

I fumbled for words. How was I supposed to explain it to Gil? I couldn't tell him about the spells. Or the knife. What I really needed was for Gil to leave me alone for once so I could sneak out to the Library of Congress.

"Nothing happened. I got the scrolls away before he touched them." I looked down at Lieutenants Virgil and Leon, who bowed, ran off, and then returned in under a minute with a soda and a glass of ice. Gil scowled at them.

"But why were the scrolls out in the first place?" Gil sank down into his favorite chair, which only seconds before had been occupied by Henry's backpack. The chair was older than the Constitution and had more patches than a quilt, but Gil refused to get rid of it.

It was a totally legitimate question. We never took down the *Book of the Dead* from the top of the bookcase. I decided to use my bad luck from earlier as an excuse. "Horus was helping me figure out a way to smite Horemheb. He thought there might be something in the *Book of the Dead*."

"And what did his godliness come up with?" Gil said.

I crossed my arms and pretended to act annoyed, which was easy. I couldn't believe Gil had known there was an immortal-killing knife in existence and had never bothered to tell me. Around my feet, the shabtis lined up in assault formation, as if they'd attack Gil at my command. I did love how they always sided with me no matter what.

"Horus came up empty, didn't he?" Gil said.

"Yep." The lie slipped off my tongue like soda. "Why? Are you sure you don't know of any ways to kill Horemheb?"

I waited, wondering what Gil would say. Maybe he would fess up. We could go after the knife and Horemheb together.

"Nope," Gil finally said.

So much for that dream.

Gil grabbed a video game controller and tossed me a second one.

I wasn't about to spend the rest of the night playing video games with him. I chucked the controller onto the coffee table. "I'm not up for playing."

"You're always up for playing," Gil said.

Maybe before I realized Gil was lying to me. How many other times had Gil lied to me and I had no idea?

"Not tonight," I said. "Too much homework."

It was a lame excuse.

"The shabtis do your homework," Gil said.

"I want to do it tonight."

"Fine. Whatever. Do your homework then." Gil threw his controller onto the futon and stormed off to his room.

No sooner had Gil's red *X*'ed door slammed shut than Colonel Cody ran over to me. He scaled the bookshelf until he was at ear level.

"Great Master," he said. "Quickly. Before the heathen emerges. The Library of Congress."

"Where in the Library of Congress?" I said. The place was bigger than my old palace.

"The cat—" Colonel Cody began.

"Horus," I corrected.

"Yes, the cat, Horus—"

"He's a god," I said.

"Yes, the god cat Horus told us of a secret room," Colonel Cody said. "Among the relics from the Library of Alexandria—"

"That library burned thousands of years ago," I said. "Everything was destroyed."

"No, Great Master," Colonel Cody said. "Many items were saved. And among these items are scrolls created during the reign of the gods. They're kept in a secret room, below the basements."

That didn't surprise me. Everything in D.C. was built on top of something else. There were basements and subbasements and secret passages below those. It was like a giant underskeleton of the city.

"We need to go now." I looked in the direction of Gil's room. Light flickered from under his black door. He was on his computer.

"We must bring the proper scroll." Colonel Cody jumped down from my shoulder and onto the coffee table without making a sound. He rifled through the *Book of the Dead* and grabbed the scroll with spell number sixty-eight, passing it my way. I folded it and tucked it under my shirt.

"Ready?" I asked Colonel Cody.

Colonel Cody snapped his fingers and four shabti majors joined him. "Ready," he said.

"Then we better hurry before Gil notices I'm gone."

I dressed in black so I could blend into the night, and snuck out trailed by five of my shabtis. I hadn't seen Colonel Cody this excited since he'd found me in Egypt back in 1922. Every other block or so, he ordered his majors to halt and drilled them on their weapons' use. I guess a hundred years of cleaning up scarab beetle shells for an ungrateful cat wasn't hard to top. It was past ten, so the streets were empty. Since we were way into October, the air was chilly, but all the energy running through my scarab heart was making me sweat, so I took off my sweatshirt and gave it to some homeless guy on the corner. He was begging next to a row of restaurants. They all had giant signs taped to the door that read:

Closed due to Failed Health Inspection

I'd eaten at most of those places. It was a good thing I never got food poisoning.

We passed by the obelisk near the Convention Center. Since the one at Dupont Circle had exploded, there were only four left. I almost reached my fingers out and touched it, just for a little bit of the scarab heart energy that ran through it, but I stopped myself. Had the Cult of Set really built them? I didn't want it to be true because they were so perfect, but as much as I hated to admit it, Horus was rarely wrong.

"We must go, Great Master," Colonel Cody said.

He was right. I wasn't here to recharge my scarab heart. It was pumped full of energy anyway. What I needed was to find out where the knife was. I turned my back on the obelisk and continued on until the Library of Congress came into view.

Spotlights shined on the library, illuminating the massive stone building in all its literary magnificence. Marble steps led to the front doors, but iron gates had been drawn closed for the night. I knew it was way past visiting hours, because I'd spent thousands of hours at the library. Not researching projects for school—I researched the world. I read history books to see what was fact and what was fiction. Because that was the thing about history—nothing you read could be believed. Like, for example, everything from my reign. History had me on the throne until I was nineteen. Nineteen! I'd been cheated out of five good years. The books didn't say anything about Horemheb casting me from the throne or colluding with the Cult of Set, either. All they focused on was the gold. And the "boy king" thing. I hated that.

The shabtis could easily have picked the locks on the iron gates, but every alarm in the place would have gone off. I'd never get to the secret room that way.

Colonel Cody snapped his fingers, and shadows cloaked the five shabtis. They couldn't turn invisible or ever change the colors they were painted, but they could bend light around themselves so normal people wouldn't notice them. And I thought being able to grow carnivorous plants was cool.

"Shall we enter first and eliminate the security?" Colonel Cody asked. He raised his hand to snap his fingers again.

"No! We aren't going to kill the guards." The shabtis did pretty much everything I wanted them to do and sometimes things I didn't. "No one gets killed. Or seriously injured. Okay?"

Colonel Cody lowered his arm. His majors relaxed their stance, but stood ready to move at his next order.

"Okay?" I said again.

Colonel Cody nodded. "Fine. No one gets killed. I swear it on the mummified body of Osiris himself."

"Or seriously injured," I added.

"Or seriously injured," he repeated.

Good. Now that we had that settled, I could break into the library.

"Where's the entrance to this secret room?" I asked.

"The cat referred to a statue," Colonel Cody said.

Nice lead, except D.C. had more statues than an old dog had warts.

"Which statue?"

"The cat said it would be where the king sits."

"What king? Osiris?" If Horus hadn't been in such a hurry to head off on his date, he could have told me himself. As far as I knew, there were no statues of Osiris anywhere near the Library of Congress. Or in D.C., for that matter.

Colonel Cody's face turned ashen. "The cat said you would know."

King. Statue. King. Statue . . .

I scanned the area, looking for anything that fit. There were a couple of naked women on horses. I diverted my eyes. There were some turtles and snakes and fish. Hardly kingly creatures. And then there was the giant statue of Neptune right in the middle of a fountain.

That was it. Neptune! He was king of the sea. Maybe not a king that Horus would consider an equal, but given the surroundings, he was the closest thing.

I waded in the water and gazed up at the giant statue of Neptune. It stood over twice as tall as me and was carved from a single piece of marble. He commanded the world from the top of a rock and was flanked by two of his minions. I climbed the rock and grabbed the statue's arms and fingers, looking for a lever or something that might reveal an entrance.

Nothing happened.

I prodded at the statue. Still nothing. And then, from under the surface of the dark water, glittering gold caught my eye. I held my breath and put my head under.

Engraved in the base of the statue and etched with gold was the Eye of Horus.

It was the most sacred representation of Horus, symbolizing what he gave up in his eternal fight with Set, or some nonsense like that. I got sick of seeing it everywhere. Horus had it plastered on all sorts of stuff back at the town house, like he was marking his territory. He must be marking his territory here, too.

I pressed my thumb into the eyeball. That was the standard way to open secret passages in tombs. Neptune and his minions slid backward, creating a chasm in the ground.

Water poured into the opening, cascading downward. It gushed by my feet, pulling at the material of my jeans. I held onto the rock base of the statue as the fountain emptied. When it finally all drained, I could see a stairway descending into the darkness.

"So that's how you get in," someone said.

I whipped around and came face-to-face with Tia.

"You!" I said. "What are you doing here?"

Tia was decked out in a bright-orange workout shirt, cargo pants and, of course, her combat boots. I wondered if she slept with them on. Her orange hair streak matched her shirt, and the number of necklaces she wore had doubled. I was surprised she wasn't hunched over from their weight.

"Why are you following me?" she said, crossing her arms. The sweet aroma of lotus blossoms filled the air, reminding me of perfume girls used to wear back in ancient Egypt.

"Following you! You're following me." I tried to ignore her scent. It brought back too many memories I kept hidden in the deepest part of my mind. Happy times, back before the priests and Horemheb revolted against me.

"Please. Don't flatter yourself." Tia started down the staircase.

"What do you think you're doing?" I asked.

"Seeing what's below," Tia said.

"But . . ."

"Are you coming or not?" she said.

I followed her inside, and pretty soon the darkness swallowed us. I would've used my scarab heart to light up the passageway if I wasn't trying to keep my immortality a secret. But Tia was more prepared than a Girl Scout. She pulled a flashlight from one of the pockets of her cargo pants and flipped it on.

"You told Henry where I live," I said. "How do you even know where I live?"

I felt a tug on the leg of my jeans. I didn't dare look. Colonel Cody knew to stay hidden, since the shabtis were under direct orders to hide from mortals. That didn't mean he didn't look for creative ways around those orders.

"I know all sorts of things about you, Tut," Tia said, making finger quotes when she said my name, causing her multitude of bracelets to jingle.

"Like what?" My scarab heart started to pump blood at the rate of a jackhammer. I needed to get control of myself.

"Well, for starters, you're Tut," she said. There went the finger quotes again, and with them, a fresh wave of her awesome perfume.

"And you're Tia. So what? You know my name." I pushed away her lotus blossom scent and kept going. The stairs went on forever. I'd counted over a hundred so far.

"Everyone knows your name," she said.

Okay, this is the part where my sensors went up. I mean, sure, everyone in the world did know my name—Tutankhamun. But nobody in the world besides Horus and Gil knew that the King Tut from ancient Egypt was actually me.

"You mean like everyone at school?" I said.

Tia laughed out loud. "Yeah, everyone at school—when they read about you in a textbook."

I sucked in a breath and held it. After three thousand years, I was a master of hidden identities. My spells had never failed.

"I don't know what you're talking about." I summoned the scent of herbs and started inaudibly intoning the spell I used to hide my identity.

Tia ignored me. "You know, I thought you'd be taller."

Holy Osiris, I got sick of people calling me short. "I'm only fourteen," I said, and I kept pushing the spell her way.

"All those statues in the museum make you look taller," Tia said. "I have to admit, I like your hair this way. It looks way better than those portraits you see in books." She stopped walking and pulled a piece of my hair from behind my ear.

I figured I'd died and gone to the Fields of the Blessed right then and there. Amun above, I had to focus. I couldn't go around having people know who I was.

"Who do you think I am, anyway?" I asked. I doubled my spell attempts.

Tia crossed her arms, making the flashlight bounce against the side wall, revealing all sorts of paintings of cats and falcons. "Duh."

Which didn't answer the question I already knew the answer to.

"What's it like to be immortal, anyway?" she asked.

I balled my hands into fists. "It's not working."

"What?"

"The spell. You're supposed to forget who I am." I knew this sounded absurd, but I didn't care. Had Horus giving me power from the *Book of the Dead* done something to my normal Osiris-given spells?

Tia narrowed her eyes. "You're trying to put a spell on me?"

Not the best way to strengthen a relationship, but that had never stopped me in the past.

"Maybe?" I said.

Fire lit up her blue eyes. "Keep your spells to yourself."

I met her eyes with fire in my own. "Then tell me how you know."

"You never told me what it's like to be immortal, King Tut," Tia said.

That was it. I gave up on the spell entirely. And an enormous weight lifted off me. For the first time in forever, I could admit my identity. My life was so much about pretending to be someone else. Someone normal and mortal. But every once in a while, I just wanted to be the real Tut.

I put my hand on the wall and, just to make sure my normal powers still worked, I made moss grow on it, covering the image of a cat that looked a lot like Horus. Really, I could make anything grow out of anywhere. Roses out of bricks. Weeds in people's gardens. My powers worked perfectly, which meant there was nothing wrong with my identity-hiding spells. So why weren't they working on Tia?

"Truthfully?" I said.

"No, I want you to lie," Tia said. "Of course, truthfully."

"Okay, truth is that sometimes it gets a little boring, but overall, it's awesome."

"What do you do with all your time?" she said as we continued downward. Lights flickered far below, like maybe there was an end to our descent. "You've been around for thousands of years, right?"

I still couldn't believe I was really talking about this. It was almost as if I'd been wanting to tell her about my life.

"I do everything," I said. "All great moments of history—I've witnessed them. The Crusades. The assassination of Julius Caesar. The building of the Great Wall of China."

"That doesn't sound even kind of boring." She tilted her head, and I couldn't help but notice the smooth skin of her neck. Great Isis, I was acting like I'd never talked to a girl before. What was wrong with me?

"Sure, when I mention the highlights. But trust me, thirty-three hundred years is a long time. I've had to get pretty creative to keep from going insane."

"Oh, really?" she said.

I reached back to the wall, but instead of making moss grow, I sprouted a lotus blossom from a crack in the stones. Once the flower reached full bloom, I plucked it and handed it to her. Her eyes widened as she took it, but then she only gave a little shrug. And here I thought it was a pretty cool trick.

"Stop showing off," she said. But I noticed she tucked the flower behind the orange streak in her hair.

Yes, I was showing off, just a little.

We descended the last few steps until we reached the bottom, ending up in a circular room about the size of my kitchen. Paintings and engravings of Horus covered the walls, showing him in both his falcon and cat forms gloriously ruling over the world. Ahead of us was a closed door with some sort of complex locking mechanism shaped in the eye of Horus. This whole place was like a monument to him. I knew Horus was vain, but this was ridiculous. He was never going to hear the end of it when I got back home.

I had no clue how to get the door open. Ten metal bars interlocked with one another, sealing it shut. My identity had already been blown. I figured there was no harm in announcing my shabtis.

I looked down. "Colonel Cody?"

"It is my deepest honor, Great Pharaoh," Colonel Cody said, emerging from the shadows.

"Great Pharaoh?" Tia said. "You're kidding me, right?"

I shrugged and tried to act normal, even though my face had to be bright red.

The other four shabtis shifted enough that the light caught their reflection. Then, forming some sort of cheerleading pyramid, with two on the bottom and two in the middle, they made a tower with Colonel Cody at the top.

"Look at them," Tia said. "They're so cute!"

Cute? They were fierce and awesome.

"Thank you, beautiful mortal girl." Colonel Cody beamed under her praise.

I'll give him credit for being perceptive.

The shabti majors poked and prodded different parts of the lock until, like some choreographed dance, the long metal bars pulled away, one by one. When the last piece of metal grinded to a halt the door slid open, revealing a tunnel lit with torches on the wall. Tia clicked her flashlight off and stuffed it back in the pocket of her cargo pants.

We started down the long tunnel ahead.

"Now tell me why you're really here," I said. No way was it some crazy fluke that Tia just happened to be hanging out at the Library of Congress after hours. She was following me.

"Why are you here?" Tia asked. The rubber soles of her combat boots slapped on each step, echoing in the silence while I tried to figure out what to say.

"Research for our project," I finally said.

"What a coincidence," Tia said. "Me, too."

"Yeah, right."

"You don't believe me? I'm offended, Tut."

"Be offended all you want," I said. "And you never told me how you knew who I was."

Tia kept pace next to me, and I noticed she was about the same height as I was. Maybe I was short. Or maybe she was tall.

"It doesn't matter," she said.

"Of course it matters."

"Why?"

There were about a million reasons. I listed them off on my fingers. "Because nobody knows who I am. Because I've never met you before this week. Because everything was just fine until you showed up."

"What's not fine?" Tia asked.

I stopped myself before mentioning Horemheb. The truth was that I knew nothing about Tia. I had no intention of trusting her. "Nothing. Everything's fine. Except that I don't believe a word you're saying."

"Good," Tia said. "That means you're smarter than I gave you credit for." But then she ruined it by adding, "Great Pharaoh."

I let it slide.

"What do you think about the gods?" Tia said, and she started fiddling with her necklaces, which were in a giant tangle.

"What do you mean, what do I think about them? They're gods."

"What do you think about all the fighting they do?" she asked.

"How do you know anything about the gods of Egypt and whether they fight or not?" I asked. Mythology, according to most of the world, was a bunch of made-up nonsense. Maybe I should just assume that Tia was not like most of the world. It might be a good starting point in figuring out who she really was.

Tia kept untangling her necklaces. They'd gotten into a giant jumble. I wasn't sure her attempts to straighten them were helping. "From all the stories. All they ever do is fight."

"Like you," I said. "Did you really get kicked out of private school for fighting?"

"Maybe I did," Tia said. "And maybe I didn't."

It was one more non-answer from her to add to the growing list.

"The gods have created an art out of bickering," I said. "It's just what they do."

"But do you ever wonder what would have happened if they didn't fight constantly?" Tia asked. "Do you ever think about how different history would have been?"

No, I never wondered. Fighting was just something the gods did. Sort of like how breathing was something people did.

"For starters, I wouldn't be here," I said. After all, the whole reason I was immortal was because of the battle between Set and Osiris. Same with Horemheb. Which brought my need for revenge back to the forefront. "Anyway, there's nothing you can do to change the gods."

"Yeah, I know," Tia said. But she almost looked sad about the whole thing.

We continued on in total silence, because I couldn't think of a response. And then I didn't have to, because we came to an arched opening.

"Tut!"

Lights blasted through the archway. We stepped inside.

"You've got to be kidding me," I said.

"Not kidding at all," someone said. And the next thing I knew, I was wrapped in a hug that would have crushed me, if I hadn't been immortal, by a guy with the head of a falcon.

Right. Head of a falcon. It was Qeb, which was short for some really long name nobody could ever pronounce. He was one of Horus's sons. Horus had four sons, and apparently we'd just found two of them.

"Let go, Qeb," I managed to say, even though my lungs had been squashed to the size of walnuts.

"Hey, who's your girlfriend?" Imsety said, swaggering over

to join us. He was the only one of Horus's sons to have a normal head, although it was completely swollen with how much he thought of himself. Aside from Qeb and his falcon head, Horus's other two sons had jackal and baboon heads.

"She's not my girlfriend," I said once Qeb let me go.

"Seriously not his girlfriend," Tia said.

Wait . . . was there some reason she wouldn't want to be my girlfriend? It's not like I was a hideous monster.

"Tia, meet Qeb and Imsety," I said. "But no matter what you do, don't trust a word they say. It will only get you in trouble."

"The last time was your fault," Imsety said. "We've been over that. You're the one who didn't stick to the plan."

I couldn't argue. There was this whole thing about a dare and a cemetery at night and Horus's favorite catnip toy. Horus had blamed me for everything. It had taken fifty years to get him back on my good side.

"But the five times before that, you guys got me in trouble," I said. It seemed like every time I ran into these two, we caused some near catastrophe.

"Is Gil still the same stick-in-the-mud he's always been?" Imsety asked.

Oh, yeah—Gil and Imsety hated each other. It was time for a change of subject. "What are you guys doing here, anyway?"

"Our job," Qeb said. "What does it look like?"

From the looks of the giant screen on the wall and the remote controls in their hands, I figured their job must be playing Mario Kart. The place looked like a bachelor pad decorated with pizza boxes and soda cans. There were a couple of sofas, a pub table, and five different gaming consoles.

"What exactly is your job?" Tia asked.

Imsety flashed a giant smile that was so completely cheesy, I couldn't believe it. I almost expected him to say, "I'm sorry. I can't hear you over the sound of how awesome I am." Instead he said, "Well, you see, our dad is Horus. You may have heard of him. He's a pretty important god. Anyway, he needed some very important guardians. And seeing as how we're so dependable and trustworthy . . ."

I let that part slide. At least I knew I was in the right place.

"Enough," I said. "We get it. If you'll just point us in the direction of the secret room you're guarding, we'll get on our way."

"No can do, little Tut," Qeb said.

"Must you always called me 'little Tut'?" I asked. I thought, after not seeing these guys for a century, they'd have gotten past that.

"It's a cute nickname," Tia said. There she went with that cute thing again. "Little Tut."

"Whatever," I said. "Where's the room?"

"You have to gain entry first," Qeb said.

"Who says?" I asked.

"Duh. The gods," Imsety said.

"Right. And you guys always listen to the rule of the gods." Never mind that they were gods themselves. Horus's sons, aside from Hapi, weren't top on the list of rule followers. I couldn't believe Horus had assigned them down here. It must have been pretty slim pickings.

"We're official rule followers now," Qeb said.

He looked like he actually believed himself.

"Fine. What do I have to do?" I figured maybe I'd have to go on some mighty quest or something. But if that's what it took to get the knife, then so be it.

Qeb clapped his hands, and lights I hadn't known existed sprang on, illuminating three ankh symbols that were taller than I was. The one on the left was a blue so deep, it looked like it was made of lapis lazuli. I wasn't going to comment on it, but it was the exact same blue as Tia's eyes. Imsety would never let me hear the end of it if I made some comment like that. The one on the right was purple crystal, like an amethyst. And the one in the middle, which was twice as tall as the other two, was made of pure gold.

Tia reached forward to touch one, but Imsety yanked her arm back.

"Careful!" he said. "It'll kill you if you touch it."

"Kill me?" She glared at me like somehow it was my fault she'd almost died.

"I told you not to trust them," I said, shooting Imsety a scowl. "What happens if I touch them? They won't kill me."

Qeb shoved his brother out of the way. "No, they won't kill you. You're supposed to play a game with them. And if you win the game, you unlock the Hall of Artifacts."

"Oooh, Hall of Artifacts. That sounds so serious," I said.

"Of course it does," Qeb said. "We're all about serious these days. Remember, we developed responsibility."

I still wasn't buying it, but arguing about it wasn't the point of this adventure. "Okay, how do I play?"

Imsety raised three fingers. "Answer three out of five questions correctly. Each correct answer unlocks one of the ankhs."

"That sounds easy enough," I said. "I'm ready."

Imsety tossed his head back and laughed, like my arrogance was out of line. I was starting to remember why he and Gil never got along. "Don't you want to know about incorrect answers?" he asked.

I shook my head. "I won't get any wrong."

He continued talking like I hadn't said a word. "First wrong answer is a freebie. Because everyone always gets at least one wrong. Second wrong answer and we shave your head."

My hand went to my hair before I could stop it. I loved my hair. After a decade, it was finally the exact length I wanted, just barely below my ears. "That's never going to happen."

"Do you have a better suggestion?" Qeb asked.

I reminded myself that these were gods we were talking about. They ripped out eyes and tore off body parts. Maybe shaving my head wasn't such a sacrifice. There were other decades. It would grow back. Things could definitely be worse. And I needed the knife.

"Go on," I said.

"Okay, then, on your third wrong answer, you get banished to another plane of existence," Imsety said.

I had no intention of getting banished anywhere. Or of

getting my head shaved. I intended to win. "Can we get on with this? It's getting late."

"Thought you'd never ask." Imsety flexed his fingers outward until they cracked. "Let's start with question number one."

A Canopic jar as round as a fishbowl magically appeared on the pub table next to him. He pulled a slip of papyrus from inside the jar and unfolded it. "Animal, vegetable, or mineral?"

Kids always played this game. "Mineral," I said, just because it was the least chosen answer.

"Correct," Imsety said, and the blue ankh shimmered and faded away. He crumpled the papyrus into a ball and tossed it at Qeb, hitting him in his falcon head.

"Wait, that was the real question?"

"Don't get cocky, Boy King," Imsety said. "They aren't all that easy. Question two." He pulled a second piece of papyrus from the oversized Canopic jar.

"Let's have it," I said.

Imsety unfolded the piece of papyrus. "How many planets are in the solar system?" he read.

I laughed out loud as images of Henry's Pluto T-shirts came to mind. I didn't care what Henry said. Pluto was not a planet.

"Eight," I said, slouching back with my arms crossed. This was going to be a piece of cake. I could smell victory.

Imsety scratched his head. "This says nine."

I yanked the piece of papyrus from his hand and crumpled it myself. "That's because it probably hasn't been updated. There are only eight planets."

Imsety narrowed his eyes at me. "I don't know. The quiz is never wrong." He looked to Tia and Qeb for some sort of confirmation.

Tia pouted. "I really want to see Tut with his head shaved."

Qeb put his hands up. "Dude, I know Pluto is a planet."

"Oh, come on, Tia," I said. "Back me up, here."

She put her hands on her hips. "Fine. There are only eight planets now. Pluto got demoted back in 2006. It's officially a dwarf planet."

The purple ankh shimmered and also vanished like the blue one had.

"No way," Qeb said. "That's not fair. I always loved Pluto. How could they demote it?"

"You guys need to get out more often," I said. I could almost imagine Qeb and Henry getting together to mourn Pluto over a spiced latte.

"Horus told us we can't leave," Qeb said.

"Then maybe watch the news?"

"We've thought about it," Imsety said. "But then Qeb will challenge me to a game, and no way can I back down from a challenge."

I could understand the logic.

"Okay, that's two right," I said. "Last one."

Imsety grabbed a third slip of papyrus and unfolded it. "What's your favorite color?"

"Blue," I said with no hesitation.

"Wrong," Imsety said, crumpling the papyrus and tossing it over his shoulder.

"What do you mean, wrong? It's my favorite color. I'm pretty sure I know what my favorite color is."

Imsety shrugged. "Sorry, little Tut. The quiz doesn't agree."

I grabbed the piece of papyrus from the ground and smoothed it out.

"Gold," I read aloud. "But that's not really a color. I mean not a traditional color. I figured you were talking about the colors of the rainbow."

Imsety buffed his fingernails on his sleeve, like this whole trivia game was some sort of minor distraction. "At no point did I specify any restrictions on the color. You got it wrong. That's your freebie."

I rolled my eyes. "Whatever. Just read the next question."

"With pleasure," Imsety said. "And remember, this time we shave your head."

"I'm not going to get it wrong."

I hoped.

He pulled a fourth piece of papyrus from the Canopic jar. After this one, there was only one piece left. He unfolded it and smoothed it out.

"Pieces of what dead king are buried in five sacred spots around Washington, D.C.?" he read.

Pieces of a dead king? I had no idea. Sure, there were tons of dead people buried around the District, but as far as I knew, none of them were kings who had been dismembered and scattered around. I ran my fingers through my hair. Sweat sprang onto my forehead. Imsety and Qeb would really shave my head. Of that I had no doubt. But if I got this wrong, I'd only have one chance left to get into the Hall of Artifacts. The trivia quiz may have been stupid, but I still had to win.

"Can you . . ." I started, thinking I could stall by asking for a clue.

"Seti the First," Tia said. "That's simple. The new obelisks are built on top of the burial sites."

Imsety crumpled the papyrus. "That's cheating. Your girlfriend can't answer for you."

"Not his girlfriend," Tia said, pointing to herself. "Remember?"

He tossed the balled-up papyrus at me. I ducked out of the way.

"It doesn't count," Imsety said. "Which means you have only one chance left."

I wasn't about to complain. I hadn't known the answer, and this way, I still had a head of hair.

"Bring it on," I said. "I'm ready."

"No cheating this time," Qeb said.

Tia made a pretend motion of zipping her mouth and tossing away a key.

Imsety pulled the final piece of papyrus from the Canopic jar. "Last question. What's the . . ." he started. "Oh, come on. This is way too easy."

I deserved something easy. My quest for vengeance was noble and just. Horemheb had to be eliminated.

"Read it."

"Fine," Imsety said. "What's the volume of a pyramid? Seriously? That's like basic pharaoh training one-oh-one."

"Darn right it is," I said. I'd learned about the great pyramids of Giza when I was six years old. My tutors had drilled me, making sure I could do all the calculations in my head. I silently sent them a prayer of thanks. "Area of the base times the height divided by three."

Imsety ripped the slip of papyrus in half and threw it to the ground. "I cannot believe we didn't even get to shave your head."

After the questions, I couldn't, either.

"Maybe next time," I said. "Not."

The final ankh—the golden one in the center—shimmered and twisted upward, pulling the entire wall with it. A dark room lay ahead. I'd won.

"Guess I won," I said.

"Well played," Qeb said. "I thought we had you there with that dead king thing."

I thought so, too, but I didn't dare voice it. The gods could play by any rules they wanted. I didn't want them to retract my victory.

"Yeah, not everyone knows about Seti the First being cut into pieces and buried under the obelisks," Imsety said. "Our dad told you, didn't he?"

Horus had never mentioned anything of the sort. I had no clue the obelisks had been built on top of Pharaoh Seti the First's body parts. Who knew?

"Yep," I lied. "You know Horus."

Full of more secrets than Imsety was full of hot air.

"You should stop by more often, little Tut," Qeb said, mussing my hair, which I was very happy to still have.

"You should drop by the town house sometime," I said. "Horus would love to see you."

"That's debatable," Qeb said. It was so hard to read what he was really thinking with that falcon head of his.

"Sure he would. Just not on the new moon." If Qeb dropped by then, Horus might kill him. Let's put it this way: new moons and Horus? Not the best of friends. During the new moon, Horus went totally blind. Not just missing-one-eye blind, but couldn't see out of the other one either. And when Horus was blind, Horus was dangerous. And pretty much crazy. He'd tried to scratch both my eyes out one time. Gil had almost pulled Horus's claws out, he'd been so mad. That had been a thousand years ago, and ever since, Horus disappeared for a few days around the new moon.

Qeb clacked his falcon beak, which made me guess he was laughing. "Right. I almost forgot about that."

I never forgot about it. The image of my eyeballs clawed out made it impossible to forget.

Ahead of us, the dark room beckoned. I couldn't risk losing entry.

"Come on." I grabbed Tia's hand and pulled her through the open doorway. And then the door lowered behind us. We were swallowed in darkness.

8

WHERE THE SHABTIS DRAW BLOOD

It's dark in here," Tia said not two seconds after the ankh door lowered behind us.

Even though I knew it was showing off, I let light erupt from my scarab heart before she could grab her flashlight. Unlit torches lined the walls.

"Sort of a cool trick," she said, "but watch this." She reached into her cargo pants pocket, and I figured she was going to grab her flashlight, but instead, she pulled a pack of matches out. I wondered what else she had stashed in her pockets. Maybe a midnight snack?

Tia lit a match and touched it to a torch. Suddenly the entire wall was on fire. One torch lit the next and then the next, as if somehow they were all connected. The room exploded with light.

It looked like a museum had been teleported inside. Gold columns—like real gold, not paint from the craft store—stretched from floor to ceiling. Statues and paintings covered every inch of wall. And shelves started just feet from where we stood and continued on, out of sight. Maybe all this stuff had come from the Library of Alexandria, and maybe at one point, it had even been catalogued. But the time of that was long gone. If Imsety and Qeb were in charge of neatness and orderliness, they'd given up ages ago.

"What are these?" Tia used the toe of her combat boot to prod a pile of stone tablets that were leaning against a column.

The symbols carved into the tablets were from back when Gil had been king of Mesopotamia, way before my time. "Sumerian accounting records."

Tia brushed her hand over one, and dust flew everywhere. "Shouldn't they be on display somewhere?"

"Do you have any idea how many tablets like this there are in the world?" I said. "The Sumerians kept track of everything."

"Can you read them?"

"Of course I can read them," I said.

"What's this one say?" she asked.

"Something about how many camels were traded for grain."

"And this one?"

"Marriage records."

"This one?"

"Are you testing me?"

"Not at all." She left the stack of tablets and moved on to some limestone blocks near the side wall. "Okay, what's this?"

It wasn't Sumerian at all. It was from my kingdom—Egypt. It only took me one look at the hieroglyphics to know what we were looking at. "The tomb of Ay. I mean, it's not put together or anything, but most of the pieces are here."

"Didn't Ay rule after you?"

She knew about Egyptian gods. I guess she knew her Egyptian history, too.

"I don't want to talk about who ruled after me," I said.

"Why not?" Tia said.

"Because he should have never been pharaoh," I said. "I was pharaoh."

"But you're immortal," Tia said. "Isn't that better?"

"It's debatable. Anyway, just stay here, okay? I don't want you looking over my shoulder."

"You can't get rid of me, Tut." Tia crossed her arms and waited, slouching in the most adorable way, while tapping the toe of her combat boot. Her streak of orange hair fell over her forehead, making it look like she was winking at me, even though I knew she wasn't.

"Yes, I can," I said. I could . . . okay, my options were nil. It wasn't like I could come back another night when she wasn't here. I needed to find the scroll to get information on the knife tonight. Tia wouldn't know what it was for, anyway.

"Just stay out of my way."

"I knew you'd give in," Tia said. She brushed the orange streak from her face, making it obvious she wasn't winking at me. She was gloating.

"I did not give in." I leaned down to ground level. "What did Horus say?" I asked Colonel Cody.

"The cat informed us to look for an invisible scroll made of gold with ink of blood," Colonel Cody said.

"You named your cat Horus?" Tia asked.

"Sort of."

It was time for spell number sixty-eight. The spell to reveal all things. I pulled the scroll from the *Book of the Dead* out from under my shirt and pressed out the wrinkles.

"The doors of the sky are open for me . . ." I began.

My scarab heart started to pound, pulsing the energy through my body. I drew on this energy. I continued the words from the spell, and the energy doubled. Tripled. It took everything I had to keep saying the words and to not get lost in how amazing the energy running through me felt.

As the last words of the spell fell from my lips, the energy gathered together and shot out of me, forming a trail. I tucked the page from the *Book of the Dead* back under my shirt and followed the trail, passing tablets and tombs and sarcophagi until I came to a marble table covered in scrolls. There was no question about it—the spell had led me to this table. I reached my hand out, moving it along the trail. It brushed against something that wasn't there; something invisible.

I wrapped my fingers around the object and it winked into existence. It was shiny gold carved with symbols painted in red—bloodred.

"You found it!" Tia said.

The trail and energy evaporated, and the piece of power

from the *Book of the Dead* that I'd just used was ripped from me. Even though I'd only had it for a matter of hours, it felt like a part of me had been stolen away. I only had two spells left.

"Yeah, look at that. I found it."

"How did you do it?" she asked.

I almost told her about Horus and the *Book of the Dead*. Almost, except something told me to keep my mouth shut.

"Just a spell I looked up at home," I said. "It's no big deal."

"Right, no big deal. So open it." Tia grabbed for the scroll.

"No." I pulled it away. I could look later, once she wasn't around.

"Yes," she said.

"No."

"Fine. Be that way," Tia said. And she pouted. And even though it killed me to admit it, she looked really cute when she pouted. So cute that all my senses must have escaped me. The next thing I knew, she'd grabbed the scroll from under my arm and unrolled it. I tried to grab it back, but I didn't want to tear it. Plus, my curiosity and desire for revenge took over, so I knelt down next to her.

The scroll was blank.

"Shouldn't there be writing?" Tia asked.

I looked to Colonel Cody. "Well?"

He facepalmed. "The cat said it would be revealed to the worthy."

"Revealed how?" Darn Horus for his half-truths and riddles. I was worthy.

"The cat did not say," Colonel Cody said.

Perfect. I figured I could take it with me back to the town house and decipher it there . . . until I saw the giant sign overhead. Written in ten different languages, including English and ancient Egyptian, were the words:

ARTIFACTS MAY NOT
UNDER ANY CIRCUMSTANCES
BE REMOVED FROM THE
HALL OF ARTIFACTS.
VIOLATORS WILL BE THROWN
INTO STASIS
FOR ALL ETERNITY!

There was a good chance it was an empty threat put in place by Imsety and Qeb, but I didn't want to risk it. Spending my immortal years in Egyptian god purgatory would ruin my plans for revenge.

"Didn't your cute little bodyguard say something about ink made of blood?" Tia asked.

Colonel Cody beamed under her praise. "The beautiful mortal girl is correct."

Tia blushed in return.

"Perhaps blood, Great Master." Colonel Cody snapped his fingers and the two green shabtis I called Major Rex and Major Mack ran off, returning moments later with a pointy tool of some kind that looked sharp enough to puncture my eardrum.

It couldn't hurt. Well, actually it could, but not that much.

Major Rex pierced my finger, and I let a drop of blood fall onto the golden scroll.

I prayed to Maat that I would be found worthy. I had to read the scroll.

Words began to take shape. *Immortal. Afterworld. Knife. Osiris.* My heart pounded. This was exactly what I'd been looking for.

Hieroglyphs of blood filled the page in front of us. Based on the style of writing and the usage of the hieroglyphs, I would have bet Horus's other eye that this scroll had been made before I'd been pharaoh. Probably before my entire dynasty. The symbol choices looked like the stuff Horus decorated his cat-scratching post with. Like the language of the gods.

Wind whipped through the room, blowing the flames in the torches. I let my mind carry me back to the ancient days—the days when Egypt had been the jewel of the world and the gods had been feared. Now they were hardly believed in, just a thing of mythology. I scanned the symbols and my brain instantly fell back into ancient Egyptian, picking out symbols that made up words.

"What's it say?" Tia asked.

That's right. I had serious doubts anyone alive could read this thing except me.

"I don't know," I lied. "The script is too old."

Except I could read every word, and it told me exactly what I needed to know.

"You read those Sumerian tablets," Tia said. "You can read anything."

"Nope. Sorry." Sure, I wanted to defend myself. To tell her I could not only read this scroll, but that I could translate our whole World Cultures textbook into this text. But my common sense held its ground.

"You're lying," Tia said. And she grabbed the scroll and ran.

I tore off after her. She ran in the opposite direction that we'd come in, almost like she knew where she was going, weaving in and out of the long rows of artifacts.

"Stop!" I called, but of course she didn't listen.

I jumped over Canopic jars and obelisks and statues and columns, trying to catch up. Tia rounded a corner and I lost sight of her.

"Where did she go?" I asked Colonel Cody.

"We'll find her," he said. He snapped his fingers and his majors ran off in four different directions.

It wasn't until I heard the snap of wood that I saw her, halfway up a rickety flight of stairs against a wall. It was another way out. Except she had the scroll. The warning from the sign flew back into my mind.

"Don't take the scroll with you!" I cried out, but either she didn't hear me or she didn't listen, because the second she got to the top and opened the door, the entire Hall of Artifacts quaked like a sonic boom had come through. I ducked as objects flew through the air from the impact. And when I looked back up, the door stood open, but there was no sign of Tia or the scroll.

9

WHERE I'M STALKED
BY THE PIZZA GUY

I ran out the same way as Tia, but there was no sign of her. I didn't want her to be cast into stasis for all of eternity, like the sign had said, but I also didn't want her to have escaped with the scroll. Both options stunk. I spent the next two hours scouring D.C. for her, dreading having to tell Horus what had happened. I didn't find her. At least if she did get away, she couldn't read the scroll. And now I knew where the knife was.

Isis had it. I cringed at the thought of visiting her. The last time I'd visited Isis, she'd tried to pull a piece of my brain out with a hook. Some mummification experiment she'd been working on, and she needed a live sample. When I'd protested, she'd laughed, calling me a ninny-faced girly-man. That had been over a hundred years ago. I had no idea where she was now, but Horus would know. Isis was his mom, after all. But he was still out on his date when I got back to the town house, and in the three hours remaining until morning rolled around, he didn't return.

Gil woke up bleary eyed, just as I was leaving for school.

"Did you go somewhere last night?" he asked.

I'd crept in. He couldn't have heard me.

"Where would I go?" I asked. As much as I wanted to, I couldn't talk to him about the knife. Horus would skin me alive.

"Where would you go?" Gil asked. And he gave me this prying look, like my entire brain was spilled out onto a serving tray in front of him.

"Nowhere," I said. "At least not without telling you. Because we don't keep secrets, right?"

"Right," Gil said. And then he ruffled my hair like I was five. "Have fun at school today."

I wasn't sure *fun* and *school* belonged in the same sentence.

We're working on our project tonight, right?" Henry said during first period. And second period. And in every single class we had together.

"Can't it wait?" I finally said when I got to World Cultures. Excuses weren't working. I just needed to say no.

"No, Tut, it can't wait. It's due in two weeks. Two weeks!"

"That's plenty of time," I said.

"Plenty of time for what?" Tia asked, dropping into her chair as if nothing had happened the night before.

"You're okay?" I said before I could stop myself.

She looked at me like my head had cracked in half like a giant egg. "Why wouldn't I be okay?"

I opened my mouth and then stopped. I couldn't really mention breaking into the Library of Congress. Or the Hall of Artifacts. Or the fact that she should be in stasis for all of eternity. And then there was the matter of the scroll she'd stolen from me. Or at least from the gods.

"You weren't supposed to take anything out of the library." I fumbled over my words. I still couldn't believe she knew who I was.

"You stole a library book?" Henry asked. "You know, librarians will come after people like you. Maybe you got away with stuff like that at your old school, but you better watch out, or you're going to get sent to juvie."

I couldn't imagine Tia at juvie. Sure, she had a reputation for trouble, but it almost seemed like it was a costume she wore. Like she wanted people to think something that wasn't really true.

"You're both crazy," Tia said.

"But . . ." I started. She knew everything about me, and I had no clue who she really was. But with Henry around, I couldn't start plying her with questions.

Seth plunked down in his seat. I covered my nose so I wouldn't have to smell him. "Where is everybody?" he asked.

Seth was right. Half our class was missing.

"It seems a handful of students have contracted a stomach flu," Mr. Plant said. "Which means I'm giving you the entire class period to work on your projects."

Project or lecture . . . I wasn't sure which was worse.

"Why do you think so many people are sick?" Henry said after Mr. Plant finished talking. "Do you think it's the curse again?"

"Enough on the curse," I said. "There is no curse."

"How can you be so sure?" Tia said, and she fixed her eyes on me. Challenged me to see how I would respond in front of Henry and Seth.

"Just a feeling," I said, praying she wouldn't reveal my identity on the school announcements. I could see it now as a special feature in the school yearbook: "King Tut Doomed to Suffer Eighth Grade Over and Over Again."

"And shouldn't we work on our projects?"

"I thought we were getting together tonight for that," Henry said.

"That's the good thing," I said. "If we work on it now, we don't have to get together tonight. Anyway, I have other plans."

"I bet you do," Tia said.

"What's up with you?" Seth asked her. "You're acting all weird and stuff."

"I'm not," she said. Except she knew she was, so she started fiddling with all the jewelry she was wearing and avoided looking at me.

Tia was one problem. Seth was another.

"What were you doing outside my town house last night?"
I narrowed my eyes at him and dared him to answer.

Seth ran his hands through his greasy hair and then wiped
them on his desk. Gods help the person who had to sit there
after him. "I don't know what you're talking about."

"Yes, you do," I said. "You were in that red van. You saw me."

"You're imagining things, Tut."

"Henry?" I said. He'd been there. He could back me up.
"Remember that red van last night? Looked like it had been
painted in blood."

Henry shook his head. "All I remember is that your house
is filled with weird things. It's like a museum."

"My stuff's not weird," I said. "And Seth was outside."

"Yeah, right," Seth said. "The last place I'd want to spend
my spare time is hanging around you."

That was probably true. Maybe I was wrong.

No, I wasn't wrong.

"You were there," I said. "I'm not crazy."

He made a cuckoo sign with his finger around his ear.
"Whatever you say, crazy boy."

I'd figure it out. Just like I'd figure out who Tia really was.

Tia sat quietly for the rest of class, while Seth continued to
assault me with his stupid little comments. Henry talked my
ear off about presentation skills and intestines in jars and mummification. He had so many of the little facts wrong, but I wasn't
about to prolong the conversation by correcting him. I endured
all three of them until the bell rang and class was over.

My phone vibrated. Sure, I wasn't supposed to have it on during school, but nobody was going to bust me for it.

It was a text from Gil. can't pick you up from school today

Gil always picked me up. I figured with the Horemheb threat, he'd be twice as overprotective as he normally was.

why not? I texted back.

I went to my locker and got to my next class before his reply came.

have something I need to do

Was it something to do with the knife? He knew about it. Was he going to look for it, too?

what? I pressed.

Another long delay.

nothing big. talk later.

And that was the end of our text conversation.

I avoided Henry after school so he wouldn't try to drag me to the library for the useless project, and hiked the six blocks home. Gil would be proud to know I was perfectly safe. Not a sign of Horemheb or the Cult of Set.

"Would Great Pharaoh care for a refreshment?" Colonel Cody asked from his prostrate position when I walked into my town house.

"Why yes, now that you mention—" I didn't have time to finish. He snapped his fingers, and Lieutenants Virgil and Leon darted off. Sometimes it's good to be pharaoh.

Horus had made it back from his date, but his lady cat, Bast, wasn't what I wanted to talk about. With Gil not home, I had a chance to get moving on the knife.

"Where does your mom live?" I asked.

"Why do you want to know?" Horus swatted at a passing beetle.

So I told him about my visit to the Library of Congress, leaving out the part about the trivia quiz. I couldn't believe I'd almost lost. I also decided to leave out the part about Tia being there and stealing the scroll. That was Qeb and Imsety's problem. I didn't want to get them in trouble. Not to mention I didn't want Horus jumping to some crazy conclusion, thinking Tia was some kind of spy or something. Which maybe she was. I don't know. Why else would she be following me around? But she couldn't possibly be working with the Cult of Set. Could she?

"Figures my mom has the knife," Horus said, distracting me from my thoughts of Tia.

"If the scroll can be believed," I said.

"Of course the scroll can be believed," Horus said. "The gods wrote it. But why does my mother always feel like she needs to be right in the middle of everything, like the world will implode if she's not involved? She acts like she's the queen of everyone. Do you remember when we moved here, how she tried to take over?"

I nodded in agreement until Horus finished his mom tirade.

"So where is she?" I asked once he'd gotten all his complaints out. With Gil gone, there was no time like the present to pay Isis a little visit. Get the knife. Cut out Horemheb's heart. My life was totally getting back on the right track.

"You know the Dynasty Funeral Homes?" Horus said.

"The ones with that stupid little jingle?" They ran a million commercials on all the local channels, mostly during shows that old people watched, like *Wheel of Fortune* and *Jeopardy*. The commercials came on so often, sometimes I couldn't get the song out of my head.

"With over fifty locations to serve you best, Dynasty Funeral Homes is where you want to rest," I sang. The shabtis clapped along with the tune. They'd heard the commercials as many times as I had.

"Those are the ones. Isis owns them." Horus took a giant sip of milk from his bowl. On my orders, the shabtis kept it filled up. Complaining about his mother must have made him thirsty.

"Seriously?"

"Seriously. And I'm sure she'd love to have you pay her a visit."

"You're not coming with me?" I asked.

Horus looked at me without blinking. "You're kidding, right? She'd point out all the things I'm doing wrong in my life. I don't have time for that kind of nonsense."

Sometimes it was hard to remember that even though Horus was a powerful god, he also had a mom to report to.

The doorbell rang.

"Expecting someone?" Horus asked.

"Great Amun, it's probably Henry," I said.

"Again?"

I scanned the town house to make sure everything looked normal. I'd stashed the *Book of the Dead* on the bookshelf, and the shabtis had repaired the feather fan.

"It's this project," I said. "He's way too enthusiastic about it."

"Enthusiastic? He almost cut my tail off last night. Reckless is a better word," Horus said. "I'll be back once he's gone." He scowled and jumped out the fire escape window.

I pointed to the closet and said to the shabtis, "Don't make a peep unless you think it's the end of the world."

"Of course, Great Master," Colonel Cody said, and they filed off and hid.

I opened the front door. It was Henry, of course. I glanced out at the street and saw the red van again. My hackles went up as I felt the occupants watching me.

"See, that's Seth," I said, pointing at the van. "You see him this time, don't you?"

Henry angled his head around so he could look. "It does look like Seth. Does he live here?"

"Great Osiris, I hope not," I said. It was bad enough having to go to school with Seth. Living in the same neighborhood would be a reason to move out.

"Great Osiris?" Henry said.

"Oh, that. I've just been getting into our project," I said. Normally I'm smart enough not to say things like that around mortals, but my game had been off this whole week.

"Great Osiris. I like it," Henry said. "Anyway, maybe Seth's girlfriend lives around here."

We both burst out laughing. There was no way Seth had a girlfriend. Still, it didn't answer the question of what Seth was doing here in the first place.

"So if I ask him about it tomorrow, you'll back me up?" I said.

"I totally got your back," Henry said, and then pushed his way into my town house like I'd invited him. He was sporting yet another Pluto shirt, but I stopped myself from commenting. I didn't have time to get into some planetary debate.

"I thought we were working on the project tomorrow," I said.

"Tut, today is the tomorrow you worried about yesterday," Henry said.

"What?" Sometimes I wondered if Henry was for real.

"The project needs to get done," he said.

He was never going to let it go. I might as well get it over with.

"Grab a water out of the fridge if you want."

While he was in the kitchen, I moved a camel seat in front of the closet. When I turned back around, Henry stared at me with one eyebrow up.

I let out a fake laugh. "The other cat's being bad. I'll keep him locked up for now."

"And where's Horus?" Henry dropped his backpack next to the futon. A bunch of scarab beetles scurried out of the way and crawled under Gil's chair. Henry scooted away from them.

"He went out to look for stinky fish," I said.

The doorbell rang.

Two visitors in one day? It was unheard of.

"Who is it?" I called, because I'd already made the mistake of opening the door once.

"Pizza delivery."

"Did you order pizza?" I asked Henry.

"No, but it is about dinnertime," Henry said, and pulled the door open.

I stepped in front of Henry. The pizza delivery guy was about Gil's age and wore a velour warm-up suit that didn't look like the uniform of any pizza place I knew. His hair was the exact same color as Seth's, except it was feathered back and fluffy instead of greasy and disgusting. I wondered if it was a coincidence that Seth was outside watching me and now there was a pizza guy who looked just like him. The pizza guy had a name-tag on with a single red block letter *B* and a thick gold necklace that looked like it was made of hand-dipped scorpions.

"We didn't order pizza." I didn't try to mask the suspicion in my voice. The red letters on the box read TEMPLE OF PIZZA. I'd never heard of it, and I knew all the pizza places around here.

"Naw, you must be wrong. We got a call to deliver this pizza here. You gonna pay or what?"

I pulled out some cash. Maybe the shabtis had ordered pizza for me. It would be just the kind of thing Lieutenant Virgil would do, since sometimes I forgot to eat.

"Nice place you got here." The pizza guy peered into my town house. "You live alone?"

"Of course not," I said. "And how'd you get here?" The only vehicle out front was the red van.

He pointed off to the side. "My bike. It's around the corner."

I felt my chest warm, like my scarab heart was going to start glowing, but I didn't care. Who'd this guy think he was to intrude on the home of a pharaoh? "Who are you?"

"Just the pizza guy." He shoved the pizza box at me and ran down the steps and out to the street. He jumped into the driver's side of the van and it peeled away. Seth grinned at me from the passenger seat.

I kicked the door shut and dropped the cardboard pizza box on the coffee table. There was no way I was trusting something Seth Cooper was involved in.

Henry didn't have the same suspicions I did. He set his water on the coffee table next to the TEMPLE OF PIZZA box.

I realized I had no appetite. Only suspicion. But Henry must've been hungry.

"I wonder what kind it is," he said, and flipped open the top.

Ten asps came pouring out.

10

WHERE I FIGHT SNAKES

That's not pizza!" Henry screamed as he jumped onto the futon like some kind of scaredy cat. I didn't blame him. Asps are only the most poisonous snakes in all of Africa. And even though their poison couldn't kill me, I jumped up beside him.

"Maybe it's one of those specialties. Like snakes and sausage."

Henry stared at me like I'd gone crazy. If the fear hadn't been so clear on his face, I would've laughed. This was the most excitement we'd had around the town house since the shabtis had set Gil's room on fire. They'd been trying to remove heathen spirits. They'd claimed it was an *accident*.

"Let your cat out," Henry managed to say as he edged up

onto the back of the futon. The snakes had made their way off the coffee table and slithered on the ground below. "He can pounce on these things and eat them for dinner."

"You know, asp really isn't bad," I said. "It's better if you drain the venom."

"Just don't tell me it tastes like chicken. Because I don't care." Henry pulled his cell phone from his pocket.

"Who are you gonna call? Asps Are Us?"

"Animal control," Henry said. "They can get rid of these things."

I grabbed his phone and tossed it across the room. "No way."

"They're gonna kill us if we don't get rid of them," Henry said. He was partially right. They'd kill him. For me, they'd only prove to be a hassle. My immortal powers healed me from minor inconveniences like snake poison. But if Henry called someone, I'd have to explain his dead body and ten asps to a bunch of officials. And I'd certainly have to move. Not to mention, I might have to drop out of school, which in itself was reason enough to let the snakes live. But the temptation of no school couldn't compete with Henry's bulging eyes.

"No authorities," I said. "I can handle them."

"You!" Henry sounded hysterical again. The snakes slithered away from the coffee table and started climbing the sides of the futon, curling around the wooden legs. "What can you do?"

I wasn't sure. It'd been six hundred years since I had to deal with asps. And even back then, there'd only been a few. My powers from Osiris were useless. What was I going to do? Tangle them in vines? They were snakes, not rodents. If Gil was around, he could have called on the power of the sun god to destroy them. But he wasn't here.

My scarab heart pounded as the energy from the *Book of the Dead* called me. It wanted me to use it. Begged to be used. And it seemed to be my only option. I jumped off the futon.

"Don't leave me here!" Henry screamed so loud the people two town houses over probably heard. "They're getting closer."

"Then jump!" I yelled.

"What!"

"Get off the futon!" I said. "Or they're going to get you."

Henry vaulted through the air in a way that would have filled Olympic gymnasts with envy.

"Follow me," I said.

I yanked the *Book of the Dead* off the bookshelf and ran for the bathroom. "Quick! Into the tub!"

Henry didn't ask any questions. I slammed the bathroom door shut behind us, and into the tub we went. Then I flipped open the golden box that held the scrolls.

"What are you doing?" Henry stared at the papyrus scrolls.

"Give me a second."

"No, really, Tut. This isn't a time for project research."

"Finally, we agree on something about the project," I said.

"Ha, ha."

"Just trust me, okay?"

Henry looked like he trusted me about as much as he'd trust a blind man to lead him across the street. But he was running short on options.

"Please don't let me die," Henry said.

I looked down at the pages. There was something about snakes in the scrolls. I could almost swear to it. I thumbed through them and, after a silent prayer to Osiris, landed on the perfect page. I guess Osiris didn't want Henry to be killed by snakes, either.

"I don't mean to rush you, but I hear them," Henry said. He grabbed one of Gil's razors and held it menacingly in one hand.

I heard the slithering, too. They'd made it under the bathroom door. "What do you think you're going to do with that razor?" I asked as I smoothed the scroll.

"I'm going to kill them," Henry said.

"With a safety razor?" A razor wasn't going to save us, but a spell from the *Book of the Dead* would.

My choices were:

(a) Spell to get rid of a snake
(b) Spell to not get bit by a snake
(c) Spell to not get eaten by a snake.

I decided on (a).

> "O Rerek-snake, take yourself off, for Geb protects me;
> get up, for you have eaten a mouse, which Re detests,
> and you have chewed the bones of a putrid cat."

Except I said it in ancient Egyptian, which sounded way cooler. The power of the *Book of the Dead* flooded out of me and the snakes burned to a crisp—all ten of them right there on the bathroom floor.

I tried to hold on to the energy as it left me—I didn't want to let it go—but it was too late. I only had one spell left.

"What did you just do?" Henry asked. "Are they—?"

"Dead? Yep. I knew there was something in the scrolls about snakes."

Henry stepped out of the bathtub and over to the crisped ashes, still holding Gil's razor. "How did you do that?"

That's when the situation majorly tanked. The bathroom door flew open and fifty shabtis poured in. Colonel Cody threw himself to the ground, even as the others began cleaning up the ashes.

"Great Master—"

"Shhhhh!" I tried to quiet him.

Colonel Cody stopped mid-sentence. I jumped out of the tub in an effort to shove the shabtis out of the bathroom. Henry looked like . . . well, like he'd just seen fifty miniature men march into the bathroom and start lying prostrate before me.

"I can explain."

Henry let out something halfway between a laugh and a snort. "You can explain why you have little men running around your town house?"

"Would you believe they're automatons?" I said.

Ten of the shabtis had little brooms and ten had little dust-pans. They swept the piles of ashes into stacks, and each stack was being dumped into the toilet and flushed. Lieutenant Roy directed the whole thing.

"Great Pharaoh, if you would let me explain—" Colonel Cody began again.

I cringed, praying maybe Henry hadn't heard.

"Pharaoh?" Henry took off his glasses and blinked rapidly, like maybe bad eyesight could explain the whole thing.

"I programmed them to say that." But even as I said it, two of the shabtis bumped into Henry's gray Chucks and tried to push them out of the way to get at a few stray ashes.

"Come on, Tut," Henry said. "They're not automatons."

"Sure they are," I said. "They're the latest models—"

But I never got the chance to finish. Horus jumped into the bathroom and hissed. "It stinks of Set in here."

On a positive note, this got Henry's attention away from the shabtis. On a negative note, well . . .

"Your cat talks?"

I glared at Horus. "He's not supposed to."

"Don't tell me he's an automaton also. And don't treat me like an idiot."

I decided retreat might be my best defense, so I moved out of the bathroom and into the kitchen. Henry and Horus followed. Using the spell from the *Book of the Dead* had left me thirstier than a humpless camel. I yanked open the fridge, pulled out a soda, and downed it in one gulp. When I went back into the family room, Horus paced from side to side, bending down to check under doors and in heating vents. He even yanked open the incinerator chute and sniffed inside. Then he whipped around and faced me.

"What in the name of Anubis happened here, Tut?" Horus said. "My protective spells should have kept Set out."

"Set? Spells?" Henry said, but both Horus and I ignored him.

"We got bad pizza," I said.

"That's an understatement." Henry sat on the futon, still holding his glasses. Out of habit, I made a pathetic attempt with my identity spells to make him forget everything he'd seen. I didn't expect it to work. This was beyond the limit of my powers. We'd crossed a point of no return.

"You used the *Book of the Dead*," Horus said like an accusation.

The departure of the energy Horus had given me left a giant hole inside me. And it wasn't coming back.

"It was the only thing I could think of," I said. "There were ten snakes, all coming at us."

"The spells are for Horemheb," Horus said. "And Set."

"Who do you think sent the snakes in the first place?" I said. "Maybe if you hadn't been avoiding Henry, you could have helped out."

Henry didn't even flinch at the "avoiding" comment. He ran his fingers through his shaggy blond hair and scanned the room with his blurry vision, like he expected the answers to all his questions to be written on the walls. The shabtis ran around, cleaning up whatever mess they could, and since the literal cat was out of the bag, I didn't bother to order them back to the closet. It was only two sodas later that Henry finally put his glasses on and spoke.

"Okay, this is going to sound like the stupidest thing I've ever said, but you're the real King Tut, aren't you?"

It was far from the stupidest thing Henry had ever said.

Horus narrowed his good eye at me and waited for my response.

"You've heard of me?" I asked.

Henry pressed his fingers to the sides of his forehead. "No. I mean yes. I mean I've heard of the pharaoh who died three thousand years ago, but it doesn't make any sense. How can you be that same person? Unless I'm going crazy." He grabbed hold of my arm. "Please tell me I'm not going crazy."

"You're not going crazy," I said. "I never died. There was this little immortality thing, and here I am, fourteen forever."

"So you're stuck in eighth grade?"

I groaned. "Only when Gil convinces me to go."

Henry gave a look that was half-skeptical, half-envious. "Which is how often?"

"Maybe every five years or so," I said.

Henry looked over at Horus. "And you're—"

Horus yawned like the fact that my identity being revealed was just another piece of the tedium he had to deal with on a daily basis. "Horus. Egyptian god. Son of Osiris. And yes, I did rip off Set's—"

"Enough, Horus," I said, cutting him off. Henry didn't need all the gory details of Egyptian mythology quarrels.

"So you have a talking god cat," Henry said. "That's pretty cool. What about the weird little clay guys? What are they?"

"Shabtis. They were placed in my tomb to serve me in the afterworld."

Henry leaned down to get a closer look at Major Rex. "He's green. And he has Egyptian writing all over him."

I nodded. "It's why they serve me. The spells written on them give me control over them."

"No way. That is awesome!" Henry said, poking at Major Rex with his index finger.

"Major Rex," Major Rex said, crossing his golden arms over his green chest. "Weapons specialist. First line of defense for the pharaoh."

Henry turned his hand palm up, like he was being introduced to a dog. Luckily, I don't think Major Rex took offense.

"Do they do your homework?" Henry asked.

"Sometimes," I lied. It was more like all the time. Except for our stupid project. Which, now that Henry knew about them, maybe I could just get the shabtis to complete for us. It's not like I needed to do the homework to learn anything. I'd been through eighth grade before.

"What are they made of? Are they fragile?" Henry asked. "Will they break?"

"Not so far," I said. It had been almost a hundred years, and I hadn't lost a single shabti.

Henry wrapped his fingers around Major Rex and lifted him up for closer examination. "I want some."

"They won't call you Great Pharaoh," I said. After all, they were my shabtis.

"I could train them," Henry said.

"I think you need to be immortal to control them," I said.

"That's a technicality," Henry said. "I'm sure there's a way around it." He set Major Rex back down.

Major Rex returned to his position guarding me.

"So I don't get it. Why are you here?" Henry asked.

"Why not? I live here," I said.

"No. I mean why aren't you back in your tomb?"

So I gave Henry the short version. The version that glossed over the facts and left out the murderous details of Horemheb killing off my entire family. This version of reality focused on a spell being cast and me living forever.

"Immortality. That's kind of cool," Henry said.

"It has its plus side."

Of course, it also had its minus side. Like Horemheb. Which put a damper on my whole mood. The week had been a complete disaster. First Horemheb had declared war on me, blowing up the obelisk only seconds after I recharged. Who knew if it would ever be safe for me to recharge my scarab heart again? Second, not one, but two people now knew my true identity: Tia and Henry. For thousands of years, it had been my best-kept secret. I'd failed miserably.

I yawned without even having to pretend I was tired. Exhausted was more like it. "You know, I'm kind of beat and my brother will probably be home any minute. Do you mind if we work on our project some other time?"

Henry stood up way too fast. "My parents will probably want me home anyway."

For Henry not to put up a fight showed just how freaked out he must be.

I yawned again. "Sounds good." My eyes were drooping. Maybe it was using two spells from the *Book of the Dead* in two days. I envied Rip Van Winkle, wishing I could sleep for one hundred years.

"Don't think you're going to sleep, Tut," Horus said, like he was reading my mind. "You have things to do."

"What kinds of things?" Henry asked. He was already halfway to the door.

"Nothing. They can wait." All I wanted to do was lie down for five minutes.

Horus jumped from his cat scratching post and landed on the ground in front of me. "They can't wait. Horemheb and Set are getting closer. Every second you wait means a second they get closer to killing you."

"Killing you?" Henry asked. Only seconds before, he'd looked as tired as I felt, but now his eyes were wide open.

I shook my head. "It's nothing."

"Really?" Henry said. "Because if there's someone trying to kill you, which, given the fact that you just had poisonous snakes delivered to your house, makes me think maybe your god cat is telling the truth, then that seems like a pretty big deal."

"Fine, yes," I said. "There is someone trying to kill me. But I've got it under control."

Horus sniffed the air again in disgust. "You have nothing

under control, Tut. And you have one spell left. You're turning what should have been a simple errand into a catastrophe."

"Cut him a little slack," Henry said.

I couldn't believe he was sticking up for me to Horus.

"Horemheb and Set aren't going to cut him any slack," Horus said. "So neither am I."

"What kind of errand is it?" Henry said. "I'll go with you."

"You're not going with me." I resigned myself to the fact that sleep wasn't in my near future. Horus was right. I had to get the knife.

"No, that's a great idea," Horus said. "Henry should go. Isis loves visitors."

"Isis?" Henry took a step backward, like Isis being real was impossible to believe. But how could it be? He was having a conversation with a talking god cat and an immortal pharaoh.

"My mother," Horus said. "She's got something Tut needs."

"Your mother's a goddess?" Henry said.

"Of course she's a goddess," Horus said, like Henry was remedial. "That's how things work. For me to be a god, my mom has to be a goddess."

Horus's condescending tone didn't even faze Henry. "Could she help us with our project?"

Seriously? The project again? At a time like this?

"I'm sure she'd be happy to," Horus said. "Isis loves projects."

And so that's how it turned out that Henry was going with me to get the sacred knife. Henry finished his soda and we were on our way.

11

WHERE I PAY A VISIT TO DEATH

I tried to leave the shabtis at home, but after the snake fiasco, Colonel Cody wasn't about to let me out of his sight.

"Great Pharaoh, you must allow us to come along," he said. "Your mortal friend will be worthless in a fight."

"Hey!" Henry said.

"Don't take offense," I said. "He's overprotective."

"What about the mortal thing?" Henry asked as we set out with our entourage of shabtis. "He makes it sound like a disease."

"I wouldn't say disease," I said, though I could see Colonel Cody's point. "More like a limitation."

"That's no better," Henry said.

We set out for Old Town, cutting across the Mall. The

shabtis marched in formation behind us, hiding behind trees and benches when they couldn't blend into the shadows. When we passed the Washington Monument, before I could stop them, palm fronds sprouted from under my feet.

"What's up with the plants?" Henry asked.

I kicked aside a few of the green leaves. "Yeah, that. You see, I have these powers. . . ."

Henry looked at me like he thought I might start growing an extra set of arms. "You're immortal *and* you have powers?"

"Sure," I said. "Osiris gave them to me. He's the god of—"

"Plants?" Henry asked.

"Kind of. He's the god of all things fertile. Which makes me able to grow plants anytime I want."

"Is that good for anything?" Henry asked. He picked up one of the palm fronds and started pulling it apart, maybe testing to make sure it was real.

"Sometimes." I almost made poison ivy grow up his pant leg just to show him how useful my powers could be, but I held back. "I can also control bugs, like all those beetles around my town house."

"Yeah, those are kind of disgusting, Tut. I didn't want to say anything, but you should clean more often."

Henry stopped talking because he tripped.

I looked down to see Colonel Cody holding the end of one of Henry's shoelaces. You don't mess with the shabtis or question their cleanliness.

"Horus likes the beetles," I said.

Henry shuddered. "What about cockroaches? They freak

me out. And they're everywhere these days. Have you noticed how many bugs there've been in the last week?"

I had noticed the increase in bugs. In the streets. In restaurants and stores. They'd even commented on it on the news, calling it the "insect revolution." Pest-control companies had to be making a fortune.

"Why is everyone so freaked out over bugs?" I said.

"Because they're nasty, dirty, filthy . . . ," Henry said. "They skitter around and crawl in your shoes. My mom found a roach in her bed the other night. She made my dad pull all the sheets off and spray insect repellent around the whole thing like a barrier."

"Did it work?" I asked.

"Only in the bedroom," Henry said. "But we found bugs in our kitchen, bathroom, and even in the pantry. My mom's convinced our maid is putting them there for some kind of twisted revenge."

"You guys should be nicer to your maid," I said.

We started across the bridge, avoiding the steady stream of cars. Given that it was Friday night, half the city was out.

"What other powers do you have?" Henry asked.

"Well, generally I can make people forget weird things that happen around me. Except it didn't work on you back at the town house."

"What do you mean?" He narrowed his eyes.

"I have this spell I use . . . ," I started.

"You tried to put a spell on me?" Henry said.

Why did people get so upset about that? It's not like I was

trying to make them do something stupid like dance in their underwear.

"It was just a little spell," I said. "So you'd forget about the snakes. And the shabtis. And Horus. But too much had happened. That's why it didn't work."

"Dude, don't put any spells on me."

Enough on the spells.

"Anyway, Gil has different powers than me," I said.

"Your brother's immortal, too?"

"He's the only other immortal I know of," I said.

Except for Horemheb. No way was I including him, since he totally didn't deserve his immortality.

"What?" Henry asked.

"What, what?" I said.

"Your face turned red."

I gritted my teeth. "Just thinking about someone I plan to kill." Okay, maybe this wasn't the smartest thing for me to say, but I didn't care. It actually felt good to get it off my chest.

To Henry's credit, he only hesitated about five seconds—his mouth opening and closing as he tried to formulate his response.

"Anyone I know?" he finally asked.

"My uncle." I spit out the word, because I hated that I was actually related to him. "He murdered my mother and father and brother."

Henry stopped walking and pulled on my shoulder so I'd stop, too. "Your own uncle did that?"

"Nice family, right?" I said, trying to laugh it off.

Henry saw right through it. "I'm sorry. That stinks."

"It's nothing."

But Henry wasn't going to let it drop. "No, really. I can't even imagine that. My only uncle gives me a new set of Mickey Mouse ears for Christmas. He has every year since I was two. And during the summers, I visit him for a week. He works at Disney World. I get to skip all the lines. And see behind the scenes."

"Maybe I can come along next summer," I said, because right now, the idea of doing something as normal as going to Disney World with a friend sounded like paradise.

"That's a great idea," Henry said.

It had been centuries since I'd really talked to anyone besides Gil or Horus, and it was nice to have a friend. Even if Henry was destined to grow old and die just like the rest of the mortals in the world.

"I need to get rid of my uncle first," I said. "That's my top priority."

"Seriously?" Henry said.

"Seriously. There's this special knife I need. It's the only way to kill an immortal."

Henry kicked a rock down the gravel path. And then he kicked another. And then he finally said, "I never signed up for killing someone."

I patted him on the shoulder. "You're not going to kill anyone. I am."

"But . . . ," he said. "What if he kills you instead?"

"Yeah, that would be a problem," I said. Because that wouldn't be revenge. That would be stupidity.

"What does Horus's mom have to do with this?" Henry asked.

"She has the knife."

"And we're going to get it?" Henry said.

"Right."

Colonel Cody and his four majors shuffled around in front of us, slipping out of the shadows. "Shall I lead onward, Great Master? Or do you intend to stand here all evening speaking with the mortal?"

It was his polite way of telling us to get a move on.

"Lead onward," I said, and we set out again.

Henry didn't say another word until we got to Old Town. Maybe if I hadn't been so focused on killing Horemheb, I would have given more effort to conversation. But the knife was within my reach. This was really going to happen.

"Dynasty Funeral Homes?" Henry said when we stopped in front of the white building. It looked like something out of a Civil War movie, with grand pillars stretching up to the roof far above and black shutters next to all the windows. "They're the ones with that stupid little jingle. Doesn't it go something like, 'With over fifty locations to serve you best, Dynasty Funeral Homes is where you want to rest.'"

"Isis owns them." I cut him off before he sang anymore. It was hard enough to keep the tune out of my head.

"I hate that jingle," Henry said. "But everyone knows it.

My own parents even preplanned their funerals through Dynasty. Isis must be making bank."

Money was not something the gods worried about. Money wasn't something I even had to worry about. With immortal powers and an endless amount of time, there were tons of ways to make money. The only time I'd lived poor was once when Gil and I were in hiding, back during the Crusades. Not an experience I ever wanted to repeat.

We climbed sixteen granite stairs to the massive front doors of the funeral home. A sign in the window read,

"NORMAL OPERATING HOURS:

8:00 A.M.–5:00 P.M. DAILY.

PLEASE USE SIDE ENTRANCE DURING NON-BUSINESS HOURS.

DEAD OR ALIVE, YOUR ETERNAL HAPPINESS IS OUR GOAL."

So we walked back down the stairs and around to the carport. An armada of ten black hearses was parked in the back. I rang the bell . . .

. . . and waited for an eternity. Finally, the lock unlatched and the door opened.

It was Tia. She was just draping a new necklace over her head. The pendant hanging from it was a lot like an ankh but was actually called a *tiet* and was, I'm sure by no coincidence, a symbol of Isis.

"What are you doing here?" I said.

"Visiting." Tia settled the necklace on top of the others and patted it in place.

"You're visiting Isis?" I asked. "How do you even know about Isis?"

"Wait, she knows about all this god stuff, too?" Henry said.

"Unfortunately," I said.

"Oh, Tut, you offend me," Tia said. "I thought we had a bond."

She'd stolen my scroll. That was no way to form a bond.

"It's been a long day," I said. "And then there were these snakes."

Henry nodded. "It's true. They were going to kill me. But then Tut pulled some ancient mumbo jumbo out of a bunch of scrolls."

Tia's blue eyes widened. "You used the *Book of the Dead* again? I thought last night was a fluke."

I didn't see any reason to mention the three spells Horus had given me. Might as well play it off. "Sure. What's the big deal?"

She looked me up and down. "It's just kind of impressive, that's all."

"I was actually pretty impressed, too," Henry said. "Or maybe I'm just happy to be alive."

"Oh, come on, you guys. I'm immortal. I have powers."

"Still," Tia said. "The gods will talk about that for centuries."

"Good. Now my life feels complete," I said.

"Anyway, I was just leaving." Tia smiled what had to be the most gorgeous smile in the world, which kind of made my head turn to mush. I saw Henry staring at her, so I elbowed him in the side.

"Wait a second," I said. "You never told me how you knew who I was."

"You're right." Tia bent down to tie the lace on her combat boots, even though it didn't look like it was untied.

"So how do you know? And who are you, really? Are you related to Isis? Are you immortal?"

"So many questions," Tia said.

"That's because you know everything there is to know about me, and I don't know anything about you."

"And that's exactly the way I like it," Tia said. "See ya, Boy King." She pushed past us and strolled away.

I totally let the "boy king" comment slide, but Henry laughed. "Boy King. I forgot about that."

"Don't you dare start saying it."

"Yeah, right," Henry said. "And I thought Great Pharaoh was the best nickname I'd ever heard."

"I can't believe Tia was here," I said. "What do you think she was doing?" I tried to keep my heart from glowing, but the whole thing was beyond annoying. Why did Tia have to be so mysterious?

"Does she know about the knife?" Henry said.

"No," I said. "I mean, maybe."

"Does she or doesn't she?" Henry said.

There it was. The truth. I didn't know what had happened to the scroll. She could have gotten it out of the Hall of Artifacts. And even if she couldn't read it, what if she knew someone who could? What if Isis read it for her and then gave her the knife?

"I hope not," I said.

"Don't underestimate her just because you think she's cute."

"Puh-lease," I said.

Henry rolled his eyes. "What? You don't think she's cute?"

"I didn't say that," I said. "But you do, too."

"Your point?" he said.

"Come on," I said, and pulled him inside. The door latched behind us. Henry and I stood in a kitchen with yellow tiled walls and a sparkling white floor. Platters of cookies cooled on the counter.

"Do you think any are chocolate chip?" Henry picked up a cookie and nibbled on it. "Because I love chocolate chip. Though I think those white macadamia nut ones are my favorites, except they have to be cooked just right. You know, where they're kind of soft and gooey on the inside and crusty on the outside. And the macadamia nuts can't be all crushed up because that's just nasty."

"Are you serious?" Now wasn't the time for cookies. We had to find Isis. I tried to concentrate, but the stupid funeral-home jingle played over the speaker system.

Just then, a guy with the head of a baboon came around the corner.

"Hapi!" I said. Of Horus's four sons, Hapi was the only one with anything resembling responsibility.

"Tut," His baboon face didn't change at all. Hapi showed about as much emotion as a potato. "It's been a long time."

"If I'd known you were so close, I would've come to visit," I said. "How come Horus never told me?"

Hapi motioned with his baboon head back in the direction he came from. "It's my granny. She's pretty reclusive."

Crazy was a better word to describe Isis, but I opted not to mention it.

"Will she talk to us?" I asked. My scarab heart skipped a beat. What if this was a dead end? Worse yet, what if she wouldn't give me the knife? I'd have to find a way to convince her.

"Sure," Hapi said. "She just saw your girlfriend. Why not you?"

"She's not my girlfriend," I said. My face burned. I didn't dare look at Henry.

Henry was more interested in Hapi than in questioning whether Tia was my girlfriend or not. "Who's the monkey?" he asked.

I tensed.

Hapi bared his teeth and snapped.

Henry inched backward and his face turned as white as a freshly bandaged mummy. The whole situation made me appreciate the fact that he was even here, sticking by my side.

"Don't call him a monkey," I whispered out of the side of my mouth. "He's a baboon. Well, just his head is. The rest of him is human."

Henry only nodded.

Maybe Hapi was feeling generous, because he didn't tear off Henry's head, or even his ears. He gave one final snarl and then relaxed his mouth.

First Horus. Now Hapi. If Henry didn't watch it, he was going to make a bad impression on all the gods.

"This is Hapi," I said.

"Nice to meet you," Henry said.

Hapi ignored him. It was time to move on.

"Can you take us to her?" I asked.

"I was heading that way anyway," Hapi said.

Hapi led us to the basement. As soon as my feet hit the last step, I knew I was in trouble. This was no regular funeral home. It was a mummification parlor. Bodies lay in open caskets all over the room, each with five Canopic jars next to them instead of four. Hooks and knives lay scattered everywhere, covered in disgusting-looking fluids. It reminded me way too much of the time Isis had threatened to use me as a lab rat. I started coughing as the smell of natron crept up my nose.

If you don't know what natron is, pray to the Egyptian god of your choice that you never have to find out. To be brief, it's the salty baking-soda powder they shove you in when they start to mummify you. Once your body hits that natron, it's all over. You stay in there until your body's shriveled into something resembling a prune, but way more leathery. But let's be straight about something. That's only the beginning. Then they pull your brains out and pulverize them.

"More visitors, Granny," Hapi said.

I tore my eyes away from the tables of disgustingness and toward Horus's mom.

"Whoa, she's intense," Henry whispered.

Intense was a perfect word for Isis. She took her role as

"mother goddess" seriously and made sure everything about her fit the image. Her dark hair was chopped into some curly bouffant do that stood a foot high on her head, and her lips were covered in bright-red lipstick. She wore a blue checked dress and a white apron, which looked like it was covered in the same stuff as all the knives around the room. And she patted Hapi on his baboon head like he was five.

"Thank you, my adorable grandson," she said. "You've always been such a good boy."

"Tell me if they bother you, Granny," Hapi said. Then he sauntered over to one of the bodies and pulled something out. It was red and puffy and looked like it belonged in menudo. Hapi shoved it into one of the Canopic jars and reached into the body again.

"It's great to see you . . ." I never knew how to address Isis. She treated me like I was one of her grandsons and insisted on friendly terms. But I just couldn't see myself addressing the most powerful goddess in the world as "Granny."

"Auntie Isis," she said. "And dear Tut, it's been far too long." She grabbed me in a giant hug, smearing whatever was on her apron all over me.

I gave her a half hug back. "It's been a long time, um, Auntie Isis."

Isis had come to visit us once, when Horus and I had first moved into the town house ninety years ago. She'd nitpicked every single thing, from the color of the walls to the arrangement of the furniture, spouting some nonsense about feng shui. Horus had done everything she requested, moving coffee tables and pictures and carpets. Or at least I'd done the moving while Horus watched. But no sooner was she out that door than we'd moved everything back. And seeing as how Isis hadn't been back to visit since, we'd kept things the way we wanted. Now she looked at me like she knew what we'd done.

"Too long," Isis said. "That rotten son of mine has kept you away, no doubt."

"No doubt," I said. Horus would spit up hairballs if he heard that. It was a good thing he wasn't here. "This is Henry, by the way."

Henry was not to be spared. Isis hugged him so hard I thought Henry might throw up. Given all the dead bodies around, he was handling it pretty well.

"It's so nice to have visitors," Isis said once she let go. "At least ones that are alive. All these corpses. They never stop coming."

"Maybe you should get into a different business if it bothers you," I said. After all, didn't mummification go out of style about the same time as the fall of the Roman Empire?

"Oh, I couldn't do that," Isis said. "If I gave up the art of mummification, it could be forgotten forever."

"And that would be a bad thing, why?" I asked. The memories of her trying to remove the piece of my brains came back full force. The world would be a much happier place with no more mummification.

Isis trilled as she laughed, like she was singing a song. "You've always had such a good sense of humor. Now to what do I owe the pleasure of your visit?"

Yes, I was here about the knife, but first . . .

"What was that girl Tia doing here?" I asked. "How do you know her?"

Please don't let Isis say the knife.

Isis *tsked* in disapproval. "I don't think you received a proper invitation to that conversation, now did you?"

Right. Crazy and well-mannered. That was Auntie Isis.

"Was it about the knife?" I asked.

Isis's entire façade fell. Her skin drained of color, and the smile that had been plastered on her powdered face turned into shock and displeasure.

"The knife?" she whispered.

I nodded. I had to force myself not to take a step backward and run out of this place.

"Do you know which one I'm talking about?" I asked.

"Oh dear," Isis said. "I've tried for so long not to think about it."

"Why not?" Henry stopped chewing his cookie, and the already cold air filled us with a chill.

I guess this is where maybe I should have given this whole meeting a little more thought. Because this was the knife that had killed Isis's husband, Osiris, after all.

"Do you know what Set did with the knife?" Isis asked. Her eyes glazed over, almost as if she were talking to herself.

I nodded, but it didn't stop her from continuing.

"He crafted it from pure gold and imbued it with spells that he claimed would bring glorious times to the world. Somehow he managed to have each one of the gods, myself included, bless it. He tricked us. And it became the most powerful weapon in existence. And then, when my husband, Osiris, was celebrating the peace of the world, Set deceived him, using the knife to cut him into fourteen pieces and scattering them around the world."

"I'm sorry," I said. Isis's eyes filled with tears. I remembered how I'd felt when I'd found out my father had died. In that moment I would have done anything to bring him back from the dead. Isis was no different.

"I found the pieces," Isis went on. "And I bandaged them together, giving my husband a proper burial."

Osiris had been the first mummy ever. The whole mummification craze started with him.

"And then I found the knife and swore revenge," Isis said, wiping her tears as her eyes filled with fire.

"But you never got revenge. Why not? If you've had the knife this long, how have you never found a way to use it against Set?" It's not like I was trying to be critical, but we were talking about thousands of years here. I was going to kill Horemheb within the week.

Isis's face hardened. "Because Ra sided against me. He said the violence had to end."

Ra was arguably the most powerful of the Egyptian gods.

"But you had the knife," I said.

"Ra said I was crazy. Me! Can you believe it?"

Yes, I could believe it. Next to me, Henry cleared his throat.

"And he took it away," Isis said.

Wait, what? Isis didn't have the knife?

"So Ra has it?" My body sagged. Here I was, so close to

revenge. And now it was all going to fall apart. Finding Ra would be impossible. Nobody knew where he was or if he even still existed.

"No, dear Tut. Ra doesn't have it."

"Then where is it?" I asked, and a sliver of hope returned.

"Ra gave it to a protector," Isis said.

"What protector?" I asked. What god could be trusted with the weapon? They all rated on the crazy scale.

Isis took out a tube of lipstick from the pocket in her apron and reapplied it. And then she smoothed her poufy hair.

"What protector?" I repeated. "Who has the knife, Auntie Isis?"

"Gilgamesh," Isis said. "He's had it for ages."

12

WHERE I SUMMON SWARMS OF INSECTS

Gil has the knife?"

I couldn't believe it. That was impossible. He wouldn't lie to me. Not for all these years. Sure, he was overprotective, but he wouldn't take it this far.

"Of course," Isis said. "Gilgamesh is the perfect protector."

I tried to clear my head, but it was futile. This just couldn't be real.

"Please tell me this is a joke." I leaned against the wall, wishing I could snap my fingers and make this whole week start again. The field trip had kicked off one disaster after another in an unending chain. My five shabtis formed their protective stance around me as Isis's words sunk in.

"It's no joke," Isis said. "Gilgamesh has the knife."

"I knew the heathen was trouble." Colonel Cody paced from one of my feet to the other. "We should kick him out of the town house."

"We're not kicking him out," I said. "And he's not a heathen." Though he was a liar.

"Who's Gilgamesh?" Henry asked.

"Where does he keep it?" I asked Isis, ignoring Henry. I'd been living with Gil for nearly three thousand years. He'd never mentioned anything about being the protector of some sacred knife, and I sure hadn't seen it around our town house.

Isis's lips twisted in a big, red-lipsticked scowl. "Sadly, I wasn't told. But if you find it and want to lend it out . . ."

"You're kidding, right?" Isis seriously wanted me to get the knife for her? I was going to get the knife for myself and kill Horemheb. That's what I was going to do. I didn't want any part of the gods' scheming and games. That could only end up bad.

"I promise to give you a proper mummification upon your death," Isis said.

That was not motivation. Not only did I not want to die, I didn't want to be mummified, either.

"Forget it, Auntie Isis," I said.

"But I need the knife," Isis said. She opened her eyes so wide, I worried her eyeballs might fall out. They pleaded with me. Masked in her eyes, I saw the same emotion that I had in mine—thousands of years of revenge, waiting to be unleashed. I wanted to kill Horemheb. Isis wanted to kill Set. We needed to do it to make things right.

"Maybe once I'm done with it," I said.

Isis patted my head. "I always knew you were a good boy. I told Horus, even though he claimed you were a pain in the—"

I grabbed Henry before she could finish. "We need to go."

"What about a demonstration first?" Isis said. She snapped her fingers. "Hapi . . ."

Hapi jogged over with two knives and a roll of bandages in his hands.

"In mummification?" Henry asked, taking a step backward, tripping on his shoelace, which was still untied from earlier.

"We've got some great new preservation techniques," Hapi said. "Check it out." He pulled something from his apron pocket that might have been an apple at one point but now looked more like a shriveled old-lady face. "See how the likeness is preserved?"

Maybe it *was* a shriveled old-lady face.

"No!" I said. "And just for the record, if I ever do die, don't pull my guts out."

"Ah, silly boy," Isis said, wrapping me in a hug. "We'll take wonderful care of you."

I decided not to push it. I had no intention of dying. My looming mummification wasn't even an issue.

"In case you change your mind," Hapi said, and he handed us each a card that read "DYNASTY FUNERAL HOMES: CALL US WHEN YOU FEEL LIKE YOU'RE ON DEATH'S DOORSTEP."

"There is one other thing I wanted to ask," Henry said.

Isis cocked her head in interest. "Yes, my child."

Just the way she said it made me shudder. But Henry was determined.

"There's this project we're working on," he said. "If we could just ask you a few questions." He pulled his notebook and a red pen out.

"Not now," I said, grabbing his arm.

Henry shrugged me off. "But this is the perfect opportunity."

"I love projects," Isis said, clapping her hands together in front of her. "Ask me anything."

"Come on, Henry."

He ignored me and poised his pen over the notebook. "One question. Tell me, Auntie Isis, how do you feel when you look at the Canopic jars? I think if we can get more of the emotions behind this death box thing, we'll get a way better grade."

I could tell him how I felt: disgusted. But he hadn't asked me.

Isis picked up a nearby Canopic jar and caressed it. It was the extra one, not one of the normal four. I didn't want to imagine what she stuffed in there.

"When I behold the beauty that is the world after death, I stand in awe of those gods who came before me. Of the empire they created. And the afterworld. Do you know what it takes to get into the afterworld, dear boy?"

Henry shook his head while jotting down her words in his notebook. "What?"

She lifted the lid from the jar and placed it on a table. From inside, she pulled out a human heart. She squeezed it so hard with her pointy red fingernails that it almost looked like it was beating.

"The heart is weighed before the gods," Isis said. "If it is found unworthy, the soul will be devoured by the crocodile goddess, Ammut."

"Good, good," Henry said, still writing. "And if it is found worthy?"

"A worthy heart gains access to the Fields of the Blessed. Eternal paradise." She stuffed the heart back in the jar and replaced the lid. Hapi took the jar from her, freeing Isis's hands so she could wipe the tears from her eyes.

"That's perfect," Henry said, closing his notebook.

"And now we're leaving," I said, dragging Henry along with me. "Bye, Auntie Isis. Bye Hapi."

"Come again," she called.

We climbed the steps back to ground level, leaving Isis and Hapi down in their basement torture chamber.

"So that was fun," Henry said. "We can totally use that in our project."

My mind was far from the project. "I can't believe Gil has it."

"Wait," Henry said. "We're talking about your brother here?"

"I can't believe it, either," I said. "As if my own uncle killing my family wasn't bad enough, now Gil's been lying to me for thousands of years?"

"I'm sorry, Tut," Henry said. And I could tell that he really meant it. Except I didn't want his pity. I wanted to find out where the knife was.

"Thanks. Maybe it's just some stupid misunderstanding."

"Maybe," Henry said, but neither of us sounded convincing.

"I need to talk to him." I pulled out my phone.

can you meet? I texted.

Gil didn't respond. So I texted again, this time with a direct message.

Just talked to Isis. Found out your secret.

I was sure Gil had more than one secret, but this ought to be enough to pique his interest.

what r u talking about? he texted back seconds later.

meet me by the merry-go-round.

Henry and I got there first. Colonel Cody insisted I stay back while the shabtis scoured the area, looking for possible threats. Given that an obelisk had blown up two feet away from me, I saw their logic. Only after they declared the merry-go-round safe did we move ahead.

Henry sat on a bench, but I was too mad to sit. I couldn't believe Gil had kept me in the dark. What else wasn't he telling me? When he came into sight, I lost all control of my powers. Bugs pulled up out of the ground—worms and beetles and gods knew what else—crawling over our shoes. Flies and bees and locusts descended on us.

Gil stopped walking. "Something wrong?"

Great Amun, yes. Something was wrong.

"So Henry and I went to visit Isis—"

"You know about Isis?" Gil asked Henry.

"I just found out," Henry said. "There was this whole incident with these snakes and some scrolls Tut pulled some mumbo jumbo out of—"

Gil's eyebrows pulled together. "You used the *Book of the Dead*, Tut?"

"That's not the point," I said. "Henry knows everything."

"How did you use the *Book of the Dead*? You don't have that ability."

Horus would disembowel me if I dragged him into this.

"It doesn't matter."

"It was Horus, wasn't it," Gil said. "I am going to take that cat and—"

"I don't want to talk about Horus," I said. "I want to talk about something Isis told me."

"Which was?" Gil said.

"The knife. Isis said you have it."

Gil's face didn't even change. "So what?"

My head pounded as blood rushed through my body. "Why didn't you tell me about it?"

"Because I'm the protector of the knife, not some kind of herald of doom," Gil said.

"But you lied to me. For thousands of years." I still couldn't believe it, even when I heard myself say it.

"I had to," Gil said. "I'm not going to just run around telling people where it is."

"Which is where?" I said.

"I'm not telling you," Gil said.

The energy from the last *Book of the Dead* spell sat at the edges of my skin, begging to be freed. "Why not? This is the perfect way to kill Horemheb."

"And kill you," Gil said. "Don't you get that? It's why the gods gave me the knife in the first place. It's too dangerous for anyone to possess."

"But I need it," I said. "Horemheb has to die."

"No, Tut," Gil said. "Not this way."

Waves of immortal energy pulsed in the air between us. I wanted to tear Gil's throat out. I wanted to make him give me the knife. I clenched my hands into fists at my sides.

"Why did your uncle kill your family in the first place?" Henry asked, breaking the invisible battle between Gil and me.

"Religion." Gil spat on the ground as if the whole subject disgusted him. "It always comes down to religion. General Horemheb was trying to wipe Tut's father's religion off the face of Egypt and instill Set as the primary god."

I tried to settle the energy inside me and focus my thoughts. There had to be some way to convince Gil to give me the knife.

Henry narrowed his eyes at Gil. "So why give you the knife? Were you a pharaoh?"

"Good question," I said. "Why you, Gil?"

Gil crossed his arms. "Because the gods chose me. That's why."

Which was no answer at all.

"The same way they chose you to protect me?" After all, that's how Gil had phrased it all those years ago.

"I swore an oath to protect you," Gil said.

For all the emotion he used, Gil might as well have said, "I've been stuck in eternal hell fixing every screwup you get yourself into."

"I don't need you babysitting me."

"Tut, the messes you get into amaze me every day," Gil said. "And just like with you, I swore an oath to protect the knife. Which is why I'll never tell you where it is. I keep my oaths."

"But why?" I said. "We could use it to our advantage. We could use it to wipe out Horemheb and the entire Cult of Set."

"Just stop, Tut," Gil said. "We're not going to wipe out the Cult of Set."

"There's a cult dedicated to Set?" Henry looked at us like we'd just told him the pyramids had been built by aliens. No, scratch that—some people did believe the pyramids had been built by aliens. But Henry actually pulled his notebook out and started writing. I grabbed his pencil and snapped it in half.

"Most gods have cults," Gil said. "Even Horus has a cult, not that he does anything to deserve it besides be an annoying, smelly cat. It's just that the Cult of Set's been really active in the last century."

"Since my tomb was opened," I said. "And now that Horemheb is back in the picture, you know he's going to want this knife, too."

"I've already thought of that," Gil said.

"We should make sure it's safe," I said.

"It's safe."

"How do you know?" Henry asked, backing me up.

Gil might not tell me where the knife was, but if he got worried enough about it, he would check on it.

"I just know. Everything is going to be fine." Gil stood up and brushed off his pants.

"I'm not reassured," I said.

"I'll take care of it," Gil said. "And we'll talk more about this later." But worry sat on the edge of his face. He was thinking about the safety of the knife.

Henry and I watched as Gil sauntered away. Once he was out of earshot, I lifted Colonel Cody from the ground and whispered in his ear. "Don't let him out of your sight. And don't let him see you following him."

13

WHERE I CURSE THE SCHOOL

If only the shabtis had cell phones so I could track them. I'd have to talk to Captain Otis about that, because the next days of waiting were torture. I'd have sooner shoved bamboo shoots under my fingernails. Colonel Cody didn't come back all weekend. Gil didn't, either. I was stuck in my town house with an angry cat. I tried to explain things to Horus, but no matter what I said, he twisted it around, making it all sound like my fault.

"Just to make sure I understand, Tut, you told Gil not only about the knife but about the *Book of the Dead*?" Horus said.

"Technically no," I said. "That's what I've been trying to tell you. I didn't say a word. He found out by accident."

"Accident," Horus growled. "Matters of the gods are never accidents."

"It's no big deal. Things will work out." I had no idea how, but I said the words to make myself feel better. It didn't work.

Horus jumped from the futon to his cat scratching post and back to the futon. He hadn't sat still since I'd come home.

"How will things work out, Tut?" Horus finally said. "Please explain it to me. Because it seems to me that you've gone a little off track from our plan."

Our plan. More like Horus's plan that he'd allowed me to be a part of. And now that things had spiraled out of control, Horus didn't know what to do.

"Gil has the knife," I said. "That was never part of the plan, and it certainly isn't my fault. The plan led me to Isis. If she still had the knife, we'd be done by now. Everything would be back to normal. But instead, things are like the opposite of normal."

Horus stopped his pacing. "I just don't understand. Why Gil? Why would the Ra give him the knife?"

Why Gil? It was a good question. And it complicated everything.

What were you talking to Isis about?" I asked Tia the second she came through the door of World Cultures on Monday.

"It's nice to see you, too," Tia said.

Henry slid in next to me, his face layered with suspicion. It helped reaffirm the fact that Tia was totally untrustworthy. I knew nothing about her.

"Seriously," I said. "How do you even know Isis? What were you doing there?"

"What were you doing there?" she asked. "You tell me your secrets. I'll tell you mine."

"You know my secrets," I whispered.

"Do I really?" she whispered back. I tried to ignore the fact that she was about two inches away from me.

"I'll find out what you were doing there," I said.

"I'd expect nothing less of you, Tut," Tia said. She used finger quotes when she said my name, like that wasn't obvious or anything.

I waited for Seth to show up next, which of course, he never did. There was no way he could explain the asp pizza. He was part of the Cult of Set. That was the only explanation.

"Where's your partner?" I asked.

"No clue. It's not my job to keep tabs on Seth Cooper." Tia fiddled with a bracelet, trying to put it around her wrist, but it kept falling onto the desk. She passed it my way and held her hand out. "Can you help me with this?"

I grabbed the bracelet and tried to open the little metal thing that clasped it, but it kept snapping out of my fingers. It was some kind of charm bracelet, with about ten different things hanging from it, so every time it fell to the desk, it made a metallic clank.

"Is this new?" I asked after my third failed attempt.

"Maybe," Tia said. "And can you hurry? My arm's falling asleep."

"Where'd you get it?"

"Isis gave it to me."

I almost had it clasped, but I pulled the bracelet back to study it. Each charm was a symbol for a different Egyptian god.

"Why'd she give it to you?" I asked as I finally fixed it around her wrist. "Are you related to Isis?"

Tia pulled her hand back. "Why do you keep asking?"

"Because he wants to know," Henry said. "So are you?"

"I refuse to answer," Tia said. And she refused to say another word for the rest of class.

Henry and I headed to science. Except our science teacher wasn't there. The door was locked, and there was a bright green note taped on the glass window.

Please report to Cafeteria for Assembly

"Assembly?" Henry said.

"Maybe we have a speaker?" I said.

"Like a famous scientist or something. That would be sweet!" Henry was four steps ahead of me before I started walking.

I caught up to him, and we shuttled off to the cafeteria, only to find twenty other classes crammed inside. Janitors were frantically trying to arrange the tables to fit us all.

"What's going on?" Henry asked one of the substitutes, some suburban housewife with a total mom haircut and mom jeans on, who looked like she might break out in hives at any second.

She pulled a tissue from her giant leather purse and wiped her face, which was covered in sweat.

"Too many teachers are out sick," she said. "Some kind of epidemic. They couldn't find enough substitutes to cover classes, so you get study hall."

Henry's eyes lit up. "We can work on our—"

I put my hand up to stop him. "Don't you dare mention the project."

"But, Tut . . . ," he began.

"Not today."

Today I had bigger things to worry about. Like why a crazy sickness seemed to be taking over the school. I left the cafeteria and Henry trailed behind me.

"Where are you going?" he asked.

"I'm looking for answers." I tried to rule out the sicknesses as coincidence . . . until we came to the gym. Yellow police tape blocked the entrance. The entire building was closed down, and health inspectors were everywhere.

"What's going on?" I asked the nearest health inspector, using my commanding pharaoh voice. Kids didn't always get the most respect, but my pharaoh voice was almost as powerful as my spells.

"Insect infestation," the health inspector said. He looked eager to answer me, like having the privilege of doing so would make his day. "We have to close the building indefinitely."

"You're kidding . . . ," I said.

"Does this mean no gym class today?" Henry asked.

"Kid, this means no gym class for the rest of the year," the health inspector said. "We haven't seen an infestation this bad since the sewers flooded decades ago."

I thought Henry might jump up and down with joy.

I wasn't quite so happy. Teachers and kids were sick. Bugs were everywhere. And everything started after the obelisk blew up. I'd seen plenty of coincidences in my years. This was not one of them.

"Is there anything else?" I asked the inspector.

He scratched his head. "Yeah, it's weird, but there's some kind of black mist that won't leave. Smells like sulfur. We've tried blowing it out with fans, but it keeps recirculating."

Black mist. Sulfur. Sickness. Crazy things going way wrong.

"It's the curse," I said to Henry once we were far enough away from the gym.

Henry grabbed my arm. "Wait. Like the curse? As in *the actual curse?*"

"Great Amun, I think so," I said, squeezing my eyes shut, as if that might make all my problems go away.

"I thought you didn't believe in the curse," Henry said.

"Oh, I believe in it, all right. I was there when it all started. See, Horemheb and I were fighting in my tomb. And then we killed each other. And then the gods brought us back to life and placed a curse on us." I remembered the black mist swirling around back in the tomb. The curse had stayed hidden for thousands of years, but with revenge so close at hand, it had resurfaced.

"You're kidding, right?"

"I wish," I said. "It first showed up when my tomb was opened, back in 1922. And then, ever since that obelisk exploded, it's been attacking the world. But I never thought it would have this much power."

"So how do you stop it?" Henry jumped out of the way as a couple of bugs scampered around his feet.

I pressed my fists to my forehead. How could I stop it? The curse was a thing of the gods. Started by them, not by me. I was as much a victim as anyone else.

"I don't know. But I need to figure it out. And it's probably safest for you to stay far away."

"But . . ."

"Trust me on this one," I said. "I'll take care of it." And then I left before Henry could argue. I skipped out of school. With the gym closed and the reported fifty kids and teachers out sick, no one was keeping track of absences.

I wasn't two steps outside the front door of the school when someone accosted me.

"Tutankhamun."

I stiffened at the sound of my full name, and goose bumps exploded on my arms. I couldn't place him at first, but then I remembered. It was the museum tour guide, complete with his white robes, flaming red hair, and freaky yellow eyes.

"What are you doing here?" I asked. "Aren't you supposed to be back at the museum?"

"I came to see you, Tutankhamun," the guy said.

Kick up the creep factor. This guy was nuts. Or . . .

"You're part of the Cult of Set!" I said. There were only two other people I'd seen with hair that red: Seth Cooper and the snake-pizza delivery guy.

"Of course, Pharaoh," the museum tour guide said.

I glanced around, but nobody was nearby to hear the word *pharaoh*.

"Who are you?" I demanded. "What do you want?"

"I'm Seti 142-A," he said. "One hundred and forty second chief of the Cult of Set, and the first of three brothers."

"Let me guess," I said. "You're related to Seth Cooper."

The look of pride that had crossed his face dimmed at the mention of Seth. "My brother, Seti 142-C."

"You guys delivered asps to my town house," I said.

"Why yes, Denounced One," Seti 142-A said.

I frowned at the use of the word *denounced*.

"I must say, we never expected you to use the *Book of the Dead*," Seti 142-A went on.

"What did you expect me to do?" I asked. "Die?"

"Of course not," Seti 142-A said. "We expected the snakes to weaken you."

I shifted my gaze, looking for the best escape. "Why were you trying to weaken me?"

Seti 142-A bowed, like talking to me was some great honor. "I'm sure I could explain everything if you would just come with me."

"I don't think so," I said. There was no way this guy was on the level.

Seti 142-A smiled, but it didn't come close to reaching his

eyes. "But you must, O Heretical One. Great Set so commanded it."

I narrowed my eyes. "Great Set?"

"The greatest of the Egyptian gods," Seti 142-A said.

"Set is hardly the greatest of the Egyptian gods, and I'm not going anywhere with you," I said, using my pharaoh voice again.

Seti 142-A put a hand over his chest. "I am but a servant of Set."

I took a step closer to him. "I don't care if you're a servant of Ra himself. Leave me alone."

"Great Set is all knowledgeable; I live to follow his orders."

I almost choked at that. The idea of having to bow down to a god as horrible as Set made my stomach turn.

"And how about Horemheb? Do you follow his orders, too? Because I have a message you can take back to Horemheb. Tell him I'm coming for him. Tell him I'm going to make him pay for everything he's done to me. Tell him . . ."

My voice trailed off when I saw Seth, aka Seti 142-C, advancing on me. He buffed up with each step he took and flexed his fingers like he was going to take me down.

"Yes, O Heretical One?" Seti 142-A said. "You were saying . . . ?"

"You're trying to stall me," I said at the same time a hand clamped down on my shoulder.

I whipped around to see the pizza delivery guy, who must be Seti 142-B. He lunged for me and I jumped backward, knocking Set 142-A to the ground. And then I took off.

They followed.

I ran through the streets of D.C., cutting corners and dashing in front of cars. I ducked into alleyways and hopped fences. But every time I looked back, one of the redheaded Seti brothers was still following.

I had to ditch them and get back to the safety of my town house, if it was really safe anymore. Horus had safety spells around it. He would have strengthened them after last night's snake incident.

I doubled my speed, tore down a metro escalator, ran through the station, and came up on the other side. Dashing behind a delivery truck, I scanned the area.

I'd lost them.

But that didn't stop me from running the rest of the way home.

No sooner had I rounded the corner when I spotted the red van parked out front. Seth opened the passenger door as I came barreling past. I jumped from the ground, vaulted over the van, stomping on the top, and landed on the other side. Then I ran inside my town house and slammed the door.

B ad day?" Horus asked.

I stood there with my back pressed to the door, panting. "Not at all. What would give you that idea?"

Horus pounced on a passing beetle. "The torn clothes. The grease smears. The way you're panting like a rhinoceros giving birth."

That would explain why ten shabtis hovered around me, spraying things at me and picking at my clothes and hair. I waved the air in front of me to get rid of the smell and hurried to the family room. I'd had to explain multiple times to the shabtis that incense-scented perfume spray isn't cool at all when you're an eighth-grade boy, no matter what century it is.

"Just another day in paradise," I said. "Could you get me a water?" I asked Lieutenant Virgil. There was no sign of Colonel Cody. I guess he and his squad hadn't made it back from trailing Gil.

"Anything to prove my worth, O Great Lord," Lieutenant Virgil said. "Your commands are what we live for."

"Doesn't that ever get old, Tut?" Horus said.

Lieutenant Virgil ran off and returned with the water.

"Never," I said. "And anyway, I would hate to disappoint them by not letting them wait on me."

Just then the vent opened and five shabtis, including Colonel Cody, climbed through.

"We have failed you, most benevolent Pharaoh," Colonel Cody said. "I shall take my life and the lives of my companions if you speak it." He climbed to the top of the coffee table, preparing to jump on the wooden floor below. I wasn't sure if his granite form would really shatter if it hit the ground. This had to be the five hundredth time he'd threatened to end his existence, but I'd always stopped him.

"No! Wait!" I said. "How have you failed?"

Colonel Cody stopped with his feet millimeters from the table's edge. "The heathen spotted us."

"Gil's not a heathen. I've told you that, like, a thousand times before," I said, even as my heart sank. If Gil had spotted the shabtis, then he'd know I was looking for the knife.

"You had the shabtis trailing Gil?" Horus had lost complete interest in the beetle he was chewing and had his one eye focused on me.

"Where did he go?" I asked, ignoring Horus's glare.

Colonel Cody bowed. "We began following the heathen lord, but he spotted us early on. I believe he led us in circles before we figured it out. We trailed him across the Potomac, through the waste water treatment plant, through the gutters and bowels of the District. It was only by the third day that it occurred to us that he may be duping us."

"So what did you do?"

Here's where Colonel Cody smiled. "We feigned disinterest. We left the heathen. Or so it seemed to him. And then, only when we were sure he was no longer looking for us did we trail him again, this time to Oak Hill Cemetery."

"Great!"

Shame covered Colonel Cody's face. "But then he spotted us again. We tried to stay hidden, Great Master. But we have failed. For this we shall end our existence."

Horus flicked his tail, maybe to give them permission to go ahead with it, but I put up my hand.

"That's not necessary," I said. This was really going to happen. Gil had to be checking on the knife. So what if he knew I was looking for it? I could work with that. Maybe even use it to my advantage.

The shabtis fell to their knees and began to cry. "Our lord is so forgiving and gracious."

I tried to put on my most benevolent smile and gloated in my moment of patronage. "Did you see the knife?"

"Not precisely," Colonel Cody said.

"What's that supposed to mean? Did you or didn't you?" I tried not to sound too harsh. I didn't need Colonel Cody offering up his death as the cost of failure again.

Too late. The shabti facepalmed. "He was consulting a map when we were spotted. And once he saw us, he ran off. "

"But you can take me back to where he was?" I said.

"It will be as you wish, Great Master," Colonel Cody said.

"Not so fast," Horus said. "Today's my day to leave."

"Leave? What are you talking about?"

"It's the new moon," Horus said.

Drat. Horus and his new moon curse.

"I'm going tonight," I said.

"Wait a couple days," Horus said. "I'll go with you."

"I'm not waiting."

"Very smart decision, Great Master," Colonel Cody said. "We don't want the heathen to move the knife."

"He won't move it," Horus said. "Just wait." And then he hissed at me, as if to drive his point home. I had to sit on my hands to keep from instinctively covering my eyes. Stupid new moon and Horus going blind. It must already be happening.

"Fine," I said. "I'll wait for you."

Which was a complete lie. I wasn't waiting for anyone.

"I'm serious, Tut," Horus said.

"So am I. I'll wait." I made a point not to promise.

I held my breath, hoping Horus wouldn't pick up on my lie. His tail had stopped moving again. Things weren't looking good.

"You better," Horus said, and then he jumped onto the fire escape and out into the night.

I let out the breath I'd been holding.

"Be ready tonight," I said to Colonel Cody.

"You won't be waiting for the cat?" he asked.

"Not a chance," I said. I'd already waited long enough for my revenge.

14

WHERE I ENTER THE REALM OF THE DEAD

The shabtis cloaked themselves in shadows and we hurried through Georgetown to Oak Hill Cemetery. Two redbrick pillars stood guard at the entrance. Stretched between them, a rusty iron gate held back the cemetery, making me feel like an uninvited guest. Thousands of dead bodies lay on the other side of the fence. Dead like I would be if I didn't get to the knife before Horemheb.

The cemetery had more obelisks than Horus had catnip toys. They were nowhere near as grand as the five—well, four, now that one had exploded—new ones around D.C., but these obelisks were ancient. They came from the days when people prepared for life after death. Like how pharaohs before me had built pyramids for their final resting places. In a way, I could see Isis's point, preserving the old ways instead of giving over to the new. There was beauty in those old ways . . . except for the mummification part.

Because the shabtis were miniature, they easily slipped through the iron bars. I scaled the fence and met them on the other side.

"This way, Master." Colonel Cody pointed toward a hill terraced with overgrown paths and covered in cracked grave markers.

We wound our way through the paths, stepping on graves as we went. That whole theory about never walking on someone's grave? It's a bunch of garbage. If graves weren't meant to be stepped on, they wouldn't be on the ground. Still, with each step I took, my anxiety grew. The cemetery felt like a bucket of creepiness had been dumped on top of it, like ghosts and goblins lurked behind every grave, waiting to jump out at unsuspecting visitors. I would have even sworn one of the little angel statues next to me moved, but when I looked, everything was normal: hands in front of her, eyes closed, praying.

"Master, you're turning green," Colonel Cody said. "Perhaps we should turn back?"

Maybe he was siding with Horus but didn't want to say so. Maybe he thought this was a bad idea, too.

I pulled my sleeve up and looked at my arm. Colonel Cody was right. My normally golden skin had a pale green pallor to it.

"We're not turning back," I said. "I'm just excited, that's all."

I would not give in to the worry that pounded through me. Everything was going to be fine. Better than fine. Perfect.

We wound through the headstones and crypts, the mausoleums and markers. Once or twice I touched an obelisk, but each one was dead. They should be filled with energy. Something in this cemetery was keeping the immortal power away.

The shabtis and I crested a hill, and I immediately dropped to the ground. Gil was at the bottom of the hill, in front of a massive mausoleum. It stood ten feet tall and had an oversized, locked iron grate keeping the world out. Gil fiddled with the lock, like he was trying to get inside but something was keeping him out. He let out a couple of choice words I can't repeat and kicked the lock. It still didn't budge.

The knife had to be inside. My fingers twitched. I couldn't wait to get my hands on it. I would finally get my revenge. Once Gil left, I could get the shabtis to unlock the gate.

"Perhaps Great Master could refrain from growing the ivy?" Colonel Cody asked. "It may draw attention."

Sure enough, vines grew around us, twisting up every grave marker and fence post, cloaking the already black night in darkness.

"I'm having a hard time keeping my powers under control," I whispered. Weeds sprouted under my feet, and bugs crawled from the ground. Branches groaned from the weight of the vines, letting out noises I'm sure could wake the dead.

Gil's head snapped my way.

I jumped behind a gravestone and held my breath, counting the seconds until he looked away. The freaky angel statues around me watched as time ticked by. All the obelisks—normally my favorite shape in the whole world—felt like bars trapping me in a pit of death. And for good reason.

The angel on my left came to life. I barely had time to roll out of the way before she flew at me.

I jumped up from my hiding spot and started running down the hill toward Gil. My cover was blown.

"Tut! Get down!" Gil shouted. "There are more of them!"

I leapt behind an obelisk. At least twenty angels swept down toward me. But they didn't look all nice and sweet like angels on greeting cards. Their teeth had transformed into fangs, and what I'd thought were tears looked more like blood. Their leathery wings flapped, sending waves of a fetid stench my way.

I jumped from one obelisk to another, evading the fanged monsters and swatting at them, using my years of rusty training. Sure, I'd trained with the palace guard back when I was pharaoh, but that was thousands of years ago.

Gil leapt to the gravestone beside me. "You followed me, Tut! Do you have any idea what a stupid thing that was to do?"

"I'm here for the knife," I said.

"You can't have it! I told you that," he said as a demon angel dove right at us. We tumbled out of the way.

I knew what Gil had told me. I didn't care.

"What are they?" I yelled to Gil.

"Some sort of shabtis!" Gil yelled back.

Great. Demon shabtis.

I grabbed a concrete vase from a headstone and swung it at one of the demon shabtis. The vase smashed. I ducked and the shabti passed overhead.

I looked down at Colonel Cody. "How do you kill a shabti?" Since they were mostly made out of clay or granite, I'd always figured you just broke them to destroy them. But the vase hadn't made a dent.

Colonel Cody fell to the ground. "I will destroy myself."

"No!" I screamed. "Not you! Them! How can I destroy them?" I'd never lost any of my shabtis. I didn't know if they were indestructible. For all I knew, Colonel Cody's vows to end his existence were empty threats.

"They can only be destroyed under a command," he said.

That sounded easy. "Die, you fiends from hell!" I screamed at the demon shabtis, but maybe I'd said it wrong, because they ignored me. Okay, they ignored the *die* part of the command. But my screaming did get their attention. Ten of the demons massed into attack formation and flew at me. Their leathery wings sliced through the air like swords.

"It's not working!" I yelled to Colonel Cody.

Gil swore and cursed the shabtis. Twelve more demon shabtis surrounded him. He was trying to hold them off with some sort of kung fu fighting moves, but I swear they were just laughing at him.

"Gil!" I screamed just as one clawed at his head, taking a swatch of his long black hair with it.

He swatted at the demon. Heat pulsed off him in waves—

the immortal powers from his patron god, Nergal—but it passed right through the shabtis.

A demon shabti came at me with both hands extended for my throat. I vaulted out of the way and landed on top of an obelisk.

"How do I command them to die?" I demanded from Colonel Cody. My shabtis had started their own attack, but the five of them weren't doing much good against the army of shrieking fiends.

"You must first get them under your control," Colonel Cody said, slicing at one of the demons with a miniature sword.

My control. Of course. They weren't my shabtis. They were somebody else's. Horemheb's. There was no doubt in my mind. They were under his control. Had his commands to kill me. They wouldn't obey me; they would only obey him. Like when my shabtis always asked before taking orders from Gil or Horus. I controlled them through the spells engraved on them.

I had no plans to die today. I started to recite from the spell to control shabtis. It was written all over them, just like with my shabtis, but I'd said it enough times that I knew it by heart.

"O shabti, allotted to me, if I be summoned . . ."

I spat out the spell as fast as I could. Demon shabtis landed on my shoulders. Ripped at my hair. They cornered me and flew at me from all angles, wings flapping and hideous fang teeth smiling.

As soon as the last word of the shabti spell was out of my

mouth, I screamed, "Die!" And this time they did. All of them. The air became a cloud of thick dust as the army of demon shabtis exploded.

Gil ran for me. Blood trailed down his face from gashes on his head. I couldn't have looked much better.

"You took your time," Gil said.

"You're welc—" My words were cut off because lightning struck the ground between Gil and me. I jumped back barely in time. Smoke curled off the burnt grass. Another bolt struck, just missing the toes of my shoes. But the lightning wasn't coming from the sky. It came from the mausoleum.

Horemheb.

Lightning crackled around him, striking the mausoleum and channeling down into the earth. Through the cloud of dust Horemheb beckoned to me, taking a step forward in challenge. I hadn't seen him since that day in the tomb, thousands of years ago, but I would never forget his face. This was the man who had murdered my father, my mother, and my brother. I'd had nightmares about him for centuries. I'd dreamt of this moment. I couldn't reverse time and make everything right. But I could kill Horemheb. Make him suffer the same way I had.

The iron grate of the mausoleum burst open as a lightning bolt struck it. Another lightning bolt struck, illuminating Horemheb in all his hideous glory.

I ran for him, tearing down the hill with Gil at my heels, but stopped as lightning blocked my path.

"Little nephew. Are you still a weakling like you were so many years ago? Or are you ready to finish what we started?"

Horemheb used the same condescending tone he'd mastered three thousand years ago. I wanted to choke him.

He was taunting me. I knew it.

"I'm ready," I said, waiting for the lightning to end.

"You'll never defeat me," he said. "You, just like your father before you, are too pathetic. Too pitiable. We can only hope the gods have pity on you when I send you to the afterworld."

That was never going to happen. I was not going to die. The knife had to be inside the mausoleum. I'd get it and kill Horemheb.

The lightning shifted, making room for me to pass. I ran for him. A fresh lightning storm erupted behind me as Horemheb ducked inside the mausoleum. I passed through the entryway seconds later. Too many seconds later.

Horemheb stood in front of a golden box. He grabbed the lid and threw it to the side where it smashed into the wall, and then from within it, he lifted a golden knife.

"Get out of the way, Tut!" Gil pushed me to the side.

But Gil wasn't going to get in the way of my revenge, either. I vaulted through the air and flattened Horemheb. He couldn't have the knife. I grabbed for the knife, but Horemheb clenched it in his hand. I had to get it. Horemheb had killed everyone I loved.

"Wait!" Horemheb said as I struggled to get the knife. "I have to tell you something, Boy King." And at his words, around us, a ring of lightning crackled in the air, separating us from the world. Gil was outside the boundary, trying to dart between the streaks of lightning with no luck.

I was on my own, which was just how I needed things to

be. I grabbed for Horemheb's wrist, but he held the knife out of my reach. I could almost smell his blood by this point.

"What?" I demanded. "What do you want to say before I kill you?"

"You don't want to kill me, Tutankhamun," Horemheb said.

I almost choked from the rage welling up in my chest. Three thousand years of rage. Time slowed down. "Of course I do."

"There are things you don't know," he said.

"You killed my family. That's all there is to know."

The general's voice pushed sanity from my mind. "It wasn't me. It was General Ay. Didn't you realize that?"

"Ay?" I struggled for the knife. General Ay had been one of my advisers when I'd been pharaoh. And after I'd disappeared from Egypt, he'd ruled.

"Yes, Ay," Horemheb said. "We were working together, but he's the one who actually killed your family. Your father. Your mother. Your brother. He killed everyone. He wanted the throne for himself. If there is anyone to take revenge on, it is General Ay."

"Don't listen to him, Tut," Gil said from outside the ring of lightning.

"You're lying!" I tried to reach the knife again. I hadn't gone through fighting demon shabtis to listen to lies from a Set-serving lunatic.

"I swear it in the name of Set himself," Horemheb said. "May he strike me down if I am speaking an untruth."

I knew enough about Egyptian gods to know you didn't

swear on their names lightly. Around us, the lightning continued to strike, but it stayed away from Horemheb. Could he be telling the truth? Was Ay really involved?

"Get away from him, Tut," Gil said, his voice tight with fear.

In that moment, the knife in Horemheb's hand started glowing and the circle of lightning vanished. Horemheb lunged at me, knife held high, ready to plunge it into my chest.

Gil pushed me to safety and dove for Horemheb, shoving him out of the way. Horemheb leapt to his feet. The knife still glowed in his hand.

"You can't protect him this time, Gilgamesh," Horemheb said. "You are powerless against me."

"I'm powerless against no one," Gil said. Fire exploded from his fingertips, surrounding Horemheb in flames.

Horemheb screamed with pain. He stumbled forward and nearly fell. Gil hit him again, and the flames doubled. Shrieks echoed off the stone walls of the mausoleum. Horemheb pulled himself to his feet and ran from the mausoleum, covered in an inferno.

Gil took off after him. The sound of squealing tires ripped through the cemetery. I looked out just in time to see the red van appear. The side door opened, and Horemheb jumped inside, still a burning ember. He was out of Gil's reach.

The van tore away. Gil chased it, but it was too late.

Horemheb had escaped.

My brain cleared from its lapse. How had I been so stupid? Of course Horemheb had killed my family, not General Ay.

That's when I felt the pain in my side. When I touched it, my hands came back with blood. Lots of it.

Gil rushed back into the mausoleum, gasping for air. "He got away," Gil said. But his expression changed to one of horror. "Tut!"

I held my hands to my side to keep the blood from spilling out. It made no difference.

"I'm not sure I feel so good," I said, falling forward.

Gil caught me under the arms. "You're fine." But nothing about his voice was convincing.

"I think I'm gonna die." Every nerve in my body seemed connected to the pain. It radiated everywhere and pulsed through me.

"You're not going to die, Tut," Gil said. "You are not going to die."

I shook my head. "I am."

"If you say it again, I swear I'll kill you myself," Gil said. He ripped his shirt off and wrapped it around my stomach. Blood seeped through within seconds.

"Sorry," I said, and I slumped to the ground.

Gil hauled me up over his shoulder. "Don't you dare give up on me."

I wanted to answer him, but everything hurt too bad to talk.

I told him I was sorry for messing things up so badly. For letting Horemheb get away with the knife.

I don't think he heard.

15

WHERE I AM ISIS'S GUINEA PIG

I woke up on the futon feeling like I'd survived the fires of hell. I struggled to open my eyes but came up short.

"I think he's waking up," I heard someone say. Was it Henry?

"Finally. If Horus gets home and finds him like this, he'll skin me alive," I heard Gil say.

I managed to widen my eyes into slits. "What's wrong with me?"

"Horemheb cut you with the knife," Gil said. He paced from one side of the family room to the other, kicking at the shabtis to get them out of his way.

Horemheb had stabbed me? It was just my luck. I'd been searching for him for three thousand years, only to let him get away with the most dangerous weapon in existence. How could I have been so stupid?

"Am I going to die?" I asked.

"Gil doesn't know," Henry said at the exact same time that Gil said, "No."

Which was not a good sign.

"Why haven't I healed?" I tried to push myself up to a sitting position, but my side exploded with pain from the effort. My scarab heart should have healed me ten times over. Panic welled up in my stomach. I felt my chest. The normal warmth that came through my skin was gone. My shabtis swarmed around me, feeling my head, rubbing my feet. Colonel Cody knelt at my side with his head bowed in prayer.

"Your scarab heart is weak because of the wound," Gil said. "It's keeping you from healing."

Perfect. I felt horrible. I'm sure I looked horrible. I forced myself to look down at my side. My normally smooth and golden skin had a six-inch-long gash crusted over with blood and oozing pus. "Has it gotten worse?"

"It's gotten way worse," Henry said.

"We tried recharging," Gil said. "But it didn't help."

I didn't remember anything about recharging.

"The shabtis carried you," Henry said. "You should have seen them carting you around through the streets of D.C., trying not to be seen."

If my side hadn't hurt so badly, the image might have been amusing. Now it was just depressing.

"What do we do?" I managed to ask.

Gil slammed his fist into the coffee table. The shabtis scattered.

"I don't know what to do," Gil said. "Tut shouldn't even be in this situation."

"Then maybe you should have told him about the knife in the first place," Henry said. "Told him where it was. Maybe even given it to him yourself."

I noticed the shabtis edge closer to Henry as he stood up for me. If I somehow actually died as a result of this stupidity, I vowed to do what I could from the afterworld to make his life easier.

Gil looked out the window, away from us. "Am I the only person in the world who understands? This is exactly why the knife had to stay hidden. Now Tut is dying and Horemheb has the knife. Things couldn't be worse."

When he put it that way, it did sound pretty bad. I guess I deserved my fate. I'd as good as let Horemheb go. Why had I even started listening to his lies? Now my side hurt like my liver was being pulled out. My future was as bright as a solar eclipse.

"Look, I'm sorry. I messed up. But isn't there something we can do to fix it?" Each word worsened the pain in my side. I'd never in all my years been hurt this badly. Sure, I'd broken bones and even lost a couple fingers and toes before. But I'd always healed. I lay back on the futon, and a few of my lower-ranked shabtis fanned me with my ostrich fan collection. I was a failure. My life was going to end here in my town house, and I'd never get revenge.

Gil lifted my shirt again and grimaced when he saw the wound. "Maybe some antibiotics will help."

To say his voice was unconvincing was a major understatement.

"What about Isis?" Henry said. He pulled the card Hapi had given him out of his back pocket. "Maybe she can help."

That's when the pain took over and I drifted off again.

I woke to the smell of incense so strong that I gagged. I opened my eyes.

I wasn't in my town house anymore. Instead, I was in the basement of the funeral home, lying on one of the mummification beds. Isis's face hovered inches from my side. Beaded necklaces fell on my stomach and chest, which the shabtis made a weak attempt to hold out of the way.

"Oh, the poor boy," Isis said, pursing her bright red lips. "This is a nasty, nasty one."

She poked at the wound with a long red fingernail.

"Ughhh!" I screamed in pain.

"Quiet!" Isis snapped. "You'll wake the dead."

I didn't care anything about the dead except that I didn't want to become one of them.

"Can you fix it?" Gil asked.

Isis whipped around to face him. "Some protector of the knife you turned out to be."

Gil transformed from my cool big brother to someone who

looked like his mother was scolding him for breaking her favorite alabaster vase.

"I had it hidden," Gil said. "It was your son who set this whole thing into motion."

"Nonsense," Isis said. "It was the defiler Set who started the feud. Who, I might add, would never have been a threat if I still had the knife to begin with. It never should have been taken away from me."

"Would you two please stop arguing?" Henry said. "Tut looks green."

"He's always looked green," Isis said, patting me on the cheek. "It's my husband's blood. Good blood."

"So green is good?" Henry asked.

"His body wants to heal," Isis said. "It just needs some encouragement. It's a very good thing you called Hapi when you did. Tut has chosen his friends wisely."

Gil glowered, but at least Henry smiled.

"So can you help or not?" Gil asked.

"Of course I can help."

Thank the gods. I wasn't going to die.

"Hapi?" Isis said, and held out her hand.

Hapi moved into my circle of vision and handed Isis two things that made my heart skip about twenty beats: a long hook and a roll of Ace bandages.

"We've been experimenting with the latest in mummification techniques," Isis said.

Hapi lifted a Canopic jar from a nearby table. I didn't want to imagine what they were going to put inside it.

"I don't want to be mummified," I tried to say, but I'm not sure what came out.

"Silly boy," Isis said. "We'll have you fixed up in no time."

She leaned toward me with the hook, poising it over my scarab heart.

I tried to pass out, but Hapi held my eyelids open. I waited for the pain. The hook delved into my chest, toward my scarab heart. I let out a howl that everyone in Old Town must've heard. They twisted it a few times, making my toenails curl so much, they probably resembled Tootsie Rolls. When they pulled the hook free, I thought it was over. But then Hapi handed Isis a knife, which she proceeded to plunge into my scarab heart.

I slipped in and out of reality. I was back in my tomb, fighting with Horemheb over the *Book of the Dead*. I watched as our blood dripped onto the scrolls, sealing our immortality. I saw Osiris giving me my scarab heart. But instead of being a somewhat normal, although green guy, this time he was wrapped as a mummy. He was trying to talk, but I couldn't hear what he was saying because the mummy wrappings were getting in the way so all it sounded like was mumbling. Energy channeled from him to me, filling my heart.

I slipped away from my tomb and Osiris and back to the funeral home and to the present.

"That should do it," Isis said. She grabbed the roll of Ace bandages and started flipping me back and forth, wrapping my side.

Energy pumped through my scarab heart, restoring my

strength. And as it was restored, my side began to heal. The pain disappeared.

I wasn't going to die after all.

"He'll be okay?" Gil said.

Isis threw the remaining bandages to Hapi. "As long as you protect him better than you did the knife. I believe that's what you're supposed to do, isn't it?"

"I'll protect him," Gil said. "And I'll get the knife back."

"You do that," Isis said, wagging a finger at him like a scolding teacher. "But trust me on this. If I ever find Ra, I will have a word with him about this knife situation. It should not be hidden away. It's a gift to be used by all. Starting with me. I should be able to claim vengeance for the death of my husband."

I didn't disagree with her at all. But Gil obviously did.

Gil's face hardened, and any signs of bowing down to Isis vanished. "If you ever do find Ra, that's a conversation I'd love to hear."

"Then we're all done here," Isis said. "Hapi, dear Grandson, would you please see our guests to the door?"

"My pleasure," Hapi said. He bared his teeth at Gil. And then at Henry. And he led us upstairs.

Henry grabbed a cookie on the way out. How he could eat in a place like this was beyond me, but that wasn't why I didn't grab a cookie. I was too busy planning my future. I was alive. Horemheb hadn't won. And there was still a chance for revenge.

16

WHERE I BURN DOWN
THE MUSEUM

I slammed the door to our town house.

"Why you?" I demanded. I figured my best tactic to not have Gil lock me up for the rest of eternity would be to get him to change sides. To help me. Horus was still on his new moon exile, which was such an inconvenience. He could have helped me convince Gil.

The shabtis who had stayed at the town house rushed over the second I came through the door. I lifted my shirt and undid the bandages to show them my side. Colonel Cody almost collapsed with relief to see nothing but a thin, red scar.

"Why what?" Gil said.

"Why did the gods pick you to watch the knife?"

Gil paced the room. "Because I'm not a god."

"I'm not a god, either," Henry said. "But it's not like I got put in charge of protecting some knife."

"And I'm immortal," Gil said.

"So is Tut," Henry said. "And he didn't have the knife, either."

It was nice to have someone over six inches tall sticking up for me.

"That's because Tut has too much vengeance in his heart," Gil said.

"And you don't?" I said. "Even after everything that happened?"

It's not like Gil's background and mine were that different. We both had people we cared about die because of the gods. Sure, Gil had started off as a pretty rotten king, unlike me. I'd always been a good pharaoh. But Gil had changed. And that didn't make the gods happy. He was no longer their puppet. So a bunch of petty Sumerian gods like Enlil and Anu got upset with Gil and cursed him. And they made his best friend, Enkidu, die.

"No, I don't carry any more vengeance," Gil said. "I put my past behind me."

I believed that like I believed in the existence of unicorns.

"Did you become immortal the same time Tut did?" Henry asked.

"Hardly," Gil said. "Tut's a baby compared to me."

"And a heathen," Colonel Cody added, nodding his head emphatically.

Gil gritted his teeth but went on. "After Enkidu died, I

went looking for immortality. I chose not to get revenge on the gods for what they did, but I also wanted to live forever. To become their equal. It was ridiculous, the things I had to go through. I died nearly one hundred times over. But finally . . ."

"Finally," I continued, "Gil ate this funny plant, and then the Sumerian god of war gave him a scarab heart."

"What kind of plant?" Henry asked. "What did it taste like?"

Gil actually cracked a grin. "Seaweed." He looked down at Colonel Cody. "And for the record, I'm not a heathen. I got my scarab heart from Nergal, who's every bit as powerful as your Egyptian gods."

I cringed, even though Horus wasn't home to hear. Horus had his own opinions of the Sumerian gods. And the Greek gods. And the Norse gods. And . . . well, you get the idea.

"Of course, Great Heathen Master," Colonel Cody said.

Have I mentioned that I love my shabtis?

"So you've had the knife all this time?" I asked.

"For thousands of years," Gil said. "I hid it each time we moved, keeping it from the gods and other immortals."

"There are no other immortals," I said.

"Are you sure?" Gil asked. "There's Horemheb."

"Besides him."

"How do you know there aren't any more?" Gil asked. "There could be others. The gods gave me the knife to protect and keep away from all immortals."

"And we all know how that turned out," Henry said.

Which brought back Gil's foul mood. Maybe Henry didn't have my back after all.

"You should have told me," I said.

"No, I shouldn't have," Gil said. "I was doing my job. And now my job is completely fouled up. This is the worst mess ever."

I couldn't really disagree. I didn't have the knife. My immortal enemy did.

"We'll get it back," I said.

"No, Tut," Gil said. "I'll get it back. You'll have no part in the knife from here on out. You never should have even known about it, not to mention tried to find it. It should have remained a thing of legend, not some prize in a scavenger hunt. Pretend it doesn't exist. Pretend you never even heard about it."

I crossed my arms, preparing to stare him down.

"Am I making myself clear here?" he asked. "Or do we need to go over this again? Because this is important. The knife is not to be used. Ever. Got it?"

So Gil wasn't going to help me. That's what I got.

"Got it," I said.

"Good. And please listen this time, for once." Gil climbed the stairs to the loft and stormed into his room, slamming the door behind him.

"I think he's upset," Henry said.

"You think?" I said, fighting to keep from running up the steps, tearing Gil's door open, and snapping back a response.

"Maybe you should give him a little space," Henry said. "He may just need a good nap."

Gil needed more than a nap. Gil needed an attitude adjust-ment.

Henry pulled my sword with the teeth off the wall, clasp-ing it way too hard.

"You're holding it wrong," I said.

He shifted it in his hands and made a swipe through the air. His glasses slid all the way down his nose from the effort. "This better?"

"You look like you're trying to hack up firewood," I said. "Let your body do the work."

Henry backed up and slashed the air a few more times. I figured he was a lost cause and clicked on the television, letting the news stream through. With all the lightning and stuff last night at the cemetery, I wondered if anything had been caught on video. But all the newscaster was talking about was some Chihuahua that could walk on its front legs.

"Horus is going to freak when he gets back, isn't he?" Henry said.

"That's putting it mildly. It's a good thing I'm immortal, because Horus will want to kill me." I changed to a different channel. This one had one of those "breaking news" banners at the bottom, and the skyline of D.C. was in the background.

Henry swung the sword around until the blade pointed down at the coffee table. Ten shabtis moved out from under it and stood ready to attack Henry if I so much as raised my pinkie.

"Should we work on our project?" Henry said.

At least he had the sense to look sheepish about asking.

"Please don't mention the project again until tomorrow," I said. "I get a day off. I've earned it."

Henry pushed his glasses up his nose. "Then fill me in on a couple details so I can work on it."

"You can't wait twenty-four hours?"

"I'm making such great progress," Henry said. "But these four heads on the Canopic jars . . . they're Horus's sons, right?"

"Right," I said, focusing more on the TV than on Henry and our project.

"And Horus is the god of what?"

"Horus is basically chief god," I said. "Since Set killed Horus's father, Osiris."

"That's who your auntie Isis was married to, right?" Henry said.

"Right." I shuddered at the thought of Isis and her hooks and bandages.

Henry replaced the sword and grabbed another one. Instead of teeth, this one had feathers hanging all over it. The feathers fluttered when he swung it, and a couple fell off when the sword stuck in the wall.

"Oops," Henry said, and tried to yank it out.

The sword wouldn't budge.

"Sorry."

"Don't worry about it," I said. The shabtis made a ladder out of themselves, standing on one another's shoulders, until they could reach it. With the tiniest of tugs, it came free from the wall.

Henry scowled as they handed it to him. "So Set's not chief god?"

"Great Amun, no!" I said. "In fact, that's the whole problem. Both he and Horus think they should rule the throne of
Egypt."

"There is no throne of Egypt," Henry said.

"Don't remind Horus of that," I said. "He still has these
grand dreams of restoring the Egyptian empire to the world.
Set probably does, too."

"That would be interesting," Henry said.

But I wasn't listening anymore.

"Can you turn up the TV?" I asked Captain Otto.

He bowed and nodded to Captain Otis, who pushed the
button on the remote control a few times.

"Reports are still coming in about the fire," the news reporter said. "But from what we know now, the modern art wing
of the Smithsonian National Gallery of Art has burned. Five
people are in critical condition from burns. Never before have
we seen such damage at any national museum."

"The art museum burned down?" Henry said.

"Shhhh . . . ," I said.

"And what of the engravings found on the site?" the anchor-
woman asked.

"Yes, experts are working on the translation as we speak,"
the news reporter said, "but there are what look like Egyptian
hieroglyphics scratched into the marble above the entryway."

The image flashed to the engravings being talked about. I
stopped breathing.

"Those look familiar," Henry said.

They should. We'd just seen them last week on our field

trip. They were the same hieroglyphics that had been carved above the entrance to the King Tut treasures exhibit. The same ones that had been engraved above the entrance to my tomb.

DEATH SHALL COME ON SWIFT WINGS TO HIM WHO DISTURBS THE PEACE OF THE KING.

On the television, black mist curled around the hieroglyphics like a thick fog.

The curse had struck again. And this time it wasn't just a warning. People had been seriously hurt. Incalculable amounts of art and history had burned.

I had to find a way to stop it. I had to save the world before the curse destroyed it. And the only option was killing Horemheb. I had to put an end to everything.

17

WHERE I TAKE THE SUBWAY STOP TO THE UNDERWORLD

I have to find out where the Cult of Set is based," I said.

Henry looked at me like I'd just told him I wanted to scale the Great Pyramid upside down. "You almost died. You're not really going running off after them, are you?"

"Of course I am," I said. "Don't you see how this is all connected? The curse exists because of us. Because of Horemheb and me. As long as we're both still alive, the curse is going to chew its way through D.C. And when it's done with D.C., it's going to attack the rest of the world. People are getting sick everywhere. And in that fire . . . people got hurt. They're going to die next. I can't let that happen. That museum thing? That's just the start. And don't forget that this is Horemheb we're talking about. If you were in my shoes, you'd want revenge the same way I do."

"I wouldn't," Henry said. But he got really interested in cleaning his glasses, which he'd just cleaned.

"Not even if they were responsible for killing your entire family? They even killed my mother," I said. "Do you have any idea what that feels like? To lose everyone? And then I was all alone. And the only person I thought I could trust—Horemheb—turned out to be the worst of all. He was my top advisor. I listened to everything he said. I knew him since I was a baby. And he betrayed me in the worst way possible. So yes, I think you would do the exact same thing."

Henry didn't reply. But with every word that came out of my mouth, I knew I was doing the right thing. I had to get my revenge even if it ended up killing me. I didn't care what Gil said. This was my sole purpose in life.

"Fine," Henry finally said. "I'm in." He put his fist out, and I bumped it in return. It was a crazy, small thing, but it felt like the first moment of true friendship I'd had in years.

"Thanks, Henry," I said.

"Are you going to tell Gil?" Henry whispered, even though the music coming from Gil's room shook the entire town house.

"I'm not stupid," I said. "I'll tell him if we find something."

More like once I had the knife in my hands and stood over the dead body of Horemheb. But not all the thoughts running through my head had to be voiced.

"How do we find the Cult of Set?" Henry asked.

That was the problem. I didn't know, but there had to be a way. Some clue I'd missed.

"Can you get me a map of D.C.?" I asked Colonel Cody. "An old one, if possible."

He beamed under my request. "It brings me infinite happiness to serve you, Great Pharaoh."

He ran off and returned moments later with the map, spreading it out over the coffee table. Four shabtis stood on the edges to keep them from curling up. The map was yellow with age and cracked in some places, but the ink was still visible.

"There's no way the Cult of Set just moved to town," I said. "They've probably been here the whole time, just like me, Gil, and Horus. Since D.C. was founded."

I grabbed a pencil and tapped it on the table, studying the map for some kind of clue to their location.

Henry flattened his bushy hair with his hands and sat down next to me so he could see the map, too. This was just the kind of thing he'd geek out over. "What about the obelisks?" he said. "You said the Cult of Set built them, right?"

"The obelisks! Of course!" I turned to Colonel Cody. "Can you get me a ruler?"

"It is my greatest—" he started.

I cut him off. "Just please hurry."

And the shabti ran off.

"So during my little Trivial Pursuit quiz at the Library of Congress, Imsety asked this one stupid question," I said. "Okay, he actually asked five stupid questions—one was even about

Pluto—but that's beside the point. Anyway, the question was about Pharaoh Seti the First, who apparently had his body chopped into five pieces and buried around D.C."

Henry looked at me like I'd told him a giant dung beetle god pushed the sun across the sky each day. Which he did. His name was Khepri. But that's a story for another time.

"Seriously?" Henry said.

"Yeah, who knew, right? And Pharaoh Seti the First? He was like this huge fan of the god Set. He started this whole Set revolution in Egypt. Turned him into some kind of rock star god. People sacrificed their children to him and everything. Anyway, you'll never guess what got built on top of the chopped-up pieces of Seti the First's body."

"The obelisks!" Henry almost bounced up and down with excitement. He was way into this. It was like a puzzle, and we were going to solve it.

I scoured the map, orienting myself. Things looked so different now. I found the location of the obelisk that had blown up last week in Dupont Circle. Since the map was old, none of the current buildings around the obelisk still existed, but the circle was still there. I drew a ring around it.

"Dude, that map's like a million years old," Henry said, cringing like I'd vandalized some sacred artifact.

"I have a hundred of these," I said, scanning the map for the location of the next obelisk. It was also at the center of a large circle. How had I not noticed this before? I circled it. The third, fourth, and fifth obelisks were the same. Each obelisk had been built on a traffic circle and each traffic circle had been built on top of the hacked-up remains of Pharaoh Seti the First, super-cheerleader of the god Set.

I grabbed the ruler from Colonel Cody and started connecting the dots. It only took seconds before a symbol started to take shape. It was a three-dimensional-looking pentacle, bigger on the left and smaller on the right.

"It almost looks like a shadow," Henry said, grabbing the pencil and the ruler. He tossed away any concern he had about defacing my map. "Like if you took the five points and extended them eastward, they would all come from a single point."

He drew the lines. I didn't dare speak because I was sure my voice would shake. I was so close.

When he finished the fifth line, I jabbed the place where they met with my index finger. "That's where the Cult of Set has to be."

"And that's where we're going?" Henry said.

"That's where we're going."

I grabbed my backpack and started shoving things into it. I'd need some sort of weapon. I yanked a small sword from the wall and tossed it into the bag. And then I tossed in a second for good measure. In went the map of D.C. in case I'd been wrong. And I took my phone, too, even though I knew Gil would be able to track me down with the GPS. I could turn off the GPS if I had to.

Henry and I crept out the fire escape. The last thing I needed was Gil hearing the door open. He'd try to stop me. I kept checking behind me, making sure he wasn't following. There was no sign of him. Maybe I should have at least left a note. Gil was going to freak for sure when he found out I was gone.

Henry and I followed the map to the source of the pentacle shadow. We ended up in the middle of Chinatown. I scanned the area, but I wasn't really sure what to look for. A giant office building with a sign that read "CULT OF SET"? A neon billboard offering free curses? Purse vendors and restaurants surrounded us, and there were enough Chinese restaurants to fill the air with the smell of grease and fried wontons. At least three restaurants advertised the best egg rolls in America. Two were closed down due to insect infestation.

"Could I interest you in a watch?" some guy wearing a gaudy fur coat and a hat with a red feather asked us, showing us a huge tray of fake Rolexes. As if I'd wear a fake Rolex.

"Not today," I said.

He slid the Rolex tray back into his cart and pulled out a different tray. "Then perhaps some jewelry?"

I was about to tell the guy where he could stick the jewelry when the charms caught my eye. The tray was filled with pendants shaped like the scepter of Set. There were about a hundred little replicas of Set's most valued possession.

"Where'd you get this stuff?" I said. We had to be close.

"So you're interested?" the guy asked, shoving the tray at me.

I pushed it away. "No, just tell me where you got them."

He took my hint and tucked the tray away in his cart. And he got a lot less friendly when he realized I wasn't going to buy anything. "Some guys sells it to me. He sells me all sorts of stuff."

"What guy?" I asked.

The salesman shrugged. "I don't know his name. He never told me. But he's got this crazy red hair. Wears clothes that look like they belong back in the eighties. Oh, and I sold him this necklace that looks like scorpions dipped in gold. He wears it all the time."

Our pizza delivery guy. Seti 142-B.

"How do I find him?" I asked. The energy inside my scarab heart tingled in anticipation. I wanted to grab the guy by the collar of his fur coat and make him tell me.

"I don't know where he lives," the guy said, backing away like he could sense my aggravation. "I always meet him outside that elevator over there." He pointed across the street to a decrepit subway elevator that was boarded up with plywood and covered in graffiti.

"Thanks." I took off running. Henry trailed at my heels. I jumped between oncoming cars, ignoring the blasting horns. I was so close. In ten seconds, I reached the elevator and started looking for a way past the boards.

"You think they're underground?" Henry said once he caught up a minute later. He'd waited for the crosswalk light to change.

With all the tunnels running belowground, there was enough room underneath D.C. for an entire city. The Cult of Set could easily be hiding down there.

"They have to be." I pried a board from the front of the elevator, exposing the button hidden below. It didn't light up when I pushed it. The elevator looked like it hadn't been used in a decade. But this was my only lead.

"I think it's broken," Henry said, pressing the elevator button a few more times. He got the same result as me.

I pried another couple of boards from the front of the elevator. Underneath, it not only looked broken, it looked abandoned. The glass windows had been shattered, and the paint was so chipped, I had no idea what color it was even supposed to be. Large gouges pockmarked the metal doors, as if someone had taken a hammer and tried to get inside.

"I think you're right." I pressed the button again, just in case. Nothing.

Except I felt something with my thumb, on the button. I bent close. Carved into the button, tiny but visible, was the shape of the scepter of Set.

I dashed back across the street to the jewelry dealer, narrowly avoiding the oncoming traffic. "How much for one of your pendants?"

The guy straightened his feather hat and smiled. "I had a feeling you'd be back. You have that look about you."

"What look is that?"

He pulled the tray of pendants out of his cart, making a show of displaying it with a wave of his hand. "That look that tells me you appreciate fine things. Like jewelry, for example."

I knew where this was going. He was trying to extract as much money from me as possible. "How much?"

"For you, I'll make you a deal," he said. "Let's say two hundred dollars and call it even."

I knew I was getting cheated, but that was the least of my concerns. I yanked my wallet out and threw two hundred dollars at him. And then I grabbed a pendant. I braved the traffic again, rejoining Henry at the elevator.

"Got it." I showed him the scepter of Set pendant that rested in my palm. And then I pressed the pendant into the elevator button.

The button lit up red.

The elevator transformed before my eyes.

The rain-battered plywood boards shimmered and became stone blocks stacked twenty-feet high. The dented metal doors turned to gold. Murals appeared painted on the stones, with all sorts of symbols and hieroglyphs. A giant iron grate covered the golden doors.

"That's something you don't see every day," Henry said.

"You can see it also?" Because nobody else walking by seemed to notice that anything was different.

"I can totally see it," Henry said, running his hands over the painted stones. "One minute it was that crummy old elevator, and now it looks like the entrance to . . ."

"To a place of the gods," I said. It was definitely Egyptian and not a normal part of the D.C. landscape. And it was exactly where the map had led us.

Henry pulled out his cell phone and started snapping pictures. "We can totally use this in our—"

"Stop," I said, putting my hand up. "Don't you dare mention it."

Henry nodded and took a few more pictures. Still, nobody around us seemed to notice it. Henry and I had broken through the illusion, but nobody else had.

Etched above the door, somebody had painted bloodred hieroglyphs.

"I'm guessing you can read that," Henry said, stashing his phone and getting his notebook and pen out.

Of course I could read it.

"'Those who enter uninvited should prepare for death'," I said. "Like that's gonna scare me." I reached for the handle on the iron grate. It was a shiny golden scepter of Set.

"You're not going down there alone," Henry said, yanking my hand back.

"Of course I am." I shook off his grip.

He stuffed his notebook into his pocket. "I'm coming with you."

I'll give Henry bonus points for bravery. With all the crazy stuff going on, for him to volunteer to head into the den of a lunatic mythological cult was saying something.

"No. You're not."

"Yes, I am," Henry said.

I didn't have time to waste arguing. I was going to have to do this the brute-force way. "Do you seriously want to be killed? Because Horemheb will be happy to arrange it."

Henry crossed his arms over his chest. "I won't be killed. I promise."

"I'm not willing to take that risk. Wait here or I swear I'll put a spell on you."

"Don't you dare."

"Then wait for me," I said. "You can be my lookout."

"No."

"I need a lookout. Please? You can text me if anyone is coming."

Henry kicked at the stone blocks with his gray high-tops as he tried to maneuver around my logic. But it was flawless. Where I was going was too dangerous for Henry. He was mortal. I wasn't going to risk his life.

"Fine," he finally said. "But if you're not back in an hour, I'm coming after you."

"Two hours." I yanked on the golden scepter of Set handle. The iron grate slid open. I stepped inside, entering the world of my enemy. No sooner did I have both feet inside than the grate slid closed. Crummy music played through hidden speakers above my head, and there was only one button to push. Which meant there was only one way to go. I jabbed it with my finger and the elevator started moving.

18

WHERE I MAKE A DATE FOR LATER

I felt like I was descending to hell. I counted to fifty before the elevator stopped. And then, when the iron grate slid open, I was dumped into total darkness. I let the smallest bit of light slip from my scarab heart. I'd ended up in some kind of tunnel with cobwebs hanging everywhere, like a haunted house. Paintings covered the walls, but they were so chipped and faded that I couldn't figure out what they were supposed to be. This must not be the main entrance. Hopefully I could keep the fact that I was now officially in the den of the enemy a secret.

I tried to text Henry to let him know where I was, but I had zero bars of coverage. The bright side of this was that Gil wouldn't be able to track my phone to know where I was, either.

The tunnel ended at a giant chasm. Around the side curved

a wooden staircase that had more steps missing than denture wearers had holes in their gums. I moved from step to step, hopping over the missing ones . . . until I jumped, and a step shattered underneath me. I managed to catch myself on another step, but it shattered, too, and I fell all the way to the bottom. I landed in a puddle of greasy water that stank of dead fish, just like the Potomac. But it wasn't very deep, so I managed to wade out.

A river ran through the room and I followed it to where it dumped out into some kind of underground grotto. The river stretched from end to end of the giant cavern. Columns reached to the ceiling, painted in vivid blues and reds, and torches lined the walls, lighting the whole place up like fireworks on the Fourth of July. Murals decorated the cavern walls, and unlike the ones back in the tunnel, these looked freshly painted. Most of them showed Set in all his hideous godliness holding a giant eyeball in his right hand and a scepter in his left.

Horus was never going to believe this. I'd found the home base of the Cult of Set.

The sound of voices floated my way. I barely had time to duck behind one of the humongous columns before three people sauntered into the cavern: Seti 142-B, Seth Cooper . . . and Tia.

Tia! What was she doing here?

"You lost track of him?" she said, slapping Seth on the arm. "You were supposed to be watching him."

Great Osiris, she had to be talking about me.

"You should have tried to get him in your van," she said.

Our pizza delivery guy, Seti 142-B, brushed invisible dust

off his shirt, like the mere act of talking to Tia disgusted him. "Yeah, sorry we aren't equipped with your girly charms."

"You're not equipped with a brain," Tia said. "You realize our brother's going to be furious."

Our brother? Wait, Tia couldn't possibly be related to these two. Could she? She looked nothing like them. They were slimy like weasels, and Tia was adorable. Yes, I realized thinking about Tia's cute factor wasn't the main issue here. The bigger issue was that Tia was involved with the Cult of Set. After seeing her at Isis's, I'd thought maybe she worked for Isis. But Set? It was wrong on so many levels.

"I have an idea," Seth said.

"Your first one," Tia said. "We should have a party to celebrate."

He scowled at her. "Maybe if you manage to lure Tut here, Horemheb won't mummify you."

Mummify! Was he serious? Okay, so even though the facts pointed to Tia being part of the Cult of Set, that didn't mean I wanted to see her get mummified. I didn't want to see anyone get mummified . . . except Horemheb. But I stayed quiet and kept hidden behind the column.

"If anyone needs to be mummified, it's you," Tia said. "I can't believe we're related."

I couldn't, either. I wasn't sure what shocked me more: the threat of Tia's mummification or the fact that Tia actually shared DNA with these two.

"Would you two just stop bickering and get on with it," B said. "Check the river level and let's get back to his town house."

"What if he won't come with us?" Seth said.

"Then Horemheb will cut your heart out instead," B said.

Wonderful. At least I knew their plans for me. One thing was for sure: I couldn't let them know I was already here. Maybe my strolling right into their lair wasn't such a great idea.

Seth stuck a measuring tape into the water. It disappeared beneath the dark surface.

"Maybe one more day," he said.

One more day for what?

"Which means no more delaying. We need to get Tut today," B said.

Um, no. Not if I had anything to say about it.

I shifted the tiniest bit and my foot accidentally scraped against the sandy ground. It had to be almost inaudible, but Tia's eyes flicked in my direction.

I held my breath and tried to make myself invisible. No, I didn't have powers of invisibility, but it couldn't hurt to wish for it.

"You guys better get going," she said to her brothers. Which meant either I'd been wrong and she hadn't heard me, or she wasn't going to turn me in. At least not yet.

"You're not coming?" B asked.

She shook her head. "I'm going to check the sarcophagus."

Wait, sarcophagus? Nothing about a sarcophagus made me happy.

"Whatever," Seth said. "Enjoy your last days on Earth, Little Sis."

Okay, so my older brother and I had argued, but I now

realized it could have been way worse. I watched the Seti brothers leave through the tunnel they'd come out of, and then Tia spun in my direction and stomped with her combat boots over to the column I hid behind.

"What are you doing here?" she said. "Are you a total moron?"

I stepped out from behind the painted column. "It's great to see you again, too."

Tia hit me on the shoulder, which actually kind of hurt. "Seriously. You need to leave."

I was attempting not to get distracted by her, but she looked really nice. I figured it wasn't the time or place to tell her, though.

"No. I need to get the knife. I'm assuming you know about it, just like you seem to know about everything. I get it now. The whole reason you knew the answer to that trivia question about Seti the First being buried around D.C.? It's because you're a member of the Cult of Set."

Tia didn't deny a thing. I'd been totally duped.

"Tut, I'm not kidding. You are in huge danger here. Don't you get that?"

I tried to pretend she actually cared, because she was kind of acting like she did. But I couldn't get past her part in all this.

"Great Osiris, I can't believe you're really related to them," I said.

"Please don't remind me." She scuffed the ground with the toe of her boot. "And watch that name around here. It's grounds for execution."

"What? Osiris?"

"Shhh . . . ," Tia said, glancing around like someone might be listening. But the cavern was empty. We were alone.

"Osiris. Osiris. Osiris," I said. "Look, I said it three times and I'm still alive."

Tia looked at me like I was acting like a five-year-old. Maybe I was.

"It's your life," she said.

"You forget I'm not a fan of Set. Unlike you. You're seriously one of them?"

"Things aren't exactly how they look," she said.

Her phone buzzed. How did she get cell coverage when my phone wasn't good for anything except playing solitaire? I checked it again, but still had no signal.

"What's it say?" I said as she read the screen.

Tia stuffed her phone in a pocket of her cargo pants. "I need to get back. And you need to leave. Now." She pointed in the direction I'd come from.

I had no intention of leaving.

"Wait," I said. "Do you know where the knife is?"

"No."

She'd answered way too quickly.

"You're lying."

"Look," Tia said. "I need to finish up here and get back, or Horemheb will come check on me himself."

Just his name made me almost choke on my own bile.

"Tell me, please," I said. I wasn't beneath begging. This was an immortal lifetime of revenge we were talking about.

"No."

Tia hurried over to the other side of the cavern and ended up in front of a giant sarcophagus. It stood on a platform twelve steps off the ground and was carved of solid granite. The lid lay to the side. Tia climbed the steps and dipped some sort of test tube into the coffin. And she pulled out what could only be natron. I forced myself not to breathe.

"What's that for?" I asked.

"Nothing," Tia said.

Her brothers had mentioned mummification. Was Tia really going to get mummified? Maybe this was her sarcophagus.

I climbed halfway up the steps to join her. "If you help me get the knife, I promise I'll make it up to you. I'll help you get out of here, if you're trying to escape. I can hide you."

Tia fixed her eyes on me. "Hide me? Are you kidding? I can leave anytime I want."

"But I heard them. They're going to mummify you."

Tia scowled. "No, they aren't. But come to think of it, there is something you can help me with."

"What?" I said.

She put a lid on the test tube full of natron. I held my breath.

"How about this?" Tia said. "Stay here, right by the river. I'll be back in an hour. You help me with one small little thing, and then I'll show you where the knife is."

"How do I know you're not lying?" I said.

Tia crossed her arms, making all her bracelets jingle. "Because I'm irresistible?"

"And I thought I was the humble one."

"Right," Tia said. "I'm sure humility is the first thing you learn as pharaoh."

Her statement, though sarcastic, was dead-on. Learning that my place in life was above the common person was part of pharaoh training. I'd always tried to be humble, but when you're the most important person in an entire country, it's difficult.

The thing was that I did want to trust Tia. I wanted to believe she was different from her brothers. Because something about her told me this was the case. She hadn't turned me in. And even though she was clearly part of the Cult of Set, she had been talking to Isis. There was something more about her. Something she kept secret. Like she had a greater purpose in life that had yet to be revealed.

"Fine," I said. I'd waited three thousand years. I could wait another hour.

Tia smiled, and it spread into her eyes and lit up her face. "Perfect. I'll be back before you know it."

Her combat boots echoed as she marched away, through an archway and down a long tunnel. I watched until I couldn't see her anymore.

And then I waited.

An hour went by.

No Tia.

I gave her five more minutes, then five more. And then I decided she wasn't coming back.

So I snuck off down the same tunnel where she'd gone.

19

WHERE I DISCOVER THE FUTURE OF THE WORLD

The tunnel ended at a door, and through the door was a hallway. All signs of the river and underground cavern disappeared. Even the humidity vanished, as if moisture was being sucked from the air. Pretty soon I was sneaking down hallways that looked like the basement of some office building, except for the fact that at every possible place imaginable, be it alcove or wall or floor, there were images of Set. Seriously, how many icons did Set need? It's not like he was a good-looking god or anything. With a head like that, I wouldn't want my face plastered all over every wall and ceiling.

I kept moving, peering in each side corridor, but most led to dead ends or storage closets. I came to an interior window and ducked under it to peek inside. It was some kind of lab, and there was an army of people in scrubs working with test tubes and needles and chemicals. I had no clue what they were doing, and I didn't want to find out.

I continued down the corridor, but when I heard voices off to my right, I turned left the first chance I got. Ahead of me was a wooden door four times as tall as I was. And no, I was not short. It reminded me of doors like we used to have back in my palace in Egypt. I crept forward and placed my ear to it, but there was no sound from inside. So I pushed on it and it swung open.

It was like I was back in ancient Egypt. I mean, everything reminded me of my palace back when I'd been pharaoh. There was a royal bed, a spotted cheetah sofa at the foot of the bed, a statue of Anubis up near the headboard. The curtains around the bed were drawn back and a fake skylight even cast light down from above. Torches had been lit and placed on the walls, lighting up every treasure around the place. But instead of images of me like there had been back when I was on the throne, Horemheb's face was plastered everywhere. This had to be his room. Just the thought made me want to take a shower.

My side twinged and I lifted my shirt. The red scar flared, which was weird because it should have been completely healed. It had almost vanished after Isis healed me. I pressed on the scar. At least it didn't hurt.

I shifted my attention to a golden desk that was pushed up against the far wall. Lying on top of it was a full-color drawing of a pyramid about half the size of the Great Pyramid of Giza. It glistened in gold, and at its peak sat a crystal larger than a sarcophagus. The strangest thing about it—no, scratch that. There were two really strange things about it. First, the date at the top right of the drawing read, YEAR ONE: FIRST REVIVAL DYNASTY. And second, there were some hieroglyphs sketched around the base of the pyramid. Most of them were general stuff anyone could find in the *Book of the Dead*. But the one that caught my eye was this one:

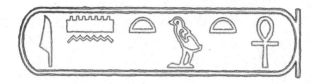

I knew these hieroglyphs as well as I knew my own name, and for a good reason. They were my name. *Tutankhamun*. The pyramid was for me.

I lifted the top drawing and found more spread across the desk. My scarab heart skipped as I recognized the giant golden pyramid as the main feature on the sketches. But the sketches were of more than just the pyramid. They showed an entire city with the pyramid at its center. And not just any city. They showed Washington, D.C. I'd lived here long enough to recognize it anywhere—even with all sorts of Egyptian structures drawn overtop already existing buildings. The pyramid was on the Mall near the Archives building, and where Capitol Hill currently stood was drawn an obelisk twice as high as the Washington Monument. On the side of the obelisk a giant scarab had been inscribed. And where the White House normally sat just north of the giant Ellipse park was a palace with all kinds of columns and Egyptian statues instead.

Did the Cult of Set seriously think they could build Egyptian stuff all over the District?

With each second that passed, the unease doubled inside me. The Cult of Set was creepy, sure. But this place, with its natron-filled sarcophagus and subterranean medical laboratory, felt sinister. There was so much going on here, and I had no idea what it all was.

I had to find the knife, eliminate Horemheb, and then get the heck out of here.

The door opened. I jumped halfway across the room, scattering the sketches everywhere.

"Scared?" Tia asked.

Thank Amun it was only her. Horemheb catching me here could not end up good. At least not until I got the knife.

I tried to calm my heart—which had also jumped out of control. "I don't get scared."

Tia raised an eyebrow. "Not even of Set?"

"Please. I'm an immortal. What would I have to worry about?"

"Getting your heart cut out?" she said.

Yeah, there was that.

She pulled me from the room and shut the door behind us. "What part of stay by the river didn't you understand?" she asked after she led me to a side hallway off the main corridor.

"You were late," I said. "I got bored."

She balled her hands into fists of frustration. "Not so smart, Tut. Did it even occur to you once that there might be a security system around here?"

Um, no. So I hadn't given it a thought. I'd been too focused on the knife.

I pressed my palm to my forehead. Security could be on their way here right now. "Do your brothers know I'm here?"

"Not yet," she said. "I managed to sabotage the video footage."

"I guess I should thank you for that?"

"Yes, you should." Tia whipped her head around, looking behind us to make sure no one was following. I got a huge whiff of her lotus blossom perfume. Just the scent of it helped clear my mind of my growing list of problems.

"Um, thanks," I said, and then I noticed her hair. "Wasn't the streak in your hair blue earlier?"

Tia reached up and grabbed it, almost like she was trying to cover it. "Maybe."

"It's orange now," I said, stating the obvious.

"Yeah, so what about it?"

"Were you coloring your hair?" I said. "Is that why you were late? You left me by the river with your crazy brothers running around trying to capture me, and you went off to color your hair?"

Tia lowered her hand and met my eye. "I color it every day. If I skipped, they might notice. And if they noticed, they might think something was wrong. And if they thought something was wrong, it might make them suspicious."

She'd obviously given the whole hair-coloring thing lots of thought. And seeing as how she was allegedly trying to help me, I decided not to press the issue.

"It looks nice," I said, forcing myself not to look down, even though my whole face heated up.

Tia's mouth sweetened into an amazing smile. "Thanks, Tut."

"You're welcome," I said, clearing my throat. "So are you going to show me where the knife is, or what?"

She leaned toward me, maybe a little closer than she needed to. Or maybe that was my imagination. "I said I would. But first you have to promise to help me."

I attempted to get my brain back on the task at hand. "With what?"

"A quest."

I busted out laughing. "Oh, come on. What kind of quest?"

Tia didn't laugh. "A quest to reunite the gods."

I realized she was serious. Not to mention ridiculous.

"What do you mean, reunite the gods?" I said. "Half of them hate each other, and the other half think that half don't deserve to be gods in the first place. Controversy is a pillar of their existence."

"Exactly!" Tia's face beamed with excitement as she spoke. "They need to put all that aside. They need to be reunited. And the time for that is now. This is the dawn of a new age."

I narrowed my eyes. Tia was crazy if she thought her plan was even possible. "And you're the one who's going to do that?"

"Why not me?" Tia said.

"Because you're not immortal," I said.

"And that's a requirement?" Tia asked.

I figured since it was an unattainable task, there were no defined requirements.

"Okay, fine. You want to reunite the gods. What's your plan for this great reunification?"

Tia's eyes lit up and she started holding out the different pendants from around her neck. "I steal sacred items of each of the gods. You know every god has one specific item that is the primary source of their power. Each item I get, I deliver to . . . well, I can't tell you that part because I'm sworn to secrecy."

"By who?"

"Didn't you just hear me?" Tia said. "I can't tell you. Anyway, once I get all these sacred objects, the power of the gods will weaken until they have no choice but to seek them out. And when they do, the . . . person . . . I'm working with will call the gods to order and only restore their power once they agree to new terms."

"And these new terms are getting along?" It was a ridiculous plan. So ridiculous that I wondered if it could actually work.

"Exactly," Tia said, smiling because I got it. Like with the hair coloring, she'd given this god-reuniting plan a bunch of thought, too. "So are you going to help me or not?"

Helping her with her quest did mean I'd get to spend a little extra time with her. And I'd get the knife. But stealing stuff from the gods? I wasn't sure I wanted to get mixed up in that. Gods got angry. And held grudges for millennia.

Sort of like me. I'd been holding hatred against Horemheb in my heart for thousands of years. The difference was that my grudge was totally legitimate. He'd given me a reason to hate him. He'd killed my family and taken away my entire world.

"I don't know," I said. "The gods will get pretty upset if you start taking things from them."

"They'll never know who took them," Tia said. "And anyway,

you're not getting your precious little knife unless you promise to help me."

That was the important carrot being dangled in front of me.

"Fine." I figured that, since hanging around with Tia was awesome, I could at least go along with her plan.

"Perfect," she said. "Just follow my lead."

The way Tia moved made me think this wasn't the first time she'd snuck around. She evaded cameras, pointing them out as we went, and took back hallways all around the place. As the darkness closed in, I followed her in silence. When she turned, I turned. When she stopped, I stopped. The last thing I wanted to do was get lost. With the maze of corridors she led me through, I'd never find my way anywhere without her.

"Why are you so good at sneaking around?" I asked. Marble columns surrounded us at every turn, and the black tile floor was shellacked so deeply, I could see my reflection in it. And along the walls, myths had been painted—except they all seemed to show Set being victorious over some other god—most of the time Horus.

"My brothers," she said.

"You hide from them?"

"Only when they're trying to kill me."

"You're kidding. . . ."

"Do you really think so?" Tia said.

Given the whole mummification talk, I guessed she wasn't lying.

"So how many people are in your psychotic cult anyway?" I asked after we hid from five guys who were polishing the floors.

"Whatever, Tut. It's not like Horus is any better than Set."

"Set killed his brother," I said.

"Set is misunderstood."

Misunderstood was not the word I'd use to describe Set. Fratricidally sadistic was way more appropriate.

"Anyway, there are enough," she said. "At least enough for my brother's plans."

"To take over D.C.?" I laughed. "Like that's going to happen."

"Crazier things have happened in the past," Tia said. "And Seti 142-A is sure the world is ready for a change. That's why my plan has to work. We can't have Set, or any Egyptian god, for that matter, taking over D.C."

Her plan did make sense—if there was any chance it would work. I kind of liked the world just like it was—minus Horemheb. I didn't want to see it change and have the world become a plaything of the gods.

We ended up in an atrium. In the center sat a building that looked like the crown jewel of the whole complex. It towered above every other structure and reminded me a lot of an oversized Lincoln Memorial: square with giant columns and a ton of steps. Trees of all sorts lined the perimeter, placed in stone urns, each big enough for Horus's four sons to sit in. And instead of a statue of Abraham Lincoln sitting at the top of the stairs, a giant sculpture of Set stood in its place.

Over the years, I'd seen various incarnations of Set. Thank the gods I'd never seen him in all his flesh-and-blood godliness. But the incarnation in front of me now was the most ferocious, venomous, deadly image of the god I'd ever seen.

He stood thirty feet tall, had clawed hands and feet, and muscles popping out of places I never knew muscles could pop out of. He held a sickle with a blade sharp enough to slice passing dust particles in half. And his face drew my eyes and held them. The fanged teeth were bared, protruding from the snout nose.

"Nice statue," I said.

Tia immediately put her finger to her mouth in a shushing motion. I couldn't help but notice how pretty her lips were. Inwardly, I groaned. I was getting more pathetic by the second. So I filled my mind with thoughts of demolishing Horemheb. It was really going to happen. But my thoughts got the better of me, and flowers and leaves started sprouting on the trees nearby.

"What are you doing?" Tia ran to the nearest tree and clamped her hand over the new growth, attempting to hold it back. But branches and leaves pushed through her fingers.

I swore inwardly and tried to turn off my godly power. "I can't help it."

"You better learn to help it soon, or we'll get caught," she said.

"Would you get in trouble, too?" I said, trying to be funny, even as I tried to focus on controlling my supernatural powers.

Tia glared at me. "Just stop the flower thing, okay?"

"I'm trying." And I was. Ten deep breaths later, all the new growth had come to a halt.

"Good," she whispered.

I wondered how long I could keep control of the plant situation. Hopefully until I got the knife and cut out Horemheb's polluted heart. We climbed the steps, hiding in the shadows. I hoped she knew what she was doing.

"Who's there?" a voice called.

Both Tia and I froze mid-step.

"I said who's there?"

I peeked around a column, not daring to breathe. A priest wearing a fake Set head stood inside the temple, near the altar. His ears reached a foot tall each, and fangs had been painted in bright red around his mouth. On top of the altar was a golden bowl that was big enough to bathe Horus in—not that I'd ever given Horus a bath—oh, except for that one time back in ancient Mongolia, but he'd sworn me to secrecy about the whole thing. The priest took a step toward us, even though we were hidden. Behind him, ten flowers bloomed on a fig tree.

"Ungrow them." I could hardly hear Tia's words between her clenched teeth.

"I can't ungrow them," I whispered back. "Plants don't work that way."

"Is anyone there?" the priest called again.

Neither of us moved.

An excruciating minute passed. I was sure we'd be caught any second. I barely held control of my powers. They threatened to explode with each second. Finally the priest shook his Set head and turned back to the altar.

The flowers on the fig tree burst into full bloom.

The priest tensed. I forced myself not to breathe, knowing at any second he'd call out the whole Cult of Set security force. There was no way that would end in my favor.

He stepped from the altar and slowly circled the room. Tia's hand grabbed my arm and her fingernails dug into my skin. I'm not sure if she was trying to help matters or whether she was just nervous. I held my breath.

After what felt like an eternity longer than my immortal lifetime, the priest said a prayer to Set, then left the temple.

The second he was out of sight I relaxed, and in a final burst, every tree in the place blossomed. Bugs crawled from the walls, spilling out onto the floor. Flies filled the air, clustering around the lights like shadows.

"That was way too close," Tia said. "Control yourself."

"Get your fingernails out of my flesh."

Blood pooled under each of her nails. Tia instantly let go and I passed my hand over the wounds, channeling energy from my scarab heart and healing them over.

"And stop showing off," she said. But the torches around the temple gave off enough light that I could see she was impressed.

"One of the benefits of immortality," I said.

"Can you heal this?" She pulled her sleeve up and held out her arm, causing her bracelets to hang low over her hand. A red line ran from her elbow to her wrist, just barely scabbed over. It looked like someone had cut her with a knife.

"How'd you get that?" I reached out and touched it, pushing her bracelets out of the way.

"A fight," she said.

I'd lived long enough to know there was way more to it than that.

"Something to do with your quest?" I asked.

Tia nodded. "The last object I tried to steal. I almost got caught."

"What was it?" I asked, tracing my fingers over the cut on her arm.

"Did you forget about the secrecy thing?"

Her and her secrets. "Can you at least tell me if you got it?"

She scowled. "I didn't get it. But I will next time."

I let go of her arm even though I kind of enjoyed holding it. "I can't heal other people. Just myself. I'm sorry." And I really was. It was a great power, being able to heal myself. But it also felt kind of selfish. Like I should be able to do more for other people but never could.

"It's okay. It will heal on its own." Tia pulled her sleeve back down and pointed to the altar. "Anyway, your knife is up there."

"In the bowl?"

She nodded.

"But that's so easy," I said. Amun, I could have found that on my own with a little more time to look around.

"It's protected by a deadly weapon," Tia said. "So be careful."

"What kind of weapon?" I asked. Why couldn't anything be easy?

"A *deadly* one," Tia said, enunciating the word *deadly* as if to say, Didn't you hear me the first time, moron?

I rolled my eyes. "Thanks."

"Good luck," she said. "And hurry up."

I tried to still my nerves, but insects continued to pour into the room. I needed the knife. And anyway, how deadly could the weapon be? I was immortal.

When I got within two steps of the altar, I heard the voice.

"Tutankhamun."

It was so soft that I thought it was a whisper. But when it came again, I realized it wasn't even a whisper; it was in my mind.

"Tutankhamun." A red glow escaped from the bowl along with the scent of burning cinnamon.

I took another step and reached out, wanting to touch the light. I inhaled the smell, and things started to get a little fuzzy.

"Tutankhamun," the voice said again. Along with my name, it started pushing something through my mind. Or pulling. Memories began to flow.

I was back in my palace, running like a wild child through the halls, getting in the way of every servant I passed. I'd never been raised to be pharaoh. That was always going to be my brother, Smenkhkare's, job. I got to do whatever I wanted. Play in the mud. Skip out on boring formal events. Smenk, on the other hand, was the one who had all the instruction. He was the one with the prearranged marriage. He was the one who had to spend his childhood sitting in on important meetings with our father. And he was also the first one killed.

I'd been the one to discover his body. I'd run into his rooms in what was just one more attempt to get him to play with me. But when I pushed the doors open, even though it was midmorning,

Smenk was still in bed. I tried to shake him. He didn't wake. I tried harder, calling his name and trying to lift him up, but his body fell limp back to the bed. Smenk blurred in my vision and my eyes got really watery. He wouldn't get up.

I screamed at him. Kicked him. He never moved.

It was my cries that had drawn the palace guard. An investigation had been made. But no foul play had been found. I was only five at the time, and in my mind, my brother was perfect and cool and awesome. Everything a big brother should be. Except he was dead.

M y memories shifted, and I sat with my mother in the palm house. *Life sure changed after my brother's death. I had all sorts of responsibilities. All kinds of training. I was destined to be pharaoh after my father, but I had no clue how to rule a country. I had tutors for every subject possible, so education took up the bulk of each day. I had to learn manners and foreign languages and how to be a good moral judge. It hurt my head. Most of it I hated.*

My mom knew exactly how I felt and insisted I get time with her each day. We'd spend our time in the palm house, which was connected through a breezeway to the main palace. It was our special place, and when we were there, no one else was allowed in. The servants would bring us a light snack, most of which I would feed to the fish. My mom would tell me stories while I played in the pond and studied the plants. I would pretend I had important tasks to do, cataloguing the different species, just so she would stay with me a bit longer. She always went along with my games. She told me of all the magnificent things I would do when I became pharaoh. How wise and just I'd be. I believed her.

I remembered the day her voice fell silent. She'd been telling me a story about how the world was created with a cosmic egg. Even though it was a long story about religion, which had never been my favorite subject, the way my mom told it had me laughing and crying in the span of minutes. She'd just finished a particularly sad part. I thought she was taking a break. Having a sip of wine. I kept feeding the fish and hid my tears so she wouldn't think I was weak.

When she didn't begin talking again, I looked in her direction. She lay slumped over on the bench.

"Mother!" I rushed to her side.

"I don't feel so well, Tut," she said. "I need help."

It was too late by the time I got help. My mother was dead.

Horemheb had been behind it. He'd been in control of the death reports. It was no wonder foul play had never been found. I should have been suspicious because, when my tears fell into the pond, all the fish were dead, too . . . from the food I'd been feeding them.

M y mind shifted again, but this time it was no memory. I stared down at my own dead body, laid out in the sarcophagus made of granite. Natron covered every part of me except my face. Even though I was dead, my entire body ached, like all my insides had been pulled out while I was still alive. Like somehow I was dead in the sarcophagus and yet still alive.

"You will die, Tutankhamun," the voice in my head said. "You

*will fail at everything in life and then you will die. You are a fail-
ure. You are worthless. You are the reason your family is dead."*

It was my worst fear.

This wasn't real.

This wasn't going to happen.

And I'd had enough.

I pushed the images away. They came back with twice the
strength, nearly dropping me to the ground with the horror
of emotions they brought. Memories from my past and visions
from my future flooded me. I pushed harder against them.
Failure. Worthless. The words were repeated over and over again.

I was not a failure. I was not going to be a part of these visions. And I didn't have time for games.

I plunged my hands into the golden liquid. It began to coil
and twist like liquid mercury. I tried to pull my hands out, but
they were locked in place. The golden liquid seeped into my
pores. I tried to push it out, but it was no use. It burrowed inside me. And then it was gone.

At the bottom of the empty bowl lay the knife. Three gem-
stones decorated the hilt, and the blade was pure gold. The
only time I'd seen it had been in Horemheb's unworthy hand
in the cemetery.

Now it was within my reach.

I grabbed the knife and held it victoriously over my head.
I would have my revenge.

20

WHERE I STEAL THE HOLY SCEPTER OF SET

No sooner was my hand out of the bowl than the golden liquid regenerated.

Tia stared at me with wide eyes. "You're crying." She took a step forward and her arms moved out a little, like she wanted to hug me but wasn't sure if she should.

I stepped to the side, out of her reach. "It's nothing." I tucked the knife into the waist of my jeans.

"Are you sure?" She reached up like she was going to wipe my cheek.

I didn't want her pity. I wanted revenge on the person who'd made those memories part of my past in the first place.

"I'm fine," I said, willing my eyes to dry up. "Now what?"

"Tut . . ." Tia's blue eyes pulled me in. Made me want to trust her.

Gods, I just wanted to trust someone. Why did the world have to be such a difficult place filled with people who all had their own agendas?

"I promise. I got what I wanted. Now what do you need me to do?"

Tia blinked a few times, and I swear there were tears in her eyes. Or maybe I was imagining it because I wanted her to care. But she had her own agenda just like everyone else in the world.

"I need you to get the scepter of Set," she finally said. She pointed across the temple to the looming statue of Set.

The scepter was so small that I'd missed it before. Set held it in an upraised hand, resting it on his palm. Torchlight bounced off it, casting gold sparkles everywhere. It was up kind of high, but aside from that, it was just sitting there, not even bolted down. "What do you need my help for? Couldn't you just use a ladder?"

Tia looked like it pained her to admit she needed help. "Only an immortal can take the scepter from the hands of Set." She scuffed her feet, kicking a few of the overgrown leaves out of the way.

"Oh." For a second, an overwhelming feeling that she was using me set in. But then I looked at her, and her blue eyes looked into mine, and I knew I'd steal the scepter for her. Tia wasn't the kind of person who liked to ask for help. That was obvious. And her quest—this whole thing about reuniting the gods—well, at least it wasn't self-serving. She had a noble cause. She was trying to help the world. It made my whole quest for vengeance seem petty.

"Just tell me what I need to do," I said.

Relief flooded Tia's face. "Thank you, Tut." She hugged me really quick and pulled away, not meeting my eyes.

My face had to be bright red. Tia had hugged me. I tried not to think about it too much. I was still in the den of the Cult of Set. My life was in danger.

"You're welcome," I said.

"Okay, so here's what you need to do," Tia said. "Climb up onto the statue and grab the scepter. Oh, and try not to grow any more flowers, will you?"

I ignored her jibe about the flowers. She was back to her usual sarcastic self.

"That sounds easy enough," I said. "And then what?"

"Then run."

I handed her my backpack and started forward. I'm not sure how many times I turned to check the entrance. The closer I got to the statue, the more I actually wished someone would come through the door and catch me, forcing me to run away. Set was scary—like the worst mummy movie come true. When I looked up at him, I swear I saw saliva dripping from his fangs. Or maybe it was blood. I couldn't see the color in the torch-light.

"It's only a statue," I muttered, but I knew I'd probably turned green.

"Did you say something?" Tia whispered.

No way was I going to let her think I was scared of some stupid statue. Even if each step I took made my knees feel like collapsing under me.

"No, nothing," I said. But then I started to lose control, and within seconds, the trees burst into motion. Branches sprouted, twisting toward the ground under the weight of the leaves and flowers that filled them. Petals fell, blanketing the temple floor. And the tallest trees pushed at the sanctuary ceiling, groaning as they were pushed back by the beams overhead.

"Stop it!" Tia said. "The priests are going to come back."

"It's not the priests I'm worried about."

I looked Set right in the eye. Searing pain tore through my side. I collapsed onto the floor. In my whole life, I'd never felt anything like it.

"Holy Sekhmet! Are you all right?" Tia knelt on the ground next to me.

Through my tunnel vision, I saw her face—forehead creased and bottom lip pressed between her teeth. The sight of her calmed me, and the white started to fade along with the pain.

"Just give me a second."

"Are you going to die?" she asked. Maybe I was fooling myself, but I swear I saw concern on her face.

I wasn't sure how to respond. I mean, the whole thing made me feel so weak—so human. But my side hurt like I'd been bitten by a crocodile. I thought Isis's healing stuff had fixed me.

"Would that bother you?" I asked, having no idea what her answer would be. But if I'd had a list of possible responses, what she said next would have been last on the list. No, it wouldn't have even made the list.

"I guess we'll find out when they mummify you," she said.

"What!" I jolted up, pain or no pain in my side.

"Quiet!" she said. "The priests!"

"I don't care about the priests," I said. "What do you mean mummify me?"

She shrugged. "You know."

"No, I don't know," I said. "What are you talking about?"

She looked at the looming statue of Set, illuminated in full hideous glory by every torch in the room. "Just get the scepter, and then we can get out of here and talk about it."

My mouth opened, but I wasn't sure what I was going to say. Here she was talking about mummification, and she still wanted me to steal some stinking scepter for her.

"Fine." I stood up. The pain was gone, and I doubted it would be able to push past my anger and return. I glared up at the glistening teeth of the statue. Yes, Set was still scary. But I'd had about as much of this as I could take.

Set was six times as tall as me. But I was immortal. And I had no time to waste. I squatted down and sprang straight up, landing on Set's lower hand, the one he had clasped around the handle of the sickle. I scaled my way up the handle to his shoulder. From his shoulder, I climbed across his chest and out onto the arm that held the scepter. When I reached his upraised palm, I wrapped my fingers around the cold metal of the scepter.

The world around me turned to chaos.

Alarms began to blare, sounding like hyenas on steroids. Lights began to flash. I catapulted off Set's palm and landed on the ground.

"Give yourselves up to Great Set or face his terrible wrath!" an intercom voice boomed above the sound of the shrieking hyena alarms. Tia was already halfway out the door. Behind me was the sound of feet running on hard limestone. Great Osiris, the priests would be here any second.

"Run, Tut!" Tia said.

I didn't have to be told twice. The threats coming over the intercom of execution by dismemberment were enough to make me not want to get caught. My skin broke into a rash of goose bumps. It was one thing to live forever. It was another entirely to live forever cut into numerous pieces.

I tore after Tia. No way was I going to get caught now.

"Where do I find Horemheb?" I yelled as we ran. Now that I had the knife, I had to complete the job.

"You have to get out of here, Tut," Tia said, leading us left and then right and then left again. "Everyone's going to be looking for you."

"But I need to kill Horemheb."

"Not now. You got the knife. Horemheb will come to you."

Tia made a valid point. This place was pandemonium. At every turn, guards searched for us. I'd leave, and when Horemheb came looking for the knife, I'd kill him then.

"How do I get out? The river?"

"I'll show you. But you need to hide until things calm down."

"I don't want to hide like a coward. I want to fight Horemheb."

"Will you fight the entire Cult of Set?" Tia asked.

Another good point. Horemheb I could handle with the knife. But an entire security force added unneeded complications. My backpack full of supplies wasn't going to put much of a dent in them.

Tia shoved open a door. We ran inside and locked it. I could still hear the sirens, though they were dulled by the thick wooden door.

"Give me the scepter." She dropped my backpack to the ground and held her other hand out.

"You forgot to say please," I said, holding the scepter out of her reach.

"Now, Tut," she said. "Before someone decides to look in here."

I started to hand the scepter over to her but stopped. It was pretty—all shiny and gold. Would taking it away really weaken Set? Maybe I should keep it. Horus would think he'd gone to kitty heaven if I brought this thing home.

Tia reached out for it, but I pulled it back so her fingers closed over empty air.

"Not so fast." I turned it over to see the hieroglyphic engravings. "Chaos," I read, turning it to see some more. "Power. Storms."

"Now, Tut."

"The magic word?"

"Please?" Tia gritted her teeth like it pained her to lower herself to that level.

"Fine." I handed it over. Sure, Horus would like it, but I wasn't going to betray Tia. She'd trusted me. And I was not a betrayer like Horemheb.

The second Tia's hands grabbed it, I swear she glowed. But then the glow went away just as quickly.

"Happy now?" I asked. "Forget it—I don't care. What did you mean about the mummification?"

"I meant what I said." She tucked the scepter into a deep side pocket of her cargo pants. "If you get caught, they're going to mummify you. Some ceremonial thing. Great Anubis, they're even planning on building that gaudy golden pyramid to put your mummified body in."

"You think it's gaudy?" Maybe it was a stupid thing to ask, but the pyramid was actually way cool.

"Yes," Tia said. "But for what it's worth, I hope you escape."

I started to respond, but voices caught my attention. The guards weren't far away.

"Me, too," I said. "How do I get out?"

"Once things quiet down, sneak out," Tia said. "If you turn left three times, go up two flights of steps and through the set of glass doors, you'll find a storage closet. Behind all the junk inside is a ladder to the surface. Climb it and it will lead you out."

My heart pounded. I was really going to get out of here with the knife. Gil probably hadn't even noticed I was gone yet. I'd show up at the town house with the knife, and then he'd have no choice but to help me get my revenge on Horem-heb. And then, once I'd gotten my vengeance, we could both be guardians of the knife. We could hide it away forever.

"What about you?" I asked.

"I'm leaving now," Tia said, patting the pocket of her cargo pants where she'd put the scepter. "The last thing I need is me being caught in here with you."

Actually, the last thing we needed was me being caught at all.

"Will I see you again?" I said, hoping I didn't sound too much like a puppy dog.

"A girl can only hope," Tia said. And then she leaned over, and before I knew what was happening, her lips were on mine, and she was kissing me. And not just some regular, plain-papyrus kind of friend kiss like you might see in some cheesy mummy movie. This was a full-on, scarab-heart-glowing-bright-red kind of kiss. The kind I hadn't had in centuries.

I knew my scarab heart was glowing; it had basically stopped in place. I felt like it was going to burn a hole in my chest. But just as quickly as the kiss had happened, Tia pulled back.

"Catch you later." She cracked the door open and slipped through.

I pulled the door closed but, not five seconds later, it burst back open. Ten guards filed into the room. I wanted to grab my backpack, but they surrounded me. And then Seti 142-A, com-plete in his loincloth getup, pushed his way through the guards and sauntered up to me.

I tried to act casual, like I was supposed to be here even though this was not part of any good plan. "Oh, hey, Seti 142-A. Long time, no see. What's going on?"

"Oh, Former Ruler of Upper and Lower Egypt," he said. "You have decided to join us after all."

I pretended to laugh. "Funny about that. I was just on my way out. So if you'll clear your guards out of here, I'll leave you to whatever crazy cult business you have planned."

Seti 142-A pretended to laugh, too. "But Tutankhamun, you are an integral part of our plans. We can't allow you to leave."

"What is it you have planned, exactly?" I prayed he didn't say the word *mummy* in his response.

"Great Horemheb himself will cut your heart out," he said. "And then our finest craftsmen will mummify your body and provide a path for your entry into the Fields of the Blessed. It will be the dawn of a new dynasty. The people will rejoice. The world will once again be set in order."

I scooted backward—straight into a guard. When had he snuck up on me?

"I'm not so crazy about that plan," I said.

"That is irrelevant." Seti 142-A nodded at the guards. They grabbed me.

"Now if my heretical pharaoh would follow me this way. The final preparations for your ceremony have been made."

Blood rushed to my head. "What is it with you guys and mummification? Do you think that's the solution to everything? If someone doesn't fit into the equation, you just mummify them?"

"Mummification provides eternal life," Seti 142-A said, as if I'd just questioned the sun rising each morning.

"But I'm already immortal."

"True," Seti 142-A said. "But Great Horemheb insists upon cutting your heart out and devouring it, ensuring you will never reach the afterworld."

It was a horrible visual image. I wanted no part in it.

The guards yanked me down the hallway. Seti 142-A said nothing, and before I knew it, we were back in the tunnel leading to the underground river. My stomach knotted and I yanked against the guards, but there were too many. My feet felt like limestone blocks as I followed Seti 142-A. I was pretty sure I was going to throw up. Tia was nowhere to be found, but I did see Seti 142-B and Seth nearby. Seth made a giant L with his fingers on his forehead. I would have shot him the bird if guards weren't holding my arms.

Then I saw Horemheb. He stood next to the sarcophagus, dressed in a red tunic. Around him were three priests, just like I'd seen so long ago in ancient Egypt. It was like history was repeating itself. On the altar beside them sat the giant golden bowl.

Wait. Maybe they didn't know I had the knife. Maybe they thought it was still in there, submerged below the golden liquid. If I played everything right, I might actually be able to get out of this without my heart in Horemheb's stomach.

Tia strolled into the cavern then, moving over to Seth and whispering something in his ear. He laughed in response and actually smiled at her, like she'd done something right.

I opened my mouth to yell to her, but I was breathing too hard to get anything out. And then pain tore through my side, crippling me with agony. I fell to my knees, trying to fight off the pain. The guards dragged me up the steps then, because there was no way I was walking up there myself.

They lay me on the altar and held my hands and feet. Sweet incense burned all around me.

Horemheb bowed forward and started chanting all sorts of crazy things about fate and destiny and his immortal right to be the ruler of Egypt. I looked up into his ugly face—a face I'd had nightmares about for three thousand years. I had to think of something fast. If only I'd brought the scrolls from the *Book of the Dead* with me, I could use my final spell for something. But nothing was coming to mind.

"Boy King," Horemheb said once he'd finished chanting. "I have waited an eternity for this day to come."

So had I. And I was going to come out victorious. I had the knife, not him. I struggled again.

Horemheb reached toward the bowl. But instead of plunging his hand into the golden liquid, he stopped and chuckled under his breath.

"No god will help you this day, Tutankhamun," he said. And then he lifted my shirt and reached for the knife.

21

WHERE FIREBALLS
AND NATRON EXPLODE

I admit it—the situation looked pretty grim. I tried to work out a plan. It involved escaping, but that was as far as I got, because something landed on Horemheb's head. It wrapped four limbs around him and started clawing into his scalp.

"Horus!"

Horus didn't look my way. But what in the name of Amun Ra was he doing here? It was the new moon. Horus was crazy during new moons. Dangerous.

I struggled against the hands that held me and broke free. I jumped off the table and dashed down the stairs.

"Fight, Tut!" Gil said. He must've come with Horus.

I didn't stop to think. Gil was knocking out crazy cult

members, throwing balls of fire and blasting heat waves at them. I tried to keep up, calling upon swarms of killer bees and fire ants to do my bidding. Gil and I fought next to each other, just like back in the old days. Our opponents kept coming. Ten. Twenty. Fifty. They were relentless.

We kept fighting until every single one lay defeated on the ground.

On the altar Horemheb and Horus still struggled. Gil summoned his most awesome power. Fire bolts flew from his fingertips: pure fire that streaked like a laser. The sarcophagus exploded. Natron and granite flew everywhere. Horus jumped away from Horemheb's head, out of the way of the flying debris. Horemheb was not so lucky. He tumbled down the stairs and a giant piece of granite landed on top of him.

I yanked the knife from my belt. Now was my chance. Horemheb would die.

But hands grabbed me from behind.

"You can't kill him," Gil said, holding me back.

I fought against Gil. I had to get to Horemheb before he got away. "Yes, I can. Of course I can."

The harder I struggled, the tighter Gil held me. "No, Tut. I'm not kidding. You can't kill him with the knife."

Obviously Gil and I had completely different views on the matter. Horemheb had to be destroyed. It was almost all I'd thought about for three thousand years. I had the upper hand. I had the knife, and Horemheb lay helpless under the lid of the sarcophagus.

"Let me go!" I said. "I may never have this chance again."

But Gil didn't let go. Instead he pried the knife from my hands. I clawed and kicked at him to stop, but it was no use.

"Don't you get it, Tut?" Gil said. "This is why the gods gave me the knife in the first place. It can't be used for vengeance. If anyone—god, immortal, or mortal—uses the knife with negative emotion in their heart, the wrath of the gods will descend upon them. They'll be cursed. Destroyed. You can't do it."

"But I have to kill him," I said. Gil's words couldn't be true. I refused to believe them. This had to be some lie the gods fed him back when they'd given him the knife.

Gil kept the knife out of my reach even though I still struggled.

"Even if you kill him, it's not going to bring your family back," Gil said. "Nothing you do will bring them back."

"It will make me feel better." I grabbed again for the knife, hoping to catch him off guard. "You have no right to take it from me."

Gil fixed his eyes on me, and I was hypnotized under their power. "I have every right, Tut. I'm the protector."

And I knew that no matter what I said, Gil would never give in. Gil had no intention of ever letting me have it.

From behind me, granite flew into the air and Horemheb jumped to his feet. Torches toppled over from the impact, smoke filled the air, and within seconds, the whole underground cavern was immersed in flames. Something exploded across the river. The flames must have reached the torch oil. The impact and heat hit me at the same time, sending me flying forward into a wall. Stars filled my vision, but I shook my head clear.

Horus landed on the ground in front of me. His remaining eye looked feral, exactly like the time he'd tried to rip me to shreds.

"Leave now, Tut," Horus said under his breath.

"But Horemheb . . . ," I said. Horus would understand. He was the one who'd told me about the knife in the first place.

Horus advanced on me. "Leave. Now."

I didn't need to be told a third time. I'd gotten this far once. I could do it again. And next time, I wouldn't tell anyone where I was going.

"Set better prepare to die!" Horus yelled amid the crackling flames.

The only response was a shrieking like a hyena.

"Show yourself, Set!" Horus howled. "How dare you encroach on Tut?" He transformed from a cat into a giant falcon. And without another word he flew into the flames and straight for Horemheb.

"That's our cue to leave," Gil said.

"But Horus—" I started, taking a step in Horus's direction.

"Will be fine." Gil yanked my arm, pulling me back. "Now run."

We ran.

Behind us, I heard the most horrendous hissing sound in the world. Millennia of rage filled the air. Fear tore at the lining of my stomach. This was way worse than stealing the scepter from Set. This battle went beyond thrones and pharaohs. It was feral and fatal and had nothing to do with me or Horemheb. This battle was the reason for the curse. It was a battle of the gods.

"What will happen to Horus?" I asked as we ran. I thought about finding the way out that Tia had told me about, but all these hallways looked the same. I could only hope Gil knew where he was going.

"Horus coming here at all violated some kind of unwritten treaty between the two of them," Gil said as he blasted through closed doors with fireballs when they blocked our way. "Their strongholds are sacred."

"Horus has a stronghold?" I asked. Gil couldn't possibly be referring to our town house.

"All the gods have strongholds. They're supposed to be sacred. But now Horus is here, thanks to you."

"What did you expect me to do? Sit around the town house like a worthless loser?"

"I expected you to think before jumping into things and creating a disaster," Gil said, throwing another fireball through a door that looked a lot like a storage closet. It might have been the one Tia had been talking about, because at the back of it was a ladder. When we reached the ladder, we started climbing.

Gil didn't take a breath from his lecture. "And if you think I'm upset that you're here, you should have seen how Horus reacted when he found out. I'm pretty sure he's going to flail you later."

It was better than what the Cult of Set had planned for me.

Given a choice between having my heart cut out and devoured, and then being mummified, or facing Horus's wrath, I'd choose Horus any day.

We climbed to the top of the ladder and Gil pushed open a stone door that looked like it belonged at the entrance to a spooky haunted house crypt. When we came out into the evening, we were halfway across D.C., all the way over at Meridian Hill Park, near the waterfall steps.

I almost felt the ground shaking under our feet. People were walking around D.C. completely oblivious to everything going on below them. The Cult of Set had a metropolis down there. They had schemes to take over the world, yet the world above remained clueless.

"Don't you ever do something like that again," Gil said once he'd resealed our escape route. And then, before I could respond, Gil did something he hadn't done in decades. He grabbed me in a giant hug. And then he let go. And hugged me again.

"I thought you were dead," he said, and I swear he wiped at his face, though I didn't dare say anything about it.

"It was touch and go for a while," I said. "But I'm happy to report that I'm completely un-mummified."

"I missed a mummification party?" Henry stepped from the shadows. I had this weird, crazy urge to hug him because it was just that kind of moment, but I held back. No need to take it too far. So instead I punched him on the arm, and he slapped me on the back. And I figured we really were friends, whether I'd wanted us to be or not.

"It was the best party ever," I said. "Fun times for all." So much fun I could hardly wait to go back. But the next time, I couldn't make any mistakes. Osiris had given me an opportunity to do away with Horemheb, and I'd blown it. That was never going to happen again.

22

WHERE I FLOOD THE CITY

I t started raining the next day, and it didn't stop. School was canceled because the only uninfested building was knee-deep in water. Henry's parents wouldn't even let him come over because they said he'd drown if he went outside. So I sat in my town house with Gil—who hadn't left me alone since we got back—and watched flood coverage until my eyeballs hurt.

"Perhaps Great Master would prefer the television off?" Colonel Cody said. He wrung his hands like he did when he worried about my mental sanity.

I couldn't turn it off. Too much was happening. After the school flooded, next came the Smithsonian. Sandbags were carted in from Ocean City to stack up against the doors and basement windows. Museums kept more stuff in their basements than I'd had in my tomb, and it was all on the verge of being ruined. Next was the White House. By the second day, the president declared D.C. a disaster zone. His security advisors insisted on flying him off to the mountains. But he couldn't fly because the runways at the airports had all flooded, so they had to drive him out in a Humvee.

And then there was the black mist.

It filled the air with the awful scent of sulfur and swirled around everything, mixing in with the rain. Meteorologists had no idea what was causing it, but I knew.

It was the curse. My curse. Osiris and Set had placed it on my tomb. It was out of control—destroying everything in its path.

To make matters worse, by day three, Horus still wasn't back. I tried not to worry about him. He was a god. But he was also my cat. I'd grown pretty attached to him after all these years. I didn't know what I would do if he never came home.

"This is why we need to do away with Horemheb," I said to Gil.

"Because it's raining?" Gil asked. He sank back in his favorite chair and crossed his legs, like somehow the world would just right itself.

"Because of the curse," I said. "If I kill Horemheb, the curse on my tomb goes away. Everything goes back to normal."

"And if Horemheb kills you first?" Gil said.

I had to fight to keep from wrapping my hands around his Sumerian neck. But seriously. I was fourteen, not some baby. I could handle this.

"Let's just go back and finish it," I said.

"No, Tut," Gil said. "Didn't you hear what I said? The knife can't be used for vengeance. If it is, the gods will retaliate. We can't risk it."

"This has nothing to do with vengeance. All I care about is stopping the curse." I tried my hardest to sound sincere, but even I heard the desperation in my voice.

"You're a horrible liar," Gil said. "You think I'd believe for one second that you've just given up your quest for revenge."

"I have," I said, opening my eyes wide like an innocent puppy dog.

Gil shook his head. "We have to hide the knife."

"And then what? We sit back and watch the world get destroyed? Maybe make some popcorn?"

"Would Great Master care for popcorn?" Lieutenant Virgil asked, bowing before me.

"No, we'll wait for the world to end first," I said, drilling home my point. "Then we'll have popcorn. With butter and salt."

"We figure out another way to stop the curse," Gil said.

"There is no other way. It started because of the fight between Horemheb and me. And it will end with the fight between us. The fight where I come out victorious." I started pacing the room. Why did Gil have to be so stubborn? Why couldn't he just give me the knife? Wrath of the gods. As if my quest for vengeance was something I should just give up. I had to complete it.

Colonel Cody paced alongside me. "Oh, Great Pharaoh, is

there anything I can bring you to ease the pain being caused by the heathen lord?"

If only he could get me the knife.

Wait a minute . . .

Maybe he could. If I could distract Gil long enough—maybe get him out of the town house—the shabtis could find it and steal it. And then, while Gil was still gone, I could go back to the Cult of Set compound and get the revenge I'd missed before.

"No, nothing," I said. But I winked at him.

"Great Master?" Colonel Cody said.

"Seriously, nothing," I said. And I winked again.

This time understanding dawned on Colonel Cody's face. The shabti smiled like the world wasn't coming to an end. "Ah, yes. Nothing it is, then. Perhaps Great Master would enjoy some quiet time in his room reading a book?"

Great Amun, I loved my shabtis. It was almost like they could read my mind.

"That sounds perfect."

Colonel Cody crossed his arms over his chest. "Our master is more than kind. He is the most gracious ruler in the world."

From his chair, Gil groaned.

I turned to Gil to make a good show of my frustration. "This discussion isn't over. We'll talk more about it later."

After Horemheb was dead.

"It's over, Tut," Gil said.

I frowned like I was angry. I even slammed my bedroom

door to make it more convincing. And then I waited for Colonel Cody so I could tell him my plan.

After I explained everything to Colonel Cody, I grabbed a couple of scrolls from the *Book of the Dead* and tucked them under my jacket. I still had my one spell left, though I wasn't sure yet what I could do with it. The knife could kill Horemheb. The *Book of the Dead* couldn't.

I lifted my bedroom window. Rain poured in through the opening. It was like the apocalypse was coming. I jumped onto the fire escape and slammed the window closed. I took the metal steps as loudly as I could. I needed to make sure Gil would follow me.

The streets and alleys were all flooded, and the black mist was everywhere but I slogged through, knee-deep in water. I waded across the street and turned the corner. And then I waited for Gil's head to appear. He looked to my open window and let out a string of words I couldn't hear but could imagine. It was perfect. I took off at a run as best I could through all the water. It was like the flood myth recreated. I needed a boat.

Now that Gil was out of the town house, I needed to mislead him so I could get back and get the knife from Colonel Cody. My phone buzzed.

I figured it was Gil, but instead, it was a text from Henry.

ok b there soon.

I wasn't sure what he was talking about. I hadn't made any plans with him.

Gil turned the corner, spotting me, so I stuffed the phone in my pocket and kept going.

Five minutes later it buzzed again. This time it was Gil. I didn't answer because I was still too close to home for my plan to work. I did make sure my GPS was on so he could track me.

He called three more times. I finally answered when I got as far as Georgetown. "What?"

"What are you doing?" Gil said. I could barely hear him over the rain.

I ducked under a canopy so the phone wouldn't short out from the deluge.

"I'm looking for Horemheb," I lied. "I need to take care of this now, even if you won't help."

"Wait for me," Gil said, and then he hung up.

That was exactly what I couldn't do. I tossed my phone in the nearest trash can and ran back toward my town house, making sure to take the route Gil wouldn't travel. By now, the shabtis would have the knife. I'd get it and pay another visit to the Cult of Set.

No sooner had I walked into the town house when my side erupted in pain. I barely had time to close the door before I fell to the floor in a series of dry heaves. When they finally stopped, I lifted my shirt. The scar was blazing red and swollen.

I staggered to my feet and into the bathroom where I lay on the cold tile floor, letting it soothe my side. Within ten seconds, Colonel Cody stood in front of my face. He fell to the floor. "Oh, Master! How can I help you? Anything you want—please tell me." His words came out fast and fell over one another.

I held my side, still feeling the scar pulse beneath my hand. The pain had subsided—maybe just a little. "Did you get the knife?" I managed to ask, trying my best to sit up.

Colonel Cody clenched and unclenched his little hands. "Of course, Great Master. But you need help first."

I shook my head. I had to get it together. So I grabbed the sink and pulled myself to my feet.

"I'm fine. Please. I just need the knife."

Colonel Cody nodded to the shabti behind him who nodded to the shabti behind him, until the entire line of shabtis seemed to be in agreement. Within seconds, I saw the golden knife being passed from one shabti to the next until Colonel Cody held it in front of himself and bowed.

"The immortal-killing knife," he said.

That certainly put things into perspective.

"Thank you for always knowing exactly what I need and want," I said. I would've hugged the little shabti, except I didn't want to crush him.

He squeezed my finger, which was close to a hug. "It is my greatest honor to be able to serve you."

I stuffed the knife into my belt.

Colonel Cody ran in front of my foot. "I cannot let you

venture into the den of the enemy again without me, Great
Master. I could never live with myself."

I started to shake my head, to tell him no, but the concern
flooding his face wouldn't let me. I picked him up instead.

"Just you," I said. "And we need to move quickly."

Colonel Cody beamed. "Of course. Quickly it is."

I ran for the door with Colonel Cody in tow, ignoring the
pain in my side. I needed to get back to Chinatown. Back to the
elevator entrance to the Cult of Set compound. I had to hoof it,
because all the public transportation was shut down.

When we got there, the limestone block structure was gone.
There wasn't even a crummy subway elevator illusion. Instead,
the earth was paved over and topped with a giant statue . . .
of Horemheb. Rain pounded in the mud at the base of the
statue.

I sank to my knees, and Colonel Cody scurried off my
shoulder. Every single thing was working against me, from the
gash in my side to the curse smothering D.C. It was like the
gods were already retaliating for something I hadn't done.

"Won't this ever work?" I screamed at Osiris. There was nobody else around to hear me.

There was also no response from Osiris.

"He has to die!" I said. "He killed everyone!"

Nothing.

"Just a small amount of revenge. Please?"

My only answer was the unending rain and the black sulfur mist that pressed in on me from all sides.

Everything had been futile. There was no way this was ever

going to work. Even if I did find Horemheb—even if I did manage to kill him—it wasn't going to bring my family back. Nothing would. I'd be cursed by the gods forever for using the knife in vengeance, no matter how much I tried to lie to myself and say it was all about the curse. My quest wasn't noble, like Tia's quest to reunite the gods. It was selfish, just like I'd been for the last three thousand years.

Vengeance wasn't the answer. It wouldn't make anything better.

Not the answer. . . .

I had to give up. . . .

My quest had to end. . . .

No sooner had the thought passed through my mind than the rain let up. Water pooled into sewers and drained away. Overhead, the sun peeked through the clouds. The black mist, which had delved into every nook and cranny of the city, lifted. The horrific sulfur smell vanished.

"Great Master, the curse . . . ," Colonel Cody said, sniffing the air.

"It's gone." I tried to sound happy about it, but along with the curse, my quest was gone, too. I was never going to get my vengeance. I was never supposed to.

"That's good," Colonel Cody said. "We shall travel back to the town house and celebrate. Perhaps break out the vintage root beer you've been saving, though I'm still not sure we should share it with the heathen lord."

I tried to laugh because I knew Colonel Cody was attempting to make me feel better. "That sounds like a good idea."

Colonel Cody clasped his hands together. "Very nice. Should we be going then?"

"Yeah, we should," I said.

But the gods had other plans for me.

"You have serious trouble, Tut."

I whipped around and came face-to-face with Tia.

"What are you talking about?" I said.

"Horemheb."

"I don't care anymore. I'm not going to kill him. I'm going to live my life and let him live his. And as long as he stays out of my way, I never plan to see him again."

Tia bit her lower lip. "I wish it were that easy."

I'd been clenching the hilt of the knife, but I tucked it under my shirt. I couldn't kill Horemheb. I had to release him. "Didn't you hear what I said? I give up. It's over."

"It's not over," Tia said. "Horemheb will never let it be over."

My stomach turned into a ball of lead, making the pain in my side feel like nothing but a splinter. Something horrible was about to happen. I felt it in my bones. "What do you mean? Why are you here?"

Tia pointed to the Washington Monument. In the clearing sky, I saw the energy sizzling off it, pure and strong. And the lights . . . they were supposed to be red, but instead they were golden. Lightning cracked all around the top of the monument, channeling down the sides until it hit the ground.

"What's going on, Tia?" I gritted my teeth. I had to prepare for the worst.

"Horemheb's up there."

"So what? I'm not going to fight him. He can stay up there forever, as far as I'm concerned."

Tia grabbed my arm. "No, Tut. He's not alone."

I faced the god-awful feeling that slammed into my stomach.

"Who's he with?" I hated to ask, but I had to.

She grimaced as she told me. "Henry."

23

WHERE I CLIMB THE FIVE HUNDRED STEPS OF DOOM

oremheb couldn't have Henry. That couldn't be happening. My brain wanted to refuse Tia's words. But then I remembered Henry's cryptic text. ok b there soon. I'd never told him to be anywhere. It had to be Horemheb, pretending to be me.

"Please tell me you're kidding," I said.

But Tia's eyes spoke the truth. Horemheb was threatening death on those around me once again.

Where in the realm of Anubis was Horus when I needed him? I had to get up there now. I couldn't even call Gil to ask for help because I'd ditched my phone.

My brain fogged over with a hatred so dark, I was having trouble thinking. Horemheb had Henry up in the top of the

Washington Monument. Horemheb—who'd killed my father. And my mother. And my brother. He had no reason not to kill Henry. . . .

Except that he wanted the knife. And he wanted me dead. Those were my only bargaining chips.

I grabbed Colonel Cody and took off, running for the monument. I'd get in through the basement. When I got to the Smithsonian subway stop, I tore down the escalator, even though it was closed due to flooding, and hopped the gate. The tracks were filled with water, but I waded my way through until I found the door I was looking for: the one I used when I snuck into the Washington Monument after hours. I ripped the door from its hinges and sprinted inside.

It took only minutes to reach the monument, but each second that passed felt like a millennium. Why had I let myself get so close to Henry anyway? It was stupid and careless, and now he'd pay for my mistake with his life.

Once I was inside the monument, I dashed for the stairs, taking them three at a time until I reached the top.

"Perhaps we can sneak up on the betrayer, Great Master," Colonel Cody whispered in my ear.

"Good plan," I whispered back. I crept forward, trying to stay in the shadows.

But Horemheb had been expecting me.

"Our boy king joins us."

The ball in the pit of my stomach hardened at the sound.

"We've waited so patiently for you," Horemheb said.

"Tut!" I heard Henry say. "Go away!"

There was something that sounded a lot like a bone snapping, and then there was a yell. I jumped from my hiding place onto the main floor.

Henry lay against the wall holding his arm. He glared at my uncle and tried to stand.

"We thought you'd never show up, little Pharaoh," Horemheb said.

I let every bit of hatred I felt for Horemheb show on my face. I had to do something to help Henry.

"Are you okay?" I asked Henry. Which was a worthless question. Henry was in the clutches of a murderer.

"He's going to kill you," Henry said.

"The boy king knows that," Horemheb said. "He's known that for three thousand years. He's been waiting for this moment as long as I have. But before I kill you, Tutankhamun, I'm going to kill your friend."

I may have been powerless when my family died in the past, but I wasn't powerless anymore. I had the knife, and thus the upper hand.

"Shut up," I said. "You're not killing anyone."

"Of course I am. After I kill your friend, I'll kill you," Horemheb said. "You never deserved to be pharaoh. And your father, Akhenaton. Don't get me started on him. He cheated me out of my throne. I should have been pharaoh. Then we would have never had any of that religious mess. He ruined everything."

"You never deserved to rule," I said. "And you're the one who ruined everything. It all came down to you. Because you were worthless and jealous and angry that your son died. That wasn't my father's fault. Things like that happen. You can't look for excuses and blame other people. You should be thankful he's gone, because he couldn't stand to see what kind of monster his father has become."

Horemheb's face reddened like he was choking. "Don't you dare act like you're better than me, Tutankhamun. You have never been better than me. You are nothing."

I'd had enough. "Maybe I am nothing. But I'm not going to play this game any longer. I'm done. Let Henry go, and you'll never see us again."

Horemheb laughed as if I'd told a joke. "Please. I will never give up my quest for revenge. Now give me the knife."

"No."

"Careful, Great Master," Colonel Cody whispered from my shoulder.

Horemheb wrapped his fingers tightly around Henry's throat. "It's going to get hard for him to breathe."

I stood frozen in place. What could I do? There had to be a way out of this that didn't end up with Henry dead.

"I don't have it."

"You're lying, Boy King," Horemheb said between his gritted teeth. "I can sense its power."

I couldn't sense anything but my situation spiraling out of control.

"The knife. Or your little friend dies." Horemheb looked down at Henry, struggling in his arms. "Hanging out with the royal family can be dangerous."

"Let Henry go," I said. Even as it came out, I knew it sounded like a plea, because that's exactly what it was. I was not going to let this happen. Henry had done nothing to deserve this. Nothing except be my friend. And even if that meant a death sentence for me, it was not going to be one for Henry.

"What did you say?" Horemheb asked.

"Let him go, and I'll give you the knife." I pulled it out from under my shirt.

Horemheb's eyes widened. "Ah, now that's more like it."

"Don't give it to him, Tut!" Henry said. "Take the knife and run!"

I smiled inwardly. Henry had no idea. There was zero chance I'd run away and leave him here to be killed by Horemheb. The earth was more likely to implode on the spot.

Horemheb ignored Henry, licking his lips at the sight of the knife. "Bring it to me slowly."

I took a deep breath . . . and felt the scrolls from the *Book of the Dead* still tucked under my jacket. And remembered that I still had one spell left.

Maybe I couldn't kill Horemheb in vengeance. I couldn't use the knife. But I didn't have to be the one to sentence him to death. He deserved to be judged. And he would be.

In my mind, I went over the spell from the *Book of the Dead*.

I took another step toward him.

Horemheb reached for the knife.

I held it out. And in one swift motion, I slashed at him, nicking the side of his hand.

Blood sprang up from the cut. Horemheb let go of Henry,

and the cut on his hand sizzled as his exposed blood hit the air. Just like when he'd cut my side, the knife had wounded him. Not enough to kill him—but I didn't need to kill him.

Horemheb snarled at me and grabbed the knife. And then before I could stop him, he lunged out for Henry with the blade.

Henry dropped to the ground. I barely had time to see his blood before Horemheb was on me. He held the knife over my chest, directly above my scarab heart. Great Osiris, he really was going to use it.

24

WHERE I END MY IMMORTAL LIFE

R eady to die?" Horemheb asked. He shifted his grip on the knife and blood from the cut on his hand dripped down on me. I moved so that the blood would fall on my chest. And then the words came to me—the same spell I'd chanted so long ago in my tomb: "The Judgment of the Dead." It hadn't worked back then because I didn't have power over the *Book of the Dead*. But this time I did. The words to the spell were hidden in my memories. I was going to get them right. I was out of time and options. This had to work. Horemheb's blood seeped through my shirt and onto the scrolls. I chanted faster.

Behind Horemheb, the wall of the monument started to glow. Light sprang from the scrolls. I kept chanting.

"Don't waste your time," Horemheb said. "It's too late."

He thrust the knife downward.

Colonel Cody leapt from my shoulder onto Horemheb's hand, knocking his hand to the side just before the blade pierced my skin. He struggled with Horemheb, trying to pry the knife from his fingers.

Edges became distinct on the glowing wall and a portal appeared, pure gold and glittering with gems. Engraved with spells from the book itself. This was it. The spell was working. This was the door to the afterworld. When the last word dropped from my lips, the spell was complete. The portal to the afterworld was active.

"It's not too late for anything," I said.

With every bit of strength I still had, I kicked Horemheb away from me.

He flew toward the portal. Colonel Cody still struggled on Horemheb's hand, pulling at his fingers. The knife Horemheb clasped finally fell to the ground. Horemheb passed through the portal. I barely had time to see Horemheb open his mouth to scream before the portal sealed and the light extinguished. And then Horemheb was gone. He'd have to face Maat now. It was the only way to pass on to the Fields of the Blessed. She'd weigh his rotten heart and feed him to the crocodile goddess, Ammut. He would be devoured.

It was only then that I realized Colonel Cody was gone,

too. My faithful shabti. He'd passed through the portal with Horemheb. I'd never see him again. He'd given his life helping me defeat my enemy. The price was too high. My heart ached, but I didn't have time to mourn him. As the power from the spell drained from me, I jumped up and ran over to Henry.

"Great Osiris!" I knew it was useless, but I pressed my hands over his neck.

The ground below him was a pool of blood. His neck looked like someone had done a bad job of trying to cut off his head; the cut extended from just under his left ear almost to his chin.

Henry's eyes opened. "Is . . . he . . . gone?"

"Shhhh!" I said. "Don't talk. I'm going to get you to a hospital."

"You . . . did . . . it," he rasped. "Horemheb . . ."

I nodded, hoping the horror wasn't showing on my face. Not that Henry would have recognized it. I'd seen people die before. I knew what death looked like. Horemheb had delivered a fatal wound to Henry, and now he was going to die.

"We did it," I said. "I sent him to be judged by the gods."

A small smile reached Henry's white lips. "Thanks . . . for being . . . my friend."

He had a hard time getting it out, but I had a harder time listening to it. What kind of friend was I? Henry was going to die.

I slammed my fist into the ground. "It's not fair! You can't die." I couldn't believe I'd let this happen. "I never should have let us become friends!"

"No . . . ," Henry started, but stopped from the effort of it.

How could I even look him in the eye? I may as well have sliced his throat myself. If only I could heal him. At that moment, I would have done anything, and yet there was nothing I could do. . . .

. . . except . . .

I dug up every bit of faith I had.

"Please, Osiris, save him," I prayed. "Take my immortality. Take my life. But please save him." I knew it might be futile, but it was all I had left.

I had to have faith. Without faith, there was no hope. Without hope, there was nothing.

Osiris heard me.

He appeared in front of me and bent down, placing one hand on my chest and one hand on Henry. And then every bit of energy that filled my scarab heart drained from me.

25

WHERE GIL TURNS UP THE HEAT

I guess that's where Gil found us, even though I didn't wake up until the next day. I opened my eyes and found Gil hovering over me on the futon back in our town house.

"You almost died," he said. He looked like he hadn't slept in days. His dark hair hung in greasy strands, escaped from a bad attempt to be pulled back. His face was the color of rice. And the bags under his eyes could have held a gallon of water each.

My hand went to my chest. The warmth I'd known for so long was gone. My scarab heart was dead. "Are you sure I didn't die?"

"Pretty sure." Gil handed me a glass of water.

I took a long drink and set the glass on the table. Lieutenant Virgil rushed forward and filled it back to the rim. I instinctively looked around for Colonel Cody.

He wasn't there.

He'd been lost in the battle, giving his life to ensure Horemheb reached the afterworld without the knife.

Great Amun, I was going to miss the little shabti. I could almost imagine his small golden face offering to end his own existence for some ridiculous oversight. I'd counted on him for everything. He was the only one who'd never lied to me, never failed me. I'd never told him how much he meant to me. Now I'd never have the chance.

The rest of my shabti army stood at attention, with one arm crossed over the other, in concentric circles around me. They didn't move, almost like they were truly statues instead of sentient beings.

My head spun as I sank bank into the futon. "I feel horrible."

Gil tried to smile, but it couldn't seem to fully form on his face. "You looked horrible when I found you."

"Thanks," I said. "How's Henry?"

"He's fine," Gil said. "Happy to be alive."

Would it be hard for me to adjust to my drained scarab heart? Already I felt the emptiness in my chest like a hole begging to be filled. But there was nothing to fill it with. Henry needed the energy from my heart more than I did. He would have died otherwise. And anyway, I'd been immortal an awfully long time.

"You know, what you did up there—" Gil started.

I put up my hand. "I don't want to talk about it." Maybe I'd want to in the future, but right now, I felt too . . . empty. Even though I'd never have changed what I'd done for anything.

"If you ever do . . ."

I forced out a smile. "I'll let you know. Did Horus make it back yet?"

Gil's face tensed. He was actually worried about Horus, too. "I haven't heard anything from him." And then he looked away.

"What?" I shifted on the futon and felt sweat start to bead up on my forehead. I motioned Major Rex forward. He seemed to be in charge now that Colonel Cody was gone.

He ran to me and bowed. "Yes, Great Master?"

"Would you mind opening a window?"

Major Rex bowed again and snapped his fingers. It was nice to know they still loved me, even if I wasn't immortal anymore.

Two shabtis opened the window and cool air blew into the town house. But I kept sweating.

Gil let out a deep breath and spoke. "It's all my fault."

I shook my head. "Nothing's your fault."

"I'm supposed to protect you," Gil said, ignoring my words.

"No," I said. "If anyone's to blame for anything, it's me. Henry was about to die, all because I let him get too close. I should have never become friends with him in the first place."

"Tut, having friends is never something to regret," Gil said. "You're the best friend Henry's ever had."

Drowsiness was starting to cloud my mind. "How do you know that?"

"He told me," Gil said.

"When?" I asked.

"This morning while you were still asleep," Gil said. "Henry recovered quickly."

"He came by?" I asked.

Gil shook his head. "No, he called. He's afraid to come over."

"Afraid?" I narrowed my eyes. "Why?"

"Because he thinks you'll regret what you did," Gil said. "He thinks you'll be sorry and never want to see him again."

I opened my mouth to say something, but stopped. Sure, part of me did regret it. Losing my immortality. My future. But it was the only thing to do. It's what a friend would do. And I was Henry's friend.

"It's not Henry's fault," I said. "I made the decision, and even if it's a change, I'll get used to it. Maybe I should go see him." I stood up, but the change in elevation made stars spin in my head. Gil caught me and settled me back on the futon. I wiped sweat off my forehead, but our town house had gone from warm to downright hot.

"You're not going anywhere," Gil said. "This will be my last failure."

"Failure!" I said. "You never fail at anything."

Gil put on a wry smile and sighed. "I've lived my life as one constant failure after another. I ruined tons of people's lives. My best friend died because I was stupid and selfish and only thought of myself. I lost the throne. And then that kid died."

"I'm as much to blame for that as you," I said.

Gil ignored me. "I've always felt like no matter how much good I do, I'll never be able to balance it all out." He grabbed my shoulders and looked me in the eye. "Now I've failed you. And I will make this up to you, Tut. I swear it on my mother's name."

My eyelids started to droop at that point. Maybe being mortal, I'd get tired more often.

"You don't have anything to make up," I said. "And could you turn down the heat?"

"No. I don't think so."

I tried to force my eyes wide at that point, because the tone of his voice clued me in to the fact that something was seriously wrong. But heat descended on the town house. I realized, even through my drowsy mind, where it was coming from.

"What are you doing, Gil?"

Gil smiled, and clarity like I hadn't seen in ages moved onto his face. "Don't you know?"

I sat up, but the heat kept coming—from Gil. He was turning the entire town house into an oven. The shabtis ran over, ostrich fans in hand, but one look from Gil and they stopped in their tracks.

I knew what he planned to do then.

"Stop it now," I said. "This isn't what I want."

Gil held up the golden knife. "You don't have a choice. I said I'd make it up to you, and it's what I'm going to do."

Inside my chest, my human heart started to pound. And Gil's scarab heart started to glow. I fought to keep my eyes open, but the heat was too much. The last thing I remember seeing was Gil talking to the shabtis. For a moment I wondered if they wouldn't listen to him, since they thought he was a heathen. But then I realized they would. They'd want to help me as much as Gil wanted to. I opened my mouth again, thinking I could tell them to hold Gil back, but words wouldn't come out.

26

WHERE I DREAM ABOUT BUGS

had a strange dream. I was back in the monument, cutting open my chest. My side ached in my dream, but it didn't stop me. I hardly had to touch the knife to my skin before it opened. And then I reached into my chest and closed my hand around what I found inside.

In my dream, when I pulled my hand out of my chest, my heart pulsed between my fingers—my human heart. I watched it beat—over and over—hypnotized by the rhythm. And even though my human heart was no longer inside me, life poured through me.

I sort of floated over to a table that had been set up against the wall. There lay the *Book of the Dead*. I placed my beating heart in a shallow clay bowl and unrolled the scrolls. From the book, I heard a spell. I wasn't speaking it myself. Somewhere in my dream, the spell came, words in ancient Egyptian. I heard it over the sound of my beating heart. I picked up a roll of gauze and my human heart, and with swift movements, I began to wrap the heart—to mummify it.

When I finished, I shoved the wrapped heart back into my chest. Even in my dream, I gasped when I felt it reconnect. This was the start of it. I was being mummified. But here in my dream, it didn't frighten me.

Next, I picked up a Canopic jar. I wanted to see what was inside, so I lifted the lid.

Scarabs poured out and began to crawl over me. But where they crawled my skin stung, as if somehow they were digging into my flesh.

"Don't slap so hard," I heard.

Another slap.

"He's waking up."

My eyes fluttered open to see Major Rex's green face only inches away.

Slap. This time on my leg.

"Stop it!" I said.

"But, my lord, the scarabs are getting out of control," Major Rex said. "We formally request permission to annihilate the beetle population." He made sure to stand all of his six inches tall when he asked it.

"Wow, that sounds a little final," Henry said from somewhere in the room.

I rubbed my eyes, sitting up. Slap. Near my foot this time.

"You can kill half of them. No more." Fifty percent should be able to hold the population until Horus got back. *If* Horus got back. Which I really hoped he did.

"But Master," Major Rex said. "That would still leave approximately—"

I put up my hand. "Half. No more."

I looked around the town house. Gil was gone, but Henry sat on the green camel seat.

"Hey," I said carefully, not sure how he would react.

Henry ran his fingers through his mop of blond hair, pushing it off his forehead. He looked different, but I couldn't quite place why.

"Hey," he said. "You slept for a long time."

I stretched to get my blood circulating again. "I guess I was tired."

Henry shifted like he had a thorn in his bottom. Camel seats weren't the height of comfort, so I could understand.

"I wanted to thank you," he said, placing a hand over his chest. I'm not sure if he even knew he was doing it.

"It was nothing," I said.

But Henry shook his head. I guess he wasn't going to let the fact that I'd healed him and drained my scarab heart in the process go. "No, it wasn't nothing. It was everything. I'd be dead right now if it weren't for you." He looked down at his feet. "That's like the nicest thing anyone's ever done for me."

I looked down also, not sure what to say. So I decided to go for the truth. "You know, I haven't had a real friend in a long time. But then you came along, and . . . well . . . anyway, I'm glad we started hanging out." Okay, that was enough of that. I glanced around. "Where's Gil?"

"Gone."

"Gone where?"

"I have no idea," Henry said. "He took the knife and left. Didn't say where he was going."

"Did he say when he was coming back?"

Henry again gave me a look like I should know the answer. "I don't think he is ever coming back."

Panic hit me, making my chest tighten. Never coming back?

"Why would you think that?" But as the words came out, I knew. Gil's final gift to me. How had I missed it? The hole in my chest had vanished, and in its place sat a scarab heart. Gil's scarab heart.

My face must have shown my thoughts because Henry nodded.

"He did it while you were sleeping," Henry said. "And then he left."

Even with the immortality pumping through me, heaviness moved in and sat on my heart. "I told him not to do it."

"He said it was the only way to make things right," Henry said.

I sat up straight, feeling the energy pulse through me. "But now he's mortal."

"I know," Henry said. "And I think he's relieved."

I thought about everything I knew about Gil. About everything he'd said before I'd fallen asleep. Even though I knew it was what he wanted, it didn't seem fair. Why should I live when Gil would die? He didn't owe me anything.

"Do you have any side effects?" I asked, trying to take my mind off of Gil. Henry was now pumped full of immortal energy. That had to make a difference.

Henry pulled at the ends of his hair. "Everything's growing really fast. Like my nails and my hair. And my eyesight . . ."

"What about it?"

"It's perfect. No glasses. People at school won't recognize me."

That's what looked different about Henry. He didn't have his normal wire-rimmed glasses perched on his nose. That said, people would have no trouble recognizing Henry. He still wore a ridiculous Pluto T-shirt. This one read, BACK IN MY DAY, WE HAD 9 PLANETS. It was actually a pretty cool shirt.

"I'm not going back to school," I said. The sole benefit I could see of Gil not being here was that I'd never be tricked or coerced into going to school again.

"Yes, you are," Henry said. "There is no way you are ditching me. And anyway, next year is high school. You can pass as a freshman."

I knew I could. I had before on numerous occasions. I just didn't want to.

"Being a freshman guy stinks," I said. "You're at the bottom of the food chain. Every single upperclassman in the school picks on freshman guys. And the girls don't give you the time of day."

"So it really won't be any different in that regard," Henry said.

"Not in your case."

"You have to go with me," Henry said.

"I don't."

"Please?"

"I'll think about it."

Just then Horus jumped in through the fire escape window.

"I see you stopped your curse," Horus said.

"Horus!" I wanted to hug him but didn't dare. He wasn't one for extraneous emotions. But he was right. The curse was gone. It had been from the second I gave up my quest for revenge.

"You won't believe the week we had," I started.

Horus held up a paw to stop me. "Did you fight a god and almost get your eye ripped out?"

"No."

"Did you end up halfway around the world, sacked out in a gutter?"

"No."

"How about food? Have you eaten in the last week?"

"I get it, Horus. You've had a rough week, too." I looked to Major Rex, who immediately summoned some shabtis to fill Horus's bowl with milk. Waiting on Horus was below Lieutenants Virgil and Leon. They only waited on me.

"Oh, by the way," Horus said while he waited for his milk bowl to be filled. "I got summoned to the afterworld. It seems

Maat needed a jury to judge Horemheb. Something about the fact that he was an immortal and had Set protecting him."

"He did make it there, then?" I said. Relief flooded through me. Osiris and the *Book of the Dead* had not failed me.

"Nice work, Tutankhamun," Horus said, pulling out the full-name thing. For a second, I thought I heard pride in his voice. I'm sure I was mistaken.

"What did the jury say?" I knew there was no way Horemheb would ever be judged worthy of life in the Fields of the Blessed, even with Set as his benefactor, but I wanted to hear it from Horus's mouth.

"Let's just say Ammut had a tasty snack." Horus lowered his mouth and started lapping at the bowl, but raised it after a couple of seconds. Milk dripped from his tongue. "Oh, and one more thing."

"What now?" I asked.

He gave me his best pirate scowl. "Now's not the time to be ungrateful. I brought you a small souvenir. Don't say I never did anything for you." He looked to the fire escape window.

In climbed Colonel Cody!

"Great Master," Colonel Cody said, and bowed to the ground.

"Colonel Cody!" I ran to him and picked him up, hugging him to my chest. "You stupid, brave little shabti. I thought I'd never see you again! Great Osiris, I missed you." On the last words, my voice cracked. I didn't care.

"And I missed you as well, Great Master," Colonel Cody said.

"Don't ever do that again, okay?" I forced down the lump in my throat.

Colonel Cody tried to bow, but I had my fingers wrapped too tightly around him. "Very good, Great Master. Never again."

"Thank you, Horus," I said.

Horus shrugged. "He latched onto me the second I came through the door to the afterworld. Wouldn't stop begging and pleading with me. Said you would be lost without him."

That did sound like Colonel Cody.

"Persistent little bugger," Horus said. "I finally told him I'd take him with me if he promised to shut up."

Colonel Cody beamed. "It is exactly as the cat god says, Great Master. And now if you'll please put me down, I'll set your town house in order once again."

I knew it would make him the happiest, so I set him down. He ran off and immediately started giving orders.

"So what now?" Henry asked.

What now. It was a perfect question.

"We could play video games." I picked up a game remote and tossed a second one to him.

Henry stared at me like I'd left my brain at the top of the Washington Monument. "That's the best you can think of?"

"I'm not working on our project," I said. "No more."

Henry laughed. "Don't worry, Tut. I finished it while you were having your little beauty sleep."

Thank Amun. "You didn't have to do that," I said.

"It was the least I could do," Henry said. "You saved my life."

"True." There was no reason to argue with solid logic.

"You're going to go looking for him, aren't you?" Henry asked.

Was I that transparent? Or was Henry just extra observant? Because yes, I was going to find Gil. He'd given his immortality up for me. I had to at least keep him from curling up in a hole and dying.

"He'd do the same thing for me," I said.

"Any idea where he would go?" Henry asked.

I shook my head. "No. But you know what I've noticed?"

"What?"

"I'm lucky."

Henry snorted. "That's one way to look at the last few weeks."

"I'll find him," I said. "And Horus will help, won't you, Horus?"

Horus looked up with his whiskers covered in milk. "Find Gil? Why would I want to do that?"

"Because if you don't, I'll tell your mother."

Horus scowled in response.

"Do you think he'll be hard to find?" Henry asked.

I tossed the game remote onto the coffee table. "I guess we're going to find out."

27

WHERE I'M IMMORTALLY IN EIGHTH GRADE

'd like to say that's where it all ended. But school started back up and Mr. Plant was relentless. He called on Henry and me the first day back.

"Ready to present your project, boys?"

Seth and Tia? They'd vanished. Seth being gone was a blessing from the gods. Tia? I looked for her around every corner. There was no sign of her. I should have asked for her number when I had the chance.

"We're ready," Henry said, jumping up from his desk. He carted a cardboard box up to the front of the classroom that looked exactly like the funerary box—my sole contribution to the project. The shabtis had done an amazing job painting it alabaster, with dark hieroglyphs covering it in perfect script.

I followed him up, carrying the trifold display board Henry had finished while I'd been asleep. The shabtis had wanted to redo the whole thing, but Henry would have been way offended, so I made them swear not to offer again.

Mr. Plant grilled us, asking us the names of the heads on the Canopic jars, asking us what went in each one. It was almost like he was looking for a reason to give us a bad grade. But when Henry started in on how the goddess Isis must feel when she looks at a Canopic jar, even Mr. Plant wiped a tear from his eye.

Yes, we got an A.

And yes, the rest of the day went on, and then the next and the next.

I looked for Gil everywhere, thinking he'd just show up after school one day like normal to drive me home, but I never saw him. He'd disappeared. But each day that passed, I formulated a plan to find him. It was my new quest.

ACKNOWLEDGMENTS

There's no way I can possibly remember to thank everyone who helped *Tut* reach publication. If I tried, I'm sure I would forget someone. So instead I'll trace the path that led to my dream becoming a reality and see where it takes me.

First and foremost, I owe a huge thank-you to Eric Elfman. Eric believed in *Tut* from the moment I arrived at the Big Sur Writing Workshop in California. Without his enthusiasm, *Tut* could very well be locked away in a tomb forever, never to see the light of day.

Second, I am filled with gratitude to Laura Rennert, who fell in love with *Tut* at the Big Sur Writing Workshop, saw the beauty of the concept, and never gave up. Without Laura's persistence, again, *Tut* would be in that tomb. I also want to thank Lara Perkins, who, though she came later in the *Tut* story, shared Laura's persistence and belief. Also, thank you to all those who help make the Big Sur Writing Workshop such an amazing event. It remains one of my favorite writing memories ever.

Third, there is my editor, Susan Chang. Thank you, Susan, for believing in the idea of a fourteen-year-old immortal King Tut in modern times. Thank you for seeing not only the potential in the King Tut story but also the potential in me. I am so grateful for your wonderful editorial wisdom. And thank you to all the wonderful people at Tor who have helped immortalize the boy king.

There's a special place in the Fields of the Blessed for writing friends. Thank you beyond words to Jessica Lee Anderson, for always being there. Always. And thank you to Christine Marciniak, for reading *Tut* nearly as many times as I did.

Incredible communities and relationships are the fabric of

happiness. Thank you to my wonderful Texas Sweethearts & Scoundrels, my amazing co-bloggers at The Enchanted Inkpot, my fellow retreaters at the Lodge of Death, the Austin writing/blogging/bookstore community, and the Far Flung Writers. I'm so happy to celebrate all your successes.

And then there is my family, which happens to be the most wonderful family in the world. Thank you, Riley, for your continued support and belief. Thank you, Zachary, for saying you loved *Tut* even before it was revised. Thank you, Lola, for making me believe I am awesome. Thank you, Mom, for touring D.C. (and Philadelphia for the King Tut treasures) with the kids and me again and again. And thank you, Dad, for providing such a positive example of a lifetime of accomplishment.

The story of publication for *Tut* has been a long one, filled with plenty of ups and downs. I'm happy it has a happy ending and am so grateful for all the support I have received. Thank you!

A NOTE FROM THE AUTHOR

REGARDING TUT . . .

In 1976, I hopped on a big yellow school bus and headed off for a field trip to the King Tut treasures at the National Gallery of Art in Washington, D.C. I wasn't sure what to expect. Sure, there had been tons of press about the boy king, including articles in *Newsweek* and the must-hear song by celebrity Steve Martin. But as a six-year-old, field trips for me were just another day out of the classroom. Having grown up near D.C., I was spoiled. The Smithsonian was on my doorstep. It was no big deal. And then I saw the exhibit.

To say the King Tut treasures left a lasting impression on me is the understatement of the millennium. I couldn't imagine all that shiny gold buried under the sand, undiscovered for thousands of years. And the questions that were left unanswered. How did the tomb remain hidden for so long? What brought about the death of the boy king? Was the curse of King Tut real?

I was hooked. On mythology. On ancient civilizations. On King Tut.

When I started writing *Tut: The Story of My Immortal Life*, pieces from ancient history and mythology began to fall into the story. I spent copious amounts of time reading books and searching the Internet to make sure I got these pieces right. And once I had all the facts, I twisted them, just a bit, to make my story unique. It's one of the most fun parts of being an author.

REGARDING GILGAMESH . . .

First Gil showed up. In *Tut*, I don't spend much time on Gil's back story, because this book is not his tale. If you want to know more

307

about Gil or ancient Mesopotamia, check out the *Epic of Gilgamesh*. You'll find that Gil was a king. His best friend died. And he searched for immortality, which he may or may not have found. It's the stuff of legends . . . and possibly the premise for another book.

REGARDING HOREMHEB AND AY . . .

Ancient history talks of the boy king having two main advisors, Horemheb and Ay. The idea makes perfect sense. A boy who inherits the throne at nine-years-old is most likely going to need a bit of guidance. History also suggests that both these advisors may have ruled as pharaoh after the boy king's demise. I'm willing to disregard Horemheb on the throne because the idea of him locked in a tomb for three thousand years is so much more fun, but if you're curious about Egyptian pharaohs either before or after King Tut, do a little research and see what you find.

REGARDING AKHENATON . . .

King Tut's dad, Akhenaton, caused a huge religious upheaval. He made it illegal to worship any Egyptian god except his favorite one, Aten, who was represented by the disk of the sun. People were not happy. Priests were not happy. Egypt was in utter chaos. And when Akhenaton died, King Tut had to clean up the mess. It's easy to glance over this religious pandemonium as just a small footnote when reading about Egypt, but this was a major deal. And possibly a dangerous time to be pharaoh. What do you think?

REGARDING HORUS, SET, AND OSIRIS . . .

Horus, though a cat in my story, is most often seen as a falcon. He's also the son of Osiris and Isis. Mythology is filled with crazy stories about why the sun crosses the sky, how the earth was made, and where thunder comes from. There's also a crazy story about how the Egyptian god Set killed his brother Osiris. And an even crazier story of how Osiris's son, Horus, then came into being after

Osiris was already dead. Take a few minutes to read about it on the Internet. You may realize how lucky Horus was to be missing only an eye.

REGARDING THE CURSE . . .

People have a weird fascination with dark and terrible things, and the curse of King Tut tops the list. Since the tomb's discovery back in 1922, King Tut's curse has been the topic of debate. Was the curse of King Tut real? Was it caused by a fungus? Was there really an inscription above the tomb? Was the curse responsible for the death of not only a bird and a dog, but also eleven people? You decide.

REGARDING THE MUMMY . . .

Here's my challenge question for you. If King Tut was immortal, like in *Tut: The Story of My Immortal Life*, then who was the mummy that archaeologists found in the tomb? It's definitely a story for another day!

GLOSSARY

Ammut—crocodile goddess who devours unworthy hearts at the entrance to the Egyptian underworld

Amun/Amun Ra—King of the Gods

Anubis—jackal-headed god of the underworld

Bast—cat goddess

Bes—god of luck

Duamutef (Dua)—jackal-headed god; one of four sons of Horus; in mummification, protected the stomach

Hapi—baboon-headed god; one of four sons of Horus; in mummification, protected the lungs

Horus—son of Osiris and Isis; most often seen with a falcon head (but takes form of a cat in *Tut: The Story of My Immortal Life)*; lost one eye in fight with his uncle Set

Imsety—god (with a normal head); one of four sons of Horus; in mummification, protected the liver

Isis—mother goddess; mother of Horus; wife of Osiris

Khepri—dung beetle god who pushes the sun across the sky each day

Maat—goddess of justice and truth; judges the dead at entrance to Egyptian underworld

Osiris—god of fertility, death, and the afterlife; carries a crook and flail; most often depicted green and partially mummified

Qebehsenuef (Qeb)—falcon-headed god; one of four sons of Horus; in mummification, protected the intestines

Ra—god of the sun

Sekhmet—lion-headed goddess

Set—god of chaos, storms, and infertility; brother and slayer of Osiris

GLOSSARY

SUMERIAN GODS

Anu—King of the Gods

Enlil—god of storms and wind

Nergal—god of war and the sun

PEOPLE

Akhenaton—father of Tutankhamun; used to be known as Amenhotep IV; introduced monotheistic religion to Egypt which made him really unpopular

Ay—advisor to Tutankhamun while he ruled Egypt; it is thought that Ay ruled Egypt after King Tut

Enkidu—best friend of Gilgamesh back in ancient Sumer

Gilgamesh (Gil)—former Sumerian king

Horemheb—commander in chief of the Egyptian army during Tutankhamun's reign; advisor to Tutankhamun

Howard Carter—English archaeologist who discovered King Tut's tomb in 1922

Smenkhkare (Smenk)—older brother of Tutankhamun

Tutankhamun (King Tut)—Egyptian pharaoh; often called the Boy King since he took the throne when he was only nine.

PLACES

Fields of the Blessed—equivalent of heaven in the Egyptian afterlife

Valley of the Kings—valley in Egypt where over sixty tombs have been discovered, many of these for pharaohs of the Egyptian New Kingdom

THINGS

Book of the Dead—ancient Egyptian funerary text containing spells to assist a dead person on their journey through the underworld and into the afterlife

GLOSSARY

Canopic jars—jars used during mummification to hold the liver, lungs, stomach, and intestines

Eye of Horus—ancient Egyptian symbol of protection, good health, and power

Sarcophagus—a funeral box, often carved of stone, which formed the outer layer of protection for a mummy

Shabti—small figures which were placed in tombs to act as servants for the dead person in the afterlife

Ankh—ancient Egyptian symbol which represents eternal life

Tiet—ancient Egyptian symbol; often called "Knot of Isis"

KING TUT'S GUIDE TO IMMORTALITY

Hey! King Tut here, and if you've finished the book *Tut: The Story of My Immortal Life* then you probably figured out that I am immortal. True, you could have figured that out just by reading the title, but where is the fun in that? So what is immortal? Well, it means living forever, and that's a mighty long time. I've had lots of practice so far. Three thousand years give or take a few hundred. In the event you're ever thinking about becoming immortal, here are some of my best tips for making the most of your eternal life.

HOBBIES

Maybe the most important tip for a happy immortal future is having lots of hobbies. And when I say lots of hobbies, I mean hundreds and hundreds of hobbies. Always wanted to learn to play the violin? Now is the perfect time. How about solving the Rubik's Cube? Or becoming a kung fu master? With so much time on your hands, there is nothing you can't become the best in the world at doing.

MONEY

Let's face it. Having money solves many of life's simple needs. Like food. And shelter. And that new pair of running shoes you are just dying to have. If you want extra time to spend on all your hobbies, you're going to need cash so you don't have to worry about the basic necessities. The key to making money as an immortal is to think long-term and to be consistent. One day a month, take something that you consider valuable and bury it. This can be a gold coin, a piece of modern art, or even a Tickle Me Elmo doll. I suggest marking the location on a carefully guarded map. Guess what? In one hundred years, your modern art is now an antique. Your gold coin has quadrupled in value. And people will sell their firstborn in order to get the Elmo doll.

TRAVEL THE WORLD

Guess what? It is a big world out there. And you, now being immortal, can see all of it. You can follow summer around the world. You can climb the Himalayas, searching for the Abominable Snowman. You can search for the lost continent of Atlantis. And since money will never be a problem for you, you can do all this while traveling first class.

DON'T BURN BRIDGES

Simply, don't be a jerk. If you make enemies while traveling to a foreign country, it could be centuries before you can show your face there again. Learn the languages where you travel (starting with "thank you"), don't overstay your welcome, and always clean up after yourself.

LIVE LIGHT

You have lots of money. You have lots of time. Don't become a collector of junk. The last thing you want to do with all your time is drag around some ridiculous number of possessions from one place to the next. Set a limit for yourself, like one knick-knack each place you go, and stick to it. The shabtis will thank you.

Hope you enjoy immortality!

A TOMB BUILDER'S GUIDE TO DESIGNING KING TUT'S TOMB

Congratulations! You've finally gotten your dream job. You have been assigned to lead the design committee for the tomb of the great pharaoh Tutankhamun. Sure, it will be years before he passes on to the afterlife—he is only a teenager—but as any great architect knows, it is always good to be prepared for any situation. There are so many things to think about. So where to start?

SIZE

A tomb for a pharaoh should be huge! You decide it should have twenty rooms, each filled with treasures. Since the boy king is so young, you will have plenty of time to finish his tomb, so you divide the construction up into stages. The first stage will consist of the entry stairway, the entrance passageway, and four main rooms: the antechamber, the annex, the burial chamber, and the treasury. The other stages can come after you finish these rooms. After much consideration, you decide on the following measurements.

Entry stairway: 6' wide by 16 steps
Entry passageway: 6' wide by 27' deep by 7' high
Antechamber: 26' wide by 12' deep by 9' high
Annex: 15' wide by 9' deep by 9' high
Burial Chamber: 14' wide by 21' deep by 12' high
Treasury: 16' wide by 13' deep by 8' high

A TOMB BUILDER'S GUIDE

LAYOUT

You know that the layout of a tomb is important so the dead pharaoh will properly be able to reach the underworld and pass into the Fields of the Blessed. You decide that the entrance should be from the east, the same way Khepri the giant dung beetle god makes the sun rise each morning. The burial chamber should be at the northwest, and the treasury should be at the northeast. The annex should be in the southwest, and the antechamber should be in the center. You pray for guidance, and the gods seem pleased with your decisions.

PROTECTION

Great! Now that the technical stuff is out of the way, what is the best way to protect this tomb that you've built? For starters, sealed doors at all the main intersections are a must. That way, if thieves do break into the tomb, they may not have the time or equipment to make it to the really special rooms (like the burial chamber or the treasury).

After the sealed doors are in place, a curse inscribed above the entry door is always nice. Statistics show that a powerful curse can keep away over sixty percent of potential thieves. After all, who would want to bring down a curse upon themselves? For great Pharaoh Tutankhamun, you think about the curse for two weeks straight, trying to come up with the perfect words. Finally you have it!

Death Shall Come on Swift Wings to Him Who Disturbs
the Peace of the King

Once the sealed doors and the curse are solidly in place, cover the entire tomb in sand. With luck, nobody will ever find it.

TUT: THE STORY OF MY IMMORTAL LIFE
PICK YOUR OWN QUEST GAME

You are about to embark on a great adventure as King Tut, Pharaoh of Egypt. Whatever you do, don't turn back. Once you make a choice, it cannot be changed! One path may lead to you saving the world. Another may lead to your doom.

CHOOSE WISELY :)

It's a big job being Pharaoh, but somebody has to do it. And let's face it. Life as Pharaoh is awesome. People treat you like a rock star! Still, forget taking nice, leisurely walks along the Nile River. Everyone bows to you and wants you to bless their children. But it's good to be famous. You don't mind the attention.

Yet deep in Egypt there is a conspiracy, and you are the only one who can get to the bottom of it. Your people are counting on you. Egypt is counting on you. And the gods are counting on you!

Visit www.pjhoover.com/tut_games.php to see if you have what it takes to save Egypt!

317

ABOUT THE AUTHOR

P. J. HOOVER first fell in love with Greek mythology in sixth grade. After a fifteen-year bout as an electrical engineer designing computer chips for a living, P. J. decided to take her own stab at mythology and started writing books for kids and teens. When not writing, P. J. spends time with her husband and two kids and enjoys practicing kung fu, solving Rubik's Cubes, and watching *Star Trek*. She lives in Austin, Texas.

For more information about P. J. (Tricia) Hoover, please visit her website: www.pjhoover.com. P. J. is also a member of the Texas Sweethearts & Scoundrels and The Enchanted Inkpot.